HUMPTY DUMPTY
IN OAKLAND

TOR BOOKS BY PHILIP K. DICK

Voices from the Street
Humpty Dumpty in Oakland

HUMPTY DUMPTY
IN OAKLAND

PHILIP K. DICK

TOR®

A TOM DOHERTY ASSOCIATES BOOK
NEW YORK

HUMPTY DUMPTY IN OAKLAND

Copyright © 1986 by The Estate of Philip K. Dick

A Tor Book
Published by Tom Doherty Associates, LLC
175 Fifth Avenue
New York, NY 10010

www.tor.com

Tor® is a registered trademark of Tom Doherty Associates, LLC.

Library of Congress Cataloging-in-Publication Data

Dick, Philip K.
    Humpty dumpty in Oakland / Philip K. Dick.—1st U.S. ed.
        p. cm.
    "A Tom Doherty Associates book."
    ISBN-13: 978-0-7653-1690-5
    ISBN-10: 0-7653-1690-0
    1. Self-deception—Fiction. 2. San Francisco (Calif.)—Fiction. I. Title.
PS3554.I3H86 2007
813'.54—dc22

                                                                        2007020866

First U.S. Edition: October 2007

Printed in the United States of America

0 9 8 7 6 5 4 3 2 1

HUMPTY DUMPTY
IN OAKLAND

1

As he drove, Jim Fergesson rolled down the window of his Pontiac, and, poking his elbow out, leaned to inhale lungfuls of early-morning summer air. He took in the sight of sunlight on stores and pavement as he went up San Pablo Avenue at a slow pace. All fresh. All new, clean. The night machine, the whirring city brush, had come by, gathering up; the broom their taxes went to.

At the curb he parked, turned off the motor, sat for a moment lighting a cigar. A few cars appeared and parked around him. Cars moved along the street. Sounds, the first stirrings of people. In the quiet their movements set up metallic echoes from the buildings and concrete.

Nice sky, he thought. But won't last. Haze later on. He looked at his watch. Eight-thirty.

Stepping from his car he slammed the door and went down the sidewalk. On his left, merchants rolled down their awnings with elaborate arm motions. A Negro swept trash with a pushbroom across the sidewalk into the gutter. Fergesson stepped through the trash with care. The Negro made no comment . . . early-morning sweeping machine.

By the entrance of the Metropolitan Oakland Savings and Loan Company a group of secretaries clustered. Coffee cups, high heels, perfume and earrings and pink sweaters, coats tossed over shoulders. Fergesson inhaled the sweet scent of young women. Laughter, giggles, intimate words passed back and forth, excluding him and the street. The office opened and the women tripped inside with a swirl of nylons and coats . . . he glanced appreciatively back. Good for business, girl behind counter to meet people. A woman adds class, refinement. Bookkeeper? No, must be where customers can see her. Keeps the men from swearing; keeps them kidding and pleasant.

"Morning, Jim." From the barbershop.

"Morning," Fergesson said, without stopping; he held his arm behind him, fingers casually trailing.

Ahead, his garage. Up the cement incline he went, key in hand. He unlocked and with both arms raised the door; it disappeared, a clank and whirr of chains.

Critically, he surveyed his old-fashioned possession. The neon sign was off. Debris from the night lay scattered in the entranceway. He kicked a pasteboard milk carton out onto the sidewalk. The carton rolled off, caught by the wind. Fergesson put his key away and walked into the garage.

Here it began. He squinted and spat out the first stale breath that hung inside the garage. Bending, he clicked on the main power. The dead things creaked back to life. He fixed the side door open, and a little sunlight came in. He advanced on the night-light and destroyed it with a jerk of his hand. He grabbed a pole and dragged back the skylight. The radio, high up, began to hum and then to blare. He threw the fan into wheezing excitement. He snapped on all lights, equipment, display signs. He illuminated the luxurious Goodrich tire poster. He brought color, shape, awareness to the void. Darkness flew; and after the first moment of activity he subsided and rested, and took his seventh day—a cup of coffee.

Coffee came from the health food store next door. As he entered, Betty rose to get the Silex from the back. "Morning, Jim. You're in a good mood this morning."

"Morning," he said, seating himself at the counter and getting, from his trouser pocket, a dime. Sure I'm in a good mood, he thought. I've got reason to be. He started to tell Betty, but then changed his mind. No, not her. She'll hear anyhow.

It was Al he had to tell.

Through the window of the health food store he saw cars parking. People passed. Did some—did one—go into the garage? Hard to see. Last night Al had gone home in an old Plymouth, taken from the lot, green, with a banged-up fender. So he would show up today in that, unless he couldn't get it started. His wife could push him, then; they always had a couple of cars home. He would drive directly onto the lot.

"Anything else, Jim?" Betty asked, wiping the counter.

"No," he said. "I'm looking for Al. I have to go." He sipped. I got my asking price on the garage, he thought. So that's that. That's how real estate transactions are handled; you set a price, and if someone meets it, that's a contract. Ask the broker.

No, he won't make a big scene, he thought. Maybe one of those glances, out of the corner of his glasses. And grin while he puffs on his cigarette. And he won't say anything; I'll have to do all the talking. He'll get me to talk more than I want to.

"You heard about me," he said when Betty came past him once more. "Selling the garage," he said. "Because of my health."

"I didn't know that," she said. "When did that happen?" Her

old wrinkled mouth fell open. "You mean your heart? I thought that was under control. You told me that doctor had it under control."

"Sure it's under control," he said, "if I didn't kill myself working on those cars, under there flat on my back lifting up an entire transmission. Those things weigh two hundred pounds. You ever try lifting one while lying flat on your back? Lifting it over your head?"

She said, "What are you going to do instead?"

"I'll tell you what I'll do," he said. "I'll get a well-earned rest. I certainly deserve that."

"I should say so," she said. "But I think—you could have tried that rice diet, couldn't you? Did you ever try that?"

"Rice doesn't help what I've got," he said, angry at her, at the crazy health food store with its vegetables and herbs. "That stuff is for neurotic middle-aged women."

She wanted to lecture him on diet. But he picked up his cup of coffee, nodded and murmured something, and went on outside, onto the sidewalk, carrying the cup back to the garage.

A lot of sympathy from her, he thought. Advice instead; who wants that from nuts?

God, he saw the old green Plymouth parked in the lot, beside the other old cars that Al had patched up to sell. By the little house with its banner. An engine, somewhere on the lot, ran loudly, raced. He's back there, he realized. Working. Holding the cup ahead of him he passed on into the gloomy damp garage. Out of the sunlight. His steps made echoing sounds.

There stood Al.

"I sold the garage," Jim said.

"You did?" Al said. He held a crescent wrench. He still had on his cloth jacket.

"That's what I want to talk to you about," Jim said. "I was looking for you. I was amazed that the guy finally met my price; I had it way up there, as I probably told you. I think I said I was asking around thirty thousand for it, when we were discussing it a month or so ago. My broker called me at home last night."

Opening and closing the wrench with his thumb, Al stared at him. He did not look as if it meant too much to him, but the old man was not fooled. The black brows remained the same. So did the man's mouth. It did not come up, the feeling. Behind the glasses the eyes shone, kept fixed on him. He seemed to be smiling.

"You want me to croak under some car?" Jim said.

"No," Al said, after a time. He still played with the wrench.

"This doesn't affect your lot," Jim said. "You have a lease. I think that runs until April." He knew it ran until April. Five months. "Why the hell wouldn't he renew? He'll probably renew."

Al said, "Maybe he wants it."

"When he came by," Jim said, "he showed no interest in it."

"He's not going to turn the garage into anything else?"

"What can you turn a garage into?" But he did not know; he had not wanted to find out because he did not care to think about anyone else running the garage—it did not matter to him what Epstein did with it: burned it down or paved it with gold or made a drive-in out of it. And then he thought, Maybe he will make a drive-in out of it. He can use the lot for parking. So there goes Al's Motor Sales, as soon as the lease expires. But he can drive his cars somewhere else. Any vacant lot will do, anywhere in Oakland. As long as it's on a business street.

Later on he sat in his office, at the desk. Through the dusty window sunlight entered, warming and lighting up the office, the one dry spot in the garage, here with the piles of invoices, repair manuals, the calendars with nude girls advertising Test-High Bearings and Sheet Metal of Emeryville, California. He pretended to consult a chart of lubrication points for a Volkswagen.

I've got thirty-five thousand dollars, he thought, and I'm spending my time worrying because some guy who leases a lot that's part of this place is maybe going to suffer through no fault of mine. That's what people can do to you, make you feel bad when you ought to be feeling good. That God damn Al, he thought.

They all envy a man who's successful, he thought. What does he have to show for possibly ten years of work? I already owned this place when I was his age. He's just a tenant. And always will be.

I can't let it worry me, he decided, because I have plenty of worries anyhow; I have to worry about myself, my physical condition.

That comes first.

What a waste it had all been. All the work. Devotion to fixing people's cars. At any time he could have sold out and got the same amount of money. Possibly more, because now he could not wait. And he had not managed to keep it quiet, the reason for his selling. He should have kept it under his hat. But instead he had gone around trying to justify himself because he knew that certain persons would do their best to make him feel guilty. And so they had. Look at just now.

All those years, he thought. And before, trying different things. Had he learned anything? His father had wanted him to be a pharmacist. His father had owned a drugstore in Wichita, Kansas. After school he had helped his father, at first opening cartons in the stockroom, then later on waiting on customers. But he had not gotten along with his father, and he had quit and gone to work as a busboy at a restaurant. And later he was a waiter. After that he had left Kansas.

In California he and another man had operated a gas station. Running the gas pumps had been too much like working in his father's drugstore; it meant he had to talk cheerfully to people, sell them things. So he had let his partner do that; he had taken on the greasing and repairing part, in the back, out of sight. He had been good enough so that when he opened his own garage his customers had come with him. Some of them still came now, almost twenty-five years later.

It's fine for them, he said to himself. I kept their cars going. They can call me any time, day or night; they know I'll always come and tow them in or fix them where they are, broken down at the side of the road. They don't have to belong to A.A.A. even, because they have me. And I never cheated them or did work that didn't need to be done. So naturally, he thought, they'll be unhappy to hear I'm quitting. They know they'll have to go to one of those new garages where everything's clean, no grease anywhere, and some punk comes out in a white suit with a clipboard and fountain pen, *smiling*. And they tell him what's wrong and he writes it down. And some union mechanic shows up later in the day with one finger stuck up his ass and leisurely works on their car. And every minute they're paying. That slip goes into that machine, and it keeps count. They're paying while he's on the crapper or drinking a cup of coffee or talking on the phone or to some other customer. It'll cost them three or four times as much.

Thinking that, he felt anger at them, for being willing to pay all that to some lazy union mechanic they never saw and didn't know. If they can pay all that, why can't they pay it to me? he asked himself. I never charged no seven dollars an hour. Somebody else'll get it.

And yet he had made money. He always had more work than he could do, especially in the last few years. And he made money renting the lot next to the garage to Al Miller for a used-car lot. He gave Al advice on his old wrecks, and sometimes Al gave him a hand on heavy jobs which he could not manage alone. They had gotten along pretty well.

But what kind of guy is that to have to spend all day with? he asked himself. Some guy monkeying around with old cars, wrecks, maybe selling one a week. Wearing the same dirty pair of jeans month in, month out. In debt to everybody; not even able to have a phone after the phone company took it away because of non-payment. And he'll never be able to get one again, as long as he lives.

I wonder what it's like not to be able to have a phone, he thought. To have to resign yourself to giving that up.

I wouldn't give it up, he decided. I'd get together some money and pay off the bill and come to terms with them. After all, that's how they make their money: selling phone service. They'd come around.

I'm fifty-eight years old, he said to himself. I've got a right to retire, heart or no heart. Wait'll he's my age. He'll see what it's like being scared you're going to drop dead every time you pull a wheel off a car.

A terrible fantasy came to him then. One that he had made up before. He lay under a car; he felt it on him. He tried to breathe, to yell for help, but the weight flattened his chest. All he could do was lie, like a turtle or a bug, on his back. And then Al came along, into the garage as he always did, wandering through the side door with a part of a distributor.

Al came up to the car. He looked down. He saw the old man flat on his back, pinned under the car, staring up, unable to speak.

He stood for a minute. He did not even put down the part he carried. His eyes roamed around; he saw that the hydraulic jack had slipped, the most terrible thing possible. It had slipped out from under the differential or the hose had come loose or something; anyhow it had let the car down on the old man, and it might have been a couple of hours ago. The old man could only stare up at him; he could not even talk. His chest was completely broken.

The car had crushed him, but he was still alive. He pleaded silently to be released. To be helped.

Al turned and walked off, carrying his distributor part. He went out of the garage again.

Seated at his desk, Jim felt the fear, the crushing. He kept his eyes fixed on the Volkswagen lube chart; he turned his attention to the dusty window, the nude-girl calendars, the invoices, the list of parts suppliers. But he still saw himself; he saw from outside his own prone, dying, smashed, bug-like body under the car, under the—what was it?—the Chrysler Imperial. And Al walking out.

All my life, he thought. As long as I've been in the garage business; I've been scared of it. Of the jack slipping. Being alone here, nobody coming in for hours. Maybe last thing in the day, around five p.m. And nobody coming in until next day.

But then his wife would call. Worse if it was early.

Nobody would do that, he said to himself. Leave a man pinned under a car. Just to get even. Not even Al.

I can't tell about him, he thought. He doesn't show his feelings. He could go either way.

And then, thinking that, he had another fantasy, one he had never had before. He saw, as clearly as before, the same scene, with Al coming in and finding him. But this time Al running, Al pulling the car off him, running to phone; then the ambulance coming, all the noise and excitement, the doctors, the stretcher, the trip to the hospital. And Al hanging around, seeing that they all did right, seeing that he was given the right medical treatment and right away. So he recovered. It was in time.

Sure, he might do that. He can work fast. Thin guys like that, who don't carry much weight—they can really move.

But this fantasy, of Al finding him and saving him, made him feel no better. In fact it made him feel worse. But he did not know why. God damn it, he thought. I don't need him to save me; I can take care of myself. I'd a lot rather he did walk off. It's none of his business.

He put down the Volkswagen chart and opened the indexed pad by the phone. In a moment he had dialed his broker, Matt Pestevrides, and had the secretary on the line.

"Hello," he said, when he had got hold of Matt. "Listen, how long am I stuck here? Now that the sale's gone through."

"Oh, you can figure on about sixty days," Matt said in a cheerful voice. "That'll give you plenty of time to wind up your affairs. I imagine you want to say goodbye to all your customers, all your old customers who've been coming in for so long. Like myself."

"Okay," he said, and hung up. Two months, he thought. Maybe I can come in just part of the day. And I won't take in anything heavy. Just easy stuff to do; the doctor said so.

2

In front of Al's Motor Sales, Al Miller walked back and forth, his hands in his pockets.

I knew he would, Al thought. Sooner or later. He couldn't just turn it over to someone else to run. Once he couldn't run it himself he had to dump it.

What now? he asked himself. I can't patch these old jalopies up without him. I'm not that good. I'm a tinkerer, not a mechanic.

He turned and faced his lot, and the twelve cars on it. What are they worth? he asked himself. On the windshields he had written, in white poster paint, various enticing statements. "Full price $59. Good tires." And, "Buick! Automatic shift. $75." "Spotlight. Heater. Make offer." "Runs good. Seatcovers. $100." His best car, a Chevrolet, was only worth a hundred and fifty dollars. Junk, he thought. They ought to be scrapped for the parts. Not safe on the road.

Next to a '49 Studebaker, the battery charger worked away,

recharging, its black wires disappearing into the open hood of the car. It takes that to start them up, he realized. A portable battery charger. The batteries, half of them won't hold a charge all night. They're down in the morning.

Each morning when he arrived at the lot he had to get into each car and start it up and run the motor. Otherwise when someone came to look he would have nothing running to show them.

I ought to call Julie, he said to himself. This was Monday, so she was not at work. He started toward the entrance of the garage, but then halted. How can I talk from there? he asked himself. But if he crossed the street to the café and phoned from there, it would cost him ten cents. The old man always let him use the garage phone free, and so it was hard to face the idea of paying out ten cents.

I'll wait, he decided. Until she shows up here at the lot.

At eleven-thirty his wife drew up to the curb in a lot car, an old Dodge with the upholstery hanging from the roof, its fenders rusted and its front end out of alignment. She smiled at him cheerfully as she parked.

"Don't look so happy," he said.

"Does everybody have to be as gloomy as you?" Julie said, as she hopped out of the car. She had on faded jeans, and her long legs looked thin. Her hair was tied back in a pony-tail. In the mid-day sunlight her freckled, slightly orange-colored face beamed its usual confidence; her eyes danced as she strode toward him, her purse under her arm. "Have you had lunch?" she said.

Al said, "The old man sold the garage. I have to close up the lot." He heard his tone; it was as dire as possible. It was obvious even to him that he wanted to destroy her mood; he did it without guilt, too. "So don't be so jolly," he said. "Let's be realistic. I can't keep these heaps working without Fergesson. Christ, what do I know about car repair? I'm just a salesman." In his most depressed moods he thought of himself that way: as a used car salesman.

"Who'd he sell it to?" she said. Her smile remained, but it was cautious now.

"I couldn't tell you," he said.

She started at once toward the entrance of the garage. "I'll ask," she said. "I'll find out what they're going to do; you don't have sense enough to find out." She disappeared inside the garage.

Should he follow her? He did not feel much like seeing the old man again. But on the other hand, it was his job to discuss the thing, not his wife's. So he followed along, knowing that her quick, long-legged stride would get her inside well before him. And sure enough, when he entered the garage, and his eyes had had time to adjust to the dim light, he found her standing with the old man, in conversation.

Neither paid him any attention as he came slowly up.

Speaking in his usual hoarse, low voice, the old man was explaining what he had explained to Al; he went over the same ground, in almost the same words. As if, Al thought, it was a set speech he had put together. The old man told her that the choice was not his, as she well knew, because his doctor had told him he could no longer do the heavy kind of work that auto-repairing entailed, and so forth. Al listened without interest, standing so that he could look outside, at the bright midday street and the cars and people going by.

"Well, I'll tell you what I think," Julie said in her brisk voice. "This might turn out to be a good thing because possibly now he can go back to school."

At that, Al said, "Christ."

The old man regarded him, rubbing his right eye, which had become red and swollen; it had something in it, evidently. Reaching into his hip pocket he brought out a large handkerchief and began touching the corner of it to his eye. He regarded both Al and Julie with what seemed to Al to be cunning and nervousness mixed together. The old man had made up his mind; he had decided on his position, not only regarding his garage, but regarding the two of them. Whether he felt he had done right or not by them did not matter. He would not budge. Al knew him well enough to know that; the old man was too stubborn. Even Julie, with her authoritative tongue, couldn't affect him.

"I tell you," the old man mumbled. "It's a lousy life, working in this damp drafty place. It's a wonder I didn't die years ago. I'll be glad to get out of here; I deserve a vacation."

Julie said, her arms folded, "You could have included a stipulation in the sale that the new owner had to continue the lease of the lot to my husband for the same figure."

Ducking his head, the old man said, "Well, I don't know. That's up to my broker; I let him handle all that."

His wife's face had become red. Al had rarely seen her as angry as this; her hands were shaking, and that was why she had folded her arms. She was hiding her hands. "Listen," she said in a high-pitched voice. "Why don't you just die and will the garage to Al? I mean, you don't have any children, any family." She was silent then. As if, Al thought, she knew she had said something bad. And it was bad, he thought. It was unfair. The garage was the old man's. But of course Julie would never admit that; she would not be bound by facts.

"Come on," Al said to her. Taking hold of her arm he forcibly moved her away from the old man, who was mumbling something in answer, toward the entrance and the street.

"It makes me so furious," she said, as they came out into the sunlight. "He's really senile."

"Senile, hell," Al said. "He's a smart old man."

"Like an animal," she said. "Without regard to others."

"He's done a lot for me," he said.

"If you sold all the cars on the lot," she said, "how much would you get?"

"About five hundred bucks," he said. But it would be a little more than that.

"I can go back on full time," she said.

Al said, "I'll shop around for another location."

"You told me you couldn't do it without his help," she said. "You said you don't have enough capital to buy cars that you can put up for sale without—"

"I'll make a deal with another garage," Al said.

Julie said, "This is the time for you to go back to school." She halted and faced him firmly.

In her mind, he needed a college degree. He needed to go three more years—he had gone to the University of California for one year—and then he would be able to get what she called a good job. His degree would be in a practical subject; business administration had been her choice. In his one year he had had no major. He had taken only a general course, a little of this and that. It had not appealed to him and so he had not gone back.

For one thing, he did not like to be indoors. Perhaps that was why the used-car business attracted him; he could be outside all day long, in the sun. And of course he was his own boss. He could come and go as he pleased; he could open the lot at eight or nine or ten, go to lunch at one or two or three. Stay half an hour, or a whole hour, or even eat his lunch in one of the cars.

He had built a little building in the center of the lot, out of basalt blocks. It had aluminum window units which he had picked up wholesale; in fact, the wiring, too, had come wholesale, and the roofing, as well as the fixtures. It was almost a house, and he thought of it as such, a house he had built with his own hands, which belonged to him, in which he could go whenever he wanted and stay, out of sight, as long as he wanted. In it he had an electric heater, a desk, a file cabinet; he had magazines to read, and his business papers. Sometimes he had a typewriter which he rented at five dollars a month. Formerly he had had a phone, but that was gone for good.

If he moved, if he gave up the lot, he would take the house with him. It belonged to him; it was his personal property, as were the cars. Unlike the cars, it was not for sale. One other object which was not for sale and which belonged to him would go along, too. Like the house, he had built it. In the rear of the lot, out of sight, he had a car he had been working on for months. When he had any spare time he turned to it.

The car was a 1932 Marmon. It had sixteen cylinders and it weighed over five thousand pounds. In the days when it had been in running condition it had gone up to a hundred and seven miles an hour. It had been, in fact, one of the finest autos in the United States, and it had originally cost five thousand five hundred dollars.

A year ago, Al had come across the old Marmon in a shed. Its condition was deplorable, and he had, after several weeks of haggling, been able to pick up the car for one hundred and fifty dollars, including two extra tires. From what he knew about cars, he believed that when it was fully restored, the Marmon would be worth between two thousand five hundred and three thousand dollars. So, at the time, it had seemed to be a good investment. But for the past year he had been at work on the task of restoration, and it was by no means finished.

One afternoon, while he had been working on the Marmon, he had looked up to see two colored men standing watching him. A good deal of the sidewalk traffic on the street was colored, and he sold as many cars to Negroes as to whites.

"Hi," he said.

One of the Negroes nodded.

"What that?" the other asked.

Al said, "A 1932 Marmon."

"Man," the taller of the two Negroes said. Both men were young. They wore sports coats and white shirts, without ties, and dark slacks. Both seemed well-groomed. One smoked a cigarette, the taller one who had spoken. "Listen," he said. "Maybe I bring my father to look at that. He like something like that to drive him in, when he got to go to visit in Florida."

The other Negro said, "Yeh, he old dad like to ride in a car like that. We go get him; you see."

Getting to his feet, Al said, "This is a collector's car." He then tried to explain to them that the car was not for sale; at least, not in the terms that they would understand. This was not transportation, he explained. This was a treasured heritage from the past, one of the superb old touring cars; in some ways, the finest of them all. And, as he talked, he saw that as a matter of fact they did understand; they understood perfectly. It was just what the taller Negro's old dad wanted to ride to Florida in. And, thinking about it, Al could see their point. It was just that this car was almost thirty years old, and not in running condition. It had not run in fact since before World War Two.

The taller Negro said, "You get that old car to run, and maybe we buy it from you." Both men were very grave; they nodded again and again. "How much you want?" the taller Negro asked. "What you asking for that car, once you get it runnin' again?"

Al said, "About three thousand dollars." And that, certainly, was the truth. That was what it was worth.

Neither of the two men batted an eye. "That about right," the taller said, nodding. They exchanged glances, both nodding. "That about what we expect to pay," the taller Negro said. "Naturally we not pay that all at once. We work through our bank."

"That so," the other agreed. "We put about say six hundred down and the rest on time payment."

The two Negroes left presently, again telling him that they would return with the taller Negro's father. Naturally, he had not expected ever to see them again. But sure enough, the next day there they were again. This time they had with them a short, stout old Negro with vest and silver watch chain and shiny black shoes. The two younger men showed him the Marmon and explained, more or less, the situation that Al had put forth. After deliberation, the old man had come to the conclusion that the car would not do after all, and for what seemed to Al to be a supremely logical reason. The old man did not think that they would have much luck finding tires for it, especially along the highway, between major towns. So in the end the old man thanked him very formally and declined the car.

The encounter had stuck in Al's mind, possibly because after that he had seen a good deal of this particular group of Negroes. They were a family, named Dolittle, and the old gentleman with the vest and silver watch chain was well-to-do. Or at least his wife was. Mrs. Dolittle owned rooming houses and apartment buildings in Oakland. Some of them were in white neighborhoods, and she rented, through a building custodian, to whites. He had found out about this from the two younger men, and after a time he had been able to get a much better apartment for himself and Julie through these people. He and she were living there now, in a renovated three-story wooden building on 56th Street, near San Pablo; they had an upper floor, and it only cost them thirty-five dollars a month.

The reason for the low rent lay in two conditions. First, this particular building was in a non-exclusive neighborhood, which meant that there was a Negro family on the bottom floor and a Mexican boy and girl with their baby on the top floor. It did not bother him to live in the same building with Negroes and Mexicans, but the other condition did bother him; the wiring and the plumbing in the building were so bad that the Oakland city inspectors were on the verge of condemning the building. Sometimes shorts in the walls kept the power off for several days. When Julie ironed, the wall heated up too hot to be touched. All of the people in the building believed that eventually the building would burn to the ground, but most of them were out of it during the day, and they seemed to feel that because of that they were somehow safe. Once, the bottom of the hot-water heater rusted through, and water leaked out, snuffing out the gas jets and spilling across the floor so that it ruined most of Julie's rugs and furnishings. Mrs. Dolittle refused to make any sort of refund to them. They had all gone without hot water for almost a month, until at last Mrs. Dolittle had found some part-time plumber who could put in another worn-out hot-water heater for ten or eleven dollars. She had a staff of inferior workmen who could patch up the building just enough to keep the city from closing it on the spot; they kept it going day by day. It was her hope, he heard, to sell it eventually to be torn down. She thought that a parking lot might go in; there was a supermarket around the corner which was interested.

The Dolittles were the first middle-class Negroes that he had ever known or even heard of. They owned more property than anyone else that he had met since coming to the Bay Area from St. Helena, and Mrs. Dolittle—who personally ran the string of rental properties—was as mean and stingy as other landladies that he had run up against. Being a Negro had not made her any more humanitarian. She did not discriminate among the races; she ill-used all her tenants, white and dark alike. Mr. McKeckney, the Negro on the floor below, told him that she had originally been a schoolteacher. Certainly she looked like it; she was a tiny, sharp-eyed, gray-haired old woman, wearing a long coat, hat, gloves, dark stockings and high heels. It always looked to him as if she were dressed for church. From time to time she had terrible fights with other tenants in the building, and her shrill loud voice issued up from the floorboards or down from the ceiling, whichever place she was. Julie was afraid of her, and always let him deal with her. Mrs. Dolittle did not scare him, but she gave him something to ponder: the effect of property on the human soul.

Contrarily, the McKeckneys downstairs owned nothing. They rented a piano, and Mrs. McKeckney, who seemed to be in her late fifties, was learning to play on her own, from a book: *John Thompson's First Grade Piano Book*. Late at night, he heard Boccherini's Minuet, again and again, played deliberately, all notes getting equal emphasis.

During the day Mr. McKeckney sat outdoors in front of the building, on an apple crate which he had painted green. Later, someone provided him with a chair, probably the big German used-furniture merchant down the street. Mr. McKeckney sat for hours on end, nodding and saying hello to everyone who passed. At first Al was mystified by the McKeckneys' ability to survive economically; he could not make out any source of income. Mr. McKeckney never left the house and although Mrs. McKeckney was gone a good deal of the time, it was always for shopping or visiting friends or doing good works at the church. Later on, however, he learned that their children, who had grown up and left home, supported them. They lived, Mr. McKeckney told him proudly, on eighty-five dollars a month.

The little McKeckney grandson, when he came to visit, played by himself on the sidewalk or in the vacant lot at the corner. He never joined in with the gangs of kids who lived in the neighborhood year around. His name was Earl. He made almost no noise, scarcely talking even to the adults. At eight in the morning he would appear wearing wool trousers and a sweater, with a grave expression on his face. He had very light skin, and Al guessed that he was heir to a good deal of white blood. The McKeckneys left him to his own devices, and he seemed responsible enough; he kept out of the street and never set fire to anything, as did most of the neighborhood kids, white and colored and Mexican. In fact he seemed a cut above them, even aristocratic, and Al occasionally pondered as to his probable background.

Only once did he hear Earl raise his voice in anger. Across the street two bullet-headed white boys lived, both bullies, with time on their hands. They were the same age as Earl. When the mood came onto them they gathered green fruit, bottles, stones, and clods of dirt, and hurled them across the street at Earl, who stood silently on his sidewalk before his house. One day Al heard them yelling in their chilling voices: "Hey, you got an ugly mama."

They repeated that again and again, while Earl stood glowering silently back at them, his hands stuck in his pockets, his face becoming more and more stern. At last the taunts drove him to answer.

In a loud, deep voice he shouted, "Take care, little boys. Take care, little fellows, there."

It seemed to do it. The white boys went off.

Recollections, thoughts, filled Al's mind. The people who came to look at cars on his lot, kids without money, workmen who needed transportation, young couples; as he stood there in front of the garage with his wife he thought about them, not about what she was saying. She was speaking to him, now, about her own job as secretary at Western Carbon and Carbide; she was recalling to him her desire to quit entirely, someday. He would have to be making a lot more money for her to do that.

". . . You're hiding from life," Julie wound up. "You're looking at life through a tiny hole."

"Maybe so," he said, feeling glum.

"Off here in this run-down district." She gestured at the street of small stores, the barber shop, the bakery, the loan company, the bar across the street. The colon-irrigation outfit whose sign always upset her. "And I don't think I can stand living in that ratty apartment much longer, Al." Her voice had softened. "But I don't want to put pressure on you."

"Okay," he said. "Maybe what I need is to get my colon irrigated," he said. "Whatever that is."

3

That evening, as Jim Fergesson walked up the cement steps to the front door of his house, the Venetian shade behind the glass of the door shivered, moved aside; an eye, bright, wary, peeped out. And then the door swung open. There stood his wife, Lydia, chuckling aloud with pleasure, blushing to see him as she always did when he got home; it was her habit, due perhaps to her Greek origins. She ushered him inside, into the hall, talking quickly.

"Oh I'm so happy that you are finally home. What sort of a day did you have this time? Listen, do you know what I've done? In my desire to please, and I know it will please, guess what I've put on the stove for you, and it's cooking now!"

He sniffed.

Lydia said, "It's chicken; stewed chicken and spinach." She laughed as she led the way through the house ahead of him.

"I'm not hungry so much tonight," he said.

Turning, she said, "I can see you're in a bad mood."

He halted at the closet to hang up his coat. His fingers felt stiff and tired; Lydia watched with an alert, bird-quick expression.

"But now you're home, and so no reason to be in a grumbling mood," Lydia said. "Is that not right? Did something happen today?" At once her face became anxious. "Nothing happened, I trust. I know fervently that nothing in the world could happen."

He said, "I just had a little run-in with Al." Going past her he entered the kitchen. "This morning."

"Oh," she said, nodding in a somber manner, showing that she understood. Over the years she had learned to catch his moods and to reflect them, to line herself up—at least in appearance—with them, so that a communication could be brought about.

His wife was very much for that, for a full discussion of his problems; sometimes she made out things in his problems that he had missed. Lydia had gone to college. In fact she still took courses, some by mail. Being able to speak Greek, she could translate philosophers. And she knew Latin, too. Her ability to learn foreign languages impressed him, but on the other hand she had never been able to learn how to drive, even though she had gone to a driving school.

Still, she listened to what he had to say about cars, even though many of the notions made no sense to her. He had never found her unwilling to listen, no matter what the topic.

The table in the dinette had been set, and now Lydia moved about the kitchen, getting pans from the stove and transferring them to the table. He seated himself on the built-in bench and began unlacing his shoes. "Time for me to take a bath?" he said. "Before dinner?"

"Naturally," Lydia said, at once returning the pans to the stove. "You would no doubt feel much more at peace with the world if you took a bath."

So he went to the bathroom to take his bath.

Hot water roared down on him as he lay soaking; he kept the water going, more for the noise than anything else. Here, with the door shut and the steam rising and the noise, he felt relaxed. He shut his eyes and permitted himself to float a little in the almost totally filled tub. The tiles sparkled with drops of condensation. The walls, the ceiling, became damp; the bathroom fogged over, making the fixtures dim shapes, dripping and tenuous. Like a real steam bath, he thought. A Swedish steam bath, with attendants waiting, and white robes and towels. He rested his arms on the sides of the tub, and, with his toes, shut the stream of water down to a trickle; he arranged it so that the incoming water was exactly balanced by that drawn off by the spillover drain.

Here, now, away from the garage, shut in by himself in the warmth and dampness of this familiar bathroom—he had lived in this house for sixteen years—he felt no trouble. What a solid old house this was, with its hardwood floors, its glass-doored cupboards. The timbers had become like iron over the years, soaking up the anti-termite compounds that he lavished on them in the early fall. Over the outer boards coats of paint had become themselves a second house protecting the first, the inner wooden one. Even this, the enamel house which he had built up layer by layer over the years, would have been enough; after all, wasps made houses out of paper, and no one bothered them.

This was no paper house that he lived in. They can take those pigs, he thought. Those three; I got them beat all the way around. I could tell them a thing or two, even that last one, the pig that got the credit. Let me ask how long that house of his stood up. This'll be here long after. In those days, in the 'thirties, they really built. That was prewar; they didn't use any green lumber.

And, as he lay in the tub working the controls with his feet, he began to think. He thought—he let his thoughts go there—on that old topic. It came to him that there was such a thing as gain.

Yes, he thought, look what I got. I got thirty-five thousand dollars. What a lot of money.

And there's nothing I have to do, he thought. It's already in; it's in writing, a fact. Just lying here in this tub I'm waiting, and it's getting closer. I can count on it, without any work now.

So now he did not have to think of work. It had been work that had forced itself into his mind, over the years. They can take their damn cars, he thought, and stick them up their ass.

I think I'll never go back there, he decided. To the garage. I think I'll stay home.

You couldn't get me to go back there, he thought. And he looked with real anger on those who wanted to get him back; he felt real hate.

What'll I do with this money? he asked himself. This enormous sum, a sort of fortune. I'll tell you what I'll do; I'll leave it to my wife. This big sum paid to me for everything that I've done— I'll be dead, and she'll be spending it. And she doesn't even need it.

Has she stood by me? he asked himself. Worked at my side? I don't see it, if she has. It's the Oakland Public Library that she's supported, not me. It's the University of California and those professors, and especially those students in sweaters. They dress nice and keep their nails cut. They have plenty of time and training to know to do that.

At the door of the bathroom a faint noise attracted his attention. The knob turned, but the door did not open; it was locked.

"What is it?" he yelled.

"I wanted—" His wife's voice, cut off by the noise of water.

He shut off the water. "It's locked," he yelled.

"Do you have a towel?"

"Yes," he said.

After a pause she said, "Dinner is ready. I want it to be exactly right for you."

"Okay," he said. "I'll be out."

Later, he sat across from Lydia at the dining table, drinking his soup. As always, she had fixed up the table; she had put on candles, a white tablecloth, and linen napkins. She wore a little jewelry, too, a necklace. And she had on rouge. Her black eyes shone and she smiled at him, an immediate smile as soon as she saw he was looking at her.

"Why so gloomy?" she said. "Is it not a lot more happier for yourself and all mankind to adopt a more pleasant exterior?" When he did not answer, she went on, "And eventually that affects the inner person, at least according to the magnificent psychology of William James and Lang."

He said, "You got that from your course?"

Briskly, with no intention of abandoning her mood, she replied, "Yes, I got that from my course, Mr. Terrible Gloom." She would fight a good fight for happiness, he saw. Her smile was enriched by determination; it defied him. Under all conditions, behind any reaction, she kept this, the faith; he would get nowhere.

In this house, he thought, in my house, I can't even be depressed. At least, not out loud. It's not permitted. Like dirt.

Swept out the door.

She moved a little faster. Her hands flew from butter plate to coffee cup to napkin. Lots of spunk, he thought. Where does it go, when I'm pushing up daisies? I'll push up—not daisies—but skunk cabbage, he decided. Imagine her at my grave with an armload of flowers from her garden in the back, roses and stuff; and there the skunk cabbage is, growing like hell. He laughed.

"Ah," she said in a full-throated voice.

It came to his attention, watching her, that she was a lot younger than he. Of course he knew that, always had the fact available. But he did not usually dwell on it. Her hands. Still smooth. Well, she didn't have to scrub them with Dutch Cleanser four times a day. Who did the floors in the house? She had a colored girl come in twice a week; that girl did the heavy work, the dirty stuff. Lydia did only the dusting, the dishes, the shopping, fixing the meals; the rest of the time she was out learning.

"What did you learn?" he said. "Today."

"Are you interested?" she said in a merry voice.

"Sure," he said. "Since I pay for it."

"Money," she said, "is the arbiter of worth in a society of barbarians, who identify themselves by when they see a sacred tablet in the temple made of gold." Her eyes fixed themselves on him. No timidity, there.

He said, "You're going to be a pretty big-time barbarian, one of these days."

The eyes continued. Watching.

"Thirty-five thousand," he said, with such fury that she did, at last, cease smiling. "Why don't you start a fund? The Fergesson Fund for Bums. Pay bums to sleep all day." His voice rose. "In the parlor," he shouted. "On the couch." His voice, squeaky, shook. "Here in my house!"

She said nothing. Watched.

"Maybe I go see Louis Malzone," he said. "My attorney. Maybe I take the trouble to invest the money in bonds." But why? he asked himself. Because she got it in the end anyhow, for nothing, for doing nothing. And he, for all he had done; what did he get?

But he felt tired. He ate his roll, spread butter—real butter—on it. And all the time she watched.

"Describe to me this run-in you had with Al," she said.

He said nothing. He ate.

"That is responsible for this overpowering incorrect view of things as they are," she said.

At that, he laughed.

"That man," she said. "Such a deliberate waste of his life, as he reveals. And his attitude toward others for what actually lies inside his own inner reality. When he and his wife—the latter whom I care a great deal for, as you know—appeared in this house for dinner on that particular Sunday afternoon, I had an even stronger impression than ever before."

"What impression?"

Lydia said, "Are you not acquainted with my impression? Why that is I could not say. I know in the past I took pains to discuss it with you. How long is it that he has rented the lot next to you for his cars? At this point a number of years. During that period I can see in you a change. There is no coincidence. What is it that I remarked when you arrived home tonight? That you were in a bad mood. I am familiar with that mood. Formerly you did not return home so much in that mood. What is he in your life? He indicates to you the absolute stupidity, without hope. Man making himself stupid. But it is you that take onto yourself for nothing at all *responsibility*."

Looking up, he saw that she was pointing her finger at him and frowning.

"Because," she said, "he has marred his own life with doing nothing, he manages to make you feel that you owe him something, but in fact you owe him to leave. To have him leave."

Fergesson said, "Just because he dresses bad."

"What, my good dear?"

"Christ," he said. "He tripped over the God damn ashtray. What about that? All this theory stuff, and you know what it is? It's nothing but he tripped over the ashtray that first time he came here. And the way he dresses."

"Pardon me," Lydia said. "Because I know better, my good dear. That man has contempt. Tell me. What is his preference?"

He did not understand; his wife had gone into her rapid Greek kind of speech, and when she did so, when she was this way, most of what she said was lost to him.

Lydia explained, "What is the church of his faith?"

"How do I know," he said.

"None," she said.

"Maybe so," he said.

"Do you know," she said, "that what a man believes about God is actually as Freud showed his attitude toward his father? And a man who has no ability to find in himself any proper reverence in the Heavenly Father, which is a good word, has no father here on earth that he relies on? I want to know what you think about this. What makes the character in this old world of ours? The family. It is in the family that the laughing little baby grows. Who peers down at him over the edge of the blessed cradle?"

"His mother," Fergesson said.

"His mother," Lydia said, "is known to him through the tit, the source of eternal plenty."

"Okay," he said, "but he also sees her."

"He experiences her as nectar," Lydia said; "as the food of the gods. But the father he gets nothing from. There is between him and the father a separation. Whereas with the mother there is unity. Do you see?"

"No," he said.

"The father," she said, "is all society and his relation to it. Once he has that he never outgrows it. But if he doesn't have it, he can never get it."

"Get what?" he said.

Lydia said, "The trust and hope."

"I give up," he said. "You better throw in a course in English, along with the Plato."

"I know," Lydia said, "that if you had got a happier man in

with you, you would not now look forward so emptily. Another man, in your place, retiring with so much accumulated wealth—what would be in his mind? Let me see it and depict it to you, my good dear. Joy."

"Joy," he echoed, with bitterness and some amusement.

"The joy of tomorrow," his wife said.

"I'm sick," he said. "Tired and physically sick. Ask the doctor. Ask Dr. Fraat. Call him up. I mean, ask what the facts are, instead of spinning a lot of philosophy. At my expense! What am I supposed to do, start taking great books courses along with you? Reading those guys? What do you know? I'd like to see you fix any simple thing there is, like a lightcord plug. Fix that and then come to me."

"You're so much like that man," she said.

He grunted and sat rubbing his forehead.

"He is that part of you," she said. "But you are more. He is nothing but that. Nothing but defeat. Because he lacks that faith."

At last he resumed eating his dinner, drinking his soup and spooning up the stewed chicken with its cooked, soft, colorless bones.

After dinner Jim Fergesson did something that had become natural to him, in the recent years. He turned on the TV set and placed his overstuffed easy-chair before it.

Not again, his wife would have said, had she still been home. But tonight Lydia had a seminar; she had been picked up by a car—it had honked once, and out she had gone with her books, wearing her coat and low-heeled shoes. And so she was not here to say it.

His mind, however, said it for her.

On the screen, Groucho Marx insulted some man who had come up, grinning, wearing a suit. No matter what Groucho said, the man continued to grin. It was all fun. Watching, Jim Fergesson found himself stirring with restlessness. At last he shut off the set.

Is that all they have now? he asked himself. He turned the set on briefly, trying the other channels. Westerns, a panel discussion . . . he shut it off. Bunch of goofs, he thought. Especially those fairies, those grinning guys who play up to the ladies, give away dishes, kiss old ladies on the cheek. Ask moronic questions; a quiz. Good they got the big crooks, he thought. At least that's gone. Especially that one, that intellectual. What a crook he was. Lydia had liked him so much, that Van Doren. He really took them in, the old man thought. But he never took me in with those manners. That educated crap. That polished front they teach them.

Going to the closet he got his coat. He did something that, although not usual, had come to him now and then in the past. Going downstairs to the street he locked the front door of the house (too bad, if she doesn't have her key) and got into his parked car. A moment later he was driving along the dark street, in the direction of San Pablo Avenue, and his garage.

That's what college ought to do, he thought as he drove. Give you the knowledge to tell a good man when you meet one. But look at Lydia, taken in by Van Doren. And look at Alger Hiss; look at how they all fell for him because he had that refined look, that thin face, the dignity and bearing and breeding, even though he was a Communist spy . . . even Stevenson fell for him. We might have had a President who would deliver the country over to those State Department Harvard queers in their striped pants. The only man who really saw through that was old Joe, and they got him; they ganged up on him because he was too blunt. He called a spade a spade.

He thought, Joe McCarthy saw through the lies and fraud that runs this society. And how he's dead because of it.

When San Pablo Avenue appeared ahead, with its light, Jim Fergesson kept to the curb lane; he slowed his car, but not at his garage. Instead, he stopped a block away at a red neon sign: THE RING-A-DING CLUB, a bar that he visited when the mood came to him.

Quite a few people were in the bar; as he opened the door, noise spilled out over him, pleasing him. And the smells of people, the good warm smells; companionship, laughter, the racket of life—its characteristic motion and color. At the bar he found himself a place to stand, and ordered a Burgie.

There were even a few women in the bar. Mostly older, however. A glance showed him that they were shrill bags. He turned away.

By the entrance a tall middle-thirties Negro in a topcoat and tan sweater was blowing up a balloon. On the floor beside him a plump black and white springer spaniel panted and lolled its tongue. Everybody seemed to be watching the dog. The Negro blew on the balloon and it expanded; the people around him shouted different things, suggestions.

What's this? Fergesson wondered. He turned to watch.

The dog, gasping, had risen on his haunches. His eyes were fixed on the balloon, which was now as large as a melon. The balloon was colored red. The man, laughing, lifted it away from his mouth and wiped his lips with the side of his hand. He was laughing too hard to blow.

"Here," a companion said, reaching. "Give it to me, man."

"No, you let me blow it; he like it better if I blow it." The man blew again; the balloon swelled and the dog watched. Suddenly the man's shoulders heaved and he dropped the balloon. The balloon fizzled away, darting. Hands flapped at it as it bounced to the floor. The dog whined and ran at it, then away again. His round body twitched. Leaning against the wall the man laughed soundlessly, and his friends groped among the tables and chairs for the empty balloon.

"I got more," the man said, reaching into his topcoat pocket. Balloons spilled out like the fingers of gloves. "Man," he gasped, "I got all the balloons in the world; let that go: it dirty."

This time he blew up a yellow balloon. The dog's tongue went in and out and he swallowed. Strange, Fergesson thought. Why's the dog interested? He thought about his own dog, dead under the wheels of a customer's car. The dog had slept in the garage, under cars being worked on. Several years ago, now.

The yellow balloon had been blown up, and the Negro tied a knot in its neck. The dog, on his feet, whined avidly and lifted and lowered his head.

"Throw it for him," a woman urged. "Don't make him wait."

"Go on," a man at a table said.

"Yes, go on and let it go."

The Negro, raising the balloon up high, let it fall. The dog caught it on his nose and bunted it. Up went the balloon, and drifted across a table. The dog followed and again he bunted it; the balloon rose and fell and the dog kept beneath it. People got out of his way. The dog scampered in a circle, his plump body pinwheeling and his mouth open. He saw nothing but the balloon, and when he crashed into a man the man moved and the dog went on.

Fergesson said to the man next to him, "Hey, they ought to commit that dog." He began to laugh. He laughed until he felt tears coming out of his eyes; he leaned back against the bar and yelled with laughter. The dog tumbled across chairs and people's feet, lunged at the balloon, knocked it again and again into the air, and then, in his excitement, bit into the balloon and popped it.

"Yaf!" the dog wheezed, and stopped short. His eyes smeared over and he sat breathing in huge, rough gulps. He seemed dazed.

The fragments of the balloon were picked up by a young colored man in a purple shirt who examined them and then put them in the pocket of his sports coat.

"Jesus," Fergesson said, wiping his eyes. The dog has settled down to rest and the man was again blowing up a balloon. This one was blue. "There he goes again," he said to the man next to him, who also watched, grinning. "What does he do, go on all night? Doesn't he get tired?"

"That's enough," the Negro said, letting the air out of the balloon.

"No, go on," a woman said.

"One more," a man at the bar said.

"He too tired," the owner of the dog said, stuffing the balloon back into his pocket, "Later, maybe."

To the man beside him, Fergesson said, "It doesn't make sense. What's the dog get out of it?"

The man shook his head, grinning.

"It's contrary to nature," Fergesson said. "It's perverted. He probably thinks about nothing but balloons all day and night. Nothing but balloons."

"Worse than some people," the man beside him said.

"Animals have no sense," Fergesson said. "They don't know when to stop. They get an idea, and that's all there is. They never lose it."

"Instinct," the man beside him said.

The dog's owner, the tall Negro, moved from table to table with an open cigar-box. Bending, he spoke to persons and some of them dropped coins into the box. He reached the bar.

"For the dog," he said. "He want to go to school and learn a trade."

Fergesson put a dime in. "What's his name?" he said. But the Negro had gone on.

"That colored guy," the man next to Fergesson said, "probably trained him for TV. They have those dog acts on all the time."

"They used to," Fergesson said. "Not so much anymore. Now it's mostly westerns, mostly for kids. I sure can't watch them."

"You think if you saw this on TV, this dog chasing a balloon, you'd laugh?"

"Sure, I'd laugh," Fergesson said. "Didn't you see me just now? I was laughing pretty hard. That's exactly what I want to see on TV, real entertainment."

"I don't think it would be funny on TV," the man said, "on that small screen."

"I've got a twenty-six-inch screen," Fergesson said. He decided to ignore the man; sipping his beer he gazed off in the other direction.

There, in a booth, sat Al Miller. With him was his wife Julie. And with them was the Negro in the topcoat who owned the dog; the Negro was talking to them, and all three seemed to be having a good time, and to be absolutely friendly.

In fact, from the way Al was gesturing, Jim Fergesson realized suddenly that he was stoned.

This was the first time that he had seen Al really drunk. Now and then he had seen him when he had had a few drinks, such as when he had come to dinner; his coordination had been bad, but that was not like this. This was the real thing, and the old man chuckled. He turned so that he could watch. So even gloomy Al, who always went around hunched over, never joking or laughing except maybe in sarcasm—even he let down once in a while. The guy, the old man thought, was actually human after all. He thought, Maybe I'll go over and join him. What about that?

Watching, he saw that Al was trying to buy the dog from the colored man. He was offering him a check, which he had in front of him and was writing with his fountain pen. Julie was trying to pull the check away from him; she shook her head no, and scowled and talked to both men. She had one hand on Al's shoulder and the other on the Negro's.

To the old man, that seemed funny, so funny that again he began to laugh; tears again came to his eyes. He set down his drink and got to his feet. Cupping his hands to his mouth he yelled across the noisy bar, "Hey Al, that's just the business for you."

It did not seem as if Al had heard him; the business negotiations continued, both men deeply engrossed. So he yelled again.

This time Al glanced up. His glasses were missing, and his hair hung down over his eyes. Without his glasses his eyes had a weak, unfocused look; he peered about half-blindly, and then returned to the negotiations. He tore up the check with great labored twists of his fingers, scattered the pieces, got out his wallet, and began writing another check in its place.

Chuckling, the old man swung back to the bar and picked up his beer. What a business for Al Miller, he thought. The perfect business. A dog that bunted colored balloons in bars; and Al could pass the hat for the dog. He thought, So the dog can go to school instead of Al.

"Hey," he yelled, again turning. But his voice was lost in the noise. "It can go to school in your place, and get that degree."

This time Al did hear him; he saw the old man and waved his hand in greeting.

The old man slid from his spot at the bar and made his way carefully through the crowd of people over to the booth. It was really hard to hear; even when he got over to the booth he could not make out Al's words. Bending down, he rested his hand against the side of the booth, his head close to Al's.

"I couldn't hear you," Al yelled up.

"Send the dog to school," the old man said, chuckling at what he had said, at what he had thought up. "Instead of you." He winked at Julie, but she stared past him.

Al said, "Hell, I'm buying it to kill it. I hate the God damn thing. It's an abomination."

"Oh," the old man said, still laughing. He hung around for a time, but none of them paid attention to him; they were too involved in their transaction.

"This is Tootie Dolittle," Al said presently, introducing the Negro, who glanced up and nodded formally. "A relative of mine."

The old man murmured something, but did not try to shake hands.

"I guess I'll be going," he said. They had not asked him to sit down. Now his laughter had gone. It did not seem so funny, and he felt tired. I still have to get over to the garage and work, he recalled. I can't stick around here, and what the hell if they don't want me to sit down. "So long," he said.

Al nodded as the old man moved away.

I wouldn't have sat down anyhow, he thought as he pushed the door of the bar open and stepped out onto the cold sidewalk. The fresh air blew around him as he walked toward his parked car. He took several deep breaths, which cleared his head at once. Hell, he thought. When do I sit down with Negroes?

He started up his car and drove the block or so to the garage.

Soon he was beneath a Studebaker, alone in the damp partly-lit building, his radio playing from its shelf. As he unfastened the crankcase pan of the car he thought, Why am I here doing this? Lying on his back, beneath the car . . . alone in the garage, with no one even knowing he was there. What was the purpose of it?

But he continued, unscrewing the bolts. Laboring away. So the guy can have it back tomorrow? he asked himself. Obligation to my old customers? Maybe it was that. He did not know. All he knew was that he had no other place to go, no other spot to be. There was really no problem, because he came here without deliberation; he came because he had always come. When there was nothing on TV to watch, or Lydia was out and there was no one to talk to, or things were not too interesting at the Ring-a-Ding Club.

I'll work an hour or so, he decided. And then call home and see if Lydia's back. That won't be so long to work.

4

It seemed clear to Al Miller that soon he would have to give up his lot. He would be pre-empted for some grand purpose: the new owner would tear down the garage and put up a supermarket or a furniture mart or multiple-unit apartments. Such had been the pattern for several years in Oakland and Berkeley. Old buildings were being torn down, even old churches. And if old churches had to go, then surely Fergesson's garage could be thrown in. And Al's Motor Sales.

With no spirit he drove the next afternoon down San Pablo to a realtor's office, to a woman that he had dealt with in the past. It was no accident that Mrs. Lane was a Negro; he had met her through the Dolittles. She had gotten Mrs. Dolittle several of her rental properties. Her specialty was business property in the non-restricted—he added in his mind, *run-down*—part of Oakland. He knew that he could hope for nothing better. What was a used-car lot, if not the embodiment of non-restricted Oakland?

Thinking that, he entered Lane Realty and approached the varnished oak counter. To his right, on a table, was a rubber plant in a pot with a saffron bow tied around it. Beside the plant was a stack of *Saturday Evening Post*s and an ashtray.

All that Lane Realty had in the way of fixtures were a desk and a typewriter, and, on the wall, a map of the East Bay. Mrs. Lane sat at the desk typing, but when she noticed him she rose and came toward the counter, smiling.

"Good morning, Mr. Miller," she said.

"Morning," he said.

"Now what can I do for you?" Mrs. Lane had a low, smooth voice. She wore a dark dress, and on her finger she had a nice big gold ring. Her hair had been done up, and she had on lots of makeup; as always she looked impressive. She was, he thought, about forty-five or fifty. She could have been a successful matronly receptionist or club woman anywhere, he thought, except of course that she was colored. And except for the fact, too, that when she smiled she made visible gold-capped front teeth of great size; jewelry, like her ring, the left of which showed the carving of a diamond, the right a club.

Al said, "I'm looking for a new location."

"I see," Mrs. Lane said. "On San Pablo? I have a lot on Telegraph Avenue." She looked at him searchingly, to see what it was he wanted.

"I don't care where it is," Al said. "Just so it's a good location." He could think of no way to improve on that utterance; he culled his brain, but no more expressive statement came. The woman smiled at him with sympathy; beyond any doubt she wanted to help him. It was her job to do so. And her heart was in her work. He felt that.

"I guess you don't want to go too high," Mrs. Lane said. "As far as rental costs."

"No," he agreed.

"I could drive you around to that location on Telegraph," Mrs. Lane said. "You could take a look at it."

"I don't need it right away," he said. "I have around two months. There's no rush. I want to be sure I get something good."

"Yes, that's the important thing," Mrs. Lane said.

"The used-car business doesn't pay very good," he said.

"Must be like the real-estate business," Mrs. Lane said, with a smile.

Maybe so, Al thought. We're both in the same boat. Or maybe I'm doing you an injustice, putting you with me. Placing you down at such a hopeless point. A personable woman like you. What would you be if you had been born white? County chairman of the Republican party? Wife of some industrialist? And what would I be if I had been born colored? Just a jerk. Another nowhere jerk.

"Mr. Miller," Mrs. Lane said in her smooth, deep voice, "you really look sad today."

"I am," he said, agreeing to that.

"Don't look so sad," she said. "Look on the bright side." She went back to her desk and got, from the drawer, a set of car keys. "Why don't I drive you over to the location I made mention of? I be glad to show it to you."

"Maybe later," he said.

"Why not now?"

"I don't know," he said, hearing himself mumble. "I have to get back to the lot."

"You might miss out on the opportunity," she said.

"Maybe so," he said, feeling dulled and weighed down.

"Listen, Mr. Miller," she said softly, leaning her bare, round, brown arms on the counter. "You got to act or you miss out. I know that one thing I learned from my years in real estate; if you want to get somewhere, you have to take advantage of the situation and move. Do you know that?" She waited, but he said nothing; he gazed down at the floor, feeling his mind too empty for any answer. "You have to do or you be done. I mean, they do *you*. It not wrong to be live-wire." Her voice had a warm, gentle patience, almost a lecturing quality, a mother-lecturing quality. "You not going to hurt anybody. I think that what bother you; you afraid you do something wrong to somebody. Because you in a business where everybody say that anyhow."

He nodded.

Mrs. Lane said, "I talk to you before and I remark to myself and Mr. Jones, who help me here. You're a good person to work with Mr.—what his name? Mr. Fergesson. He completely honest, too. I take my car to him . . ." Her voice trailed off. "Well, I have my own mechanic."

To himself, Al thought, A Negro mechanic. She wouldn't dare take her car to Jim Fergesson, honest as he is. Because he probably wouldn't work on her car. Maybe he would, maybe he wouldn't. But she can't take the chance. It isn't worth it.

"Can I show you that location?" Mrs. Lane said, holding up her car keys.

"No," he said. "Some other time. Thanks."

As he left the real-estate office, he saw that she was watching him go; she watched him until the side of the building cut off his sight of her and hers of him.

Going back, he said, speaking across the threshold, "Maybe in another couple of days. When my plans are more jelled."

Mrs. Lane smiled at him. With compassion, he thought. Compassion and understanding. He went on then. Back to his car.

He thought, She just wants to sell me something. But he knew it was more than that; not that at all, actually. What was it, then? Love, he thought. Love for him. Big, middle-aged, good-looking, light-skinned, Negro business woman, he thought. Wants to mother me, if possible. He felt depressed, and yet, at the same time, it seemed to him as if some of his burden had departed. He did not feel as bad as before. That's a smart woman, a smart saleswoman; she knows her stuff, he thought. A real professional. I'll be back. She knows that.

That peasant-minded, shrewd, cretin-brained old asshole Fergesson has put me here, he thought. Where I have to rely on this, on some woman feeling sorry for me. Where I have nothing else to get by on; I have no other way to survive, no system of my own. I have to appeal to the soft side of some woman real-estate broker.

What I ought to do, he thought, is ruin his sale, screw up his sale forever; I ought to open a whorehouse on the lot and bring disgrace on that location. I ought to turn it into a—what, that a used-car lot isn't already?

Who looks down on me? he asked himself. Everyone? Each person?

He did not feel like going back to his lot. He started up his car, driving in no particular direction; he merely drove through the downtown Oakland traffic, enjoying the feel of the car. It was a good solid old Chrysler with leather seats. The shift would not go into reverse, however, and so he had acquired it for seventy-five dollars. But still, it was a good car. Good enough for any reasonable person. A fine highway car.

As he drove along he conjured up, inside his mind, a sales presentation which would move this particular item; he dwelt on that, to keep himself occupied.

When he got back to Al's Motor Sales he saw that the big white door of the garage was shut. The old man had closed up the garage, but not for lunch, since the Pontiac was gone. The old-fashioned cardboard sign on the doors had the hands turned so that it all read:

WILL RETURN AT 2.30

As he parked amid the cars on the lot, he saw that a second car, a nearly new Cadillac, had followed him and was parking behind him, next to his Chevrolet. He got out, and so did the driver of the Cad.

"Hello," the man called.

Al shut the door of his car and walked toward the man. The man, in his early fifties, had on a smartly-tailored business suit, tie—the narrow fashionable type of tie—and the pointed Italian style of shoes that Al saw in the ads and uptown store-windows. The man smiled at him. He had a reasonably friendly manner. His hair was curly, gray, and although somewhat long, was strikingly cut. Al felt a little awed.

"Hi," Al said. "How are you, today?" It was his standard greeting.

On his lot there surely was nothing to interest this well-dressed and obviously well-to-do man, who drove last year's Cadillac. For an instant Al felt uneasy; perhaps this was a tax agent from the State, or even from the Federal Government—a host of ideas flew through his brain as he faced the man, keeping a smile of greeting on his face.

And then he recognized the man. This was one of Fergesson's old customers. Obviously the man had brought his car around to the garage for work, and found the garage shut.

"I'm looking for Jim," the man said, in a full, impressive voice. "I see the door's shut, though." He lifted his arm and looked at a wristwatch visible by the silver cuff-link. Al gazed at both the watch and the cuff-link, and a deep, perplexing yearning came up inside him. That was something he had always wanted: a good wristwatch, the kind he had seen advertised in the *New Yorker*.

Al said, "He's probably picking up a part. Or maybe somebody broke down on the road. They call in to him instead of the A.A.A."

"I can see why," the man said.

If I had even three good cars, Al thought, I could attract customers like this. If I had anything decent to show . . . he felt gloomy, and he put his hands into his pockets, rocking back and forth on his heels and staring down at the pavement. He could think of nothing to say.

"I've been coming to him for four and a half years," the man said. "For any little thing I need, even grease jobs."

Al said, "He sold the garage."

The man's eyes widened. With dismay, he said, "No."

"That's right," Al said. His gloom increased; he found it almost impossible to speak. So he continued rocking back and forth.

"Too old?" the man said.

"Heart or something," Al murmured.

"Well, I am certainly sorry," the man said. "Really sorry. It's the end of an era. The end of the old craftsmanship."

Al nodded.

"I haven't been in for a month or so," the man said. "When did he decide? He must have just decided."

"Yes," Al said.

The man put out his hand; Al noticed it, started, drew his own hand out and shook. "My name is Harman," the man said. "Chris Harman. I'm in the record business. I run Teach Records."

"I see," Al said.

"You don't think he'll be back," Harman said, again looking

at his watch. "Well, I can't wait. Tell him I was by. I'll call him on the phone and tell him how sorry I am. Good day." Nodding, and giving a friendly wave to Al, he got back into his Cadillac, shut the door, shifted into reverse, and, in a moment, had backed from the lot and out into the San Pablo traffic. Presently the Cadillac had disappeared from sight.

Half an hour later the old man's Pontiac appeared and parked. As Fergesson got out, Al walked up to him.

"An old customer of yours came by," he said. "He was sorry to hear you sold the garage."

"Who?" Fergesson said, as he unlocked the garage door and pushed it up with both hands. With a worried expression he started into the garage. "God damn," he said, "I'm really behind, now, with that job, having to go out like that."

"Harman," Al said, following along after him.

The old man said, "Yes, a '58 Cadillac. Good-looking guy, silver hair. Around fifty."

"Owns a record line or something," Al said.

The old man switched on a trouble lamp and dragged the long rubber cord across the grease-covered floor of the garage, toward a Studebaker which was up on the hoist. "You know that brick building up on 23rd, just off Broadway? Up where those new car agencies are? Near where you branch off to get to the lake? Anyhow, his place is up there. He owns the whole building; it's all his record company. He makes records. A presser."

"So he said," Al said. He waited for a time, watching the old man lie down on his back on the flat cart with its castors; Fergesson rolled skillfully beneath the Studebaker and resumed work.

"Listen," the old man said, from beneath the car.

Al bent down.

"He makes dirty records," the old man said.

At that, Al felt his scalp crawl. "That well-dressed guy? With that car?" He could hardly believe it; in his mind he would have pictured it completely the other way. A man who made dirty records . . . it would be a short, greasy, sloppily-dressed man, with perhaps green-tinted glasses, a furtive look, bad teeth, a hoarse voice, picking his teeth with a toothpick. "No kidding," he said.

"That's only one thing he makes," the old man said. "That's just between you and me; it's not public."

"Okay," Al said, interested.

"It's not his name on it, Teach Records. It's one of those party labels, I mean, no label at all."

"How do you know?"

"He came by about a year ago. He's been coming to me to get his car fixed for years. He brought a box of dirty records and wanted me to sell them."

Al laughed. "No kidding."

"I—" The old man wheeled himself out for a moment, lying on his back and looking up at Al. "I kept the box around for a while, but it didn't do anything. There were some folders." He got laboriously to his feet. "I think I've got a couple left. Sort of dirty-joke folders advertising the records."

"I'd like to see them," Al said. He followed the old man into the office, where he stood as the old man rummaged in the over-flowing desk drawers. At last, in an envelope, the old man came onto what he wanted.

"Here." He passed the envelope to Al.

Opening the envelope, Al found some glossily-printed small folders, the size to be put out in a little heap on a counter. A drawing on the front, of a nude girl, with the words SPREE RECORDS SUMMER FUN-FEST LIST (FOR MEN ONLY), and then, inside, a list of titles. The titles themselves had nothing dirty about them.

"Songs?" he said. "Like 'Ruth Wallace'?"

"Mostly monologues," the old man said. "I listened to one. It was about Eva crossing the ice; you know, in *Uncle Tom's Cabin.*"

"Was it dirty?"

"Really dirty," the old man said. "Every word I ever heard. Some guy was reading it. Harman said it was some great comedian who writes a lot—or wrote a lot; he said the guy was dead, I think—for all the major magazines. Some really famous guy. You would have recognized the name. Bob something."

"You don't remember it?"

"No," Fergesson said.

"I'll be darned," Al said. "I never met a guy who makes dirty records, before. It's illegal, isn't it? Records like that."

"Sure," the old man said. "He makes a lot of other stuff, too. But that's all I saw, just that one thing. I think he puts out some jazz and even some classical stuff. Specialty stuff. Several lines."

Turning to the back of the folder, Al saw that there was no address. No manufacturer. "I thought he was a banker," he said. "Or a lawyer or a business man."

"He is a business man."

That was so. Al nodded.

"He makes a lot of money," the old man said. "You saw his car."

"Plenty of people drive Cads," Al said, "who don't have a bean."

"You should see his house. I have; I let him off there one day. He's got a place up in Piedmont. Practically a mansion. With trees and hedges all around it. And a wrought-iron gate. Ivy growing up the side of the house. And a really classy-looking wife. He's got at least one other car, too. A Mercedes-Benz sports car."

"Maybe not paid for," Al said. "He could have almost no equity in the house. I will admit he knows how to dress."

"And yet he's been here," the old man said, "and stood

around and talked to me, and not acted snotty; not acted like he had on a nice suit like that and was in a garage."

"Some guys have that," Al said. "A real gentleman has that. Grace. It's part of being a real aristocrat." But, he thought, not the kind of profession he had ever identified with the aristocracy. "I hope we're talking about the same guy," he said.

"Ask him when you see him again," the old man said. "He'll probably be back if he needs some work done on his car. Ask him if he doesn't sell party records."

"Maybe I will," Al said.

"He'll tell you to your face," the old man said. "He's not ashamed. It's a business. Like any other."

"Hardly that," Al said. "Hardly like any other, considering it's illegal. You could probably put the guy in jail with what you know. You better not tell anybody; I hope you aren't telling everybody you see. Didn't he say to keep it quiet?"

His face flushing, Fergesson said, "I never told anybody but you. Now I wish I hadn't told you. Get off my back." So saying, he wheeled himself under the Studebaker once more and resumed work.

"No offense," Al said. He wandered back out of the garage again, into the bright sunlight.

I could blackmail him, he thought. The idea bolted through his mind for an instant, sweeping everything away, leaving him trembling.

Obviously Harman no longer made dirty records; this was a thing out of his past. Probably in those days he had not been wealthy, well-dressed, fashionable. Maybe he had just been starting out; he had not yet arrived. This was a period in his life that he hoped to conceal forever.

Thinking that, he felt himself become cold and then even

colder; he felt his heart cease beating for a moment. That really made the blackmail business into something plausible.

Tell me to my face hell, he thought. If Harman knew I knew, he'd probably turn black and fall down in a faint.

It was a wholly new idea for making money, the blackmail idea. What had Mrs. Lane said to him? Some damn thing about you got to act or you miss out. Maybe, he thought, she's a prophetess. What's it called? A medium, looking into the future. A fortune-teller.

This was the ideal business opportunity.

It took no capital. No stock. No fixtures. No investment of any kind. Not even ads or business cards. Nor a State Tax franchise.

But blackmail was wrong. And yet, so was the used-car business. Everybody knew that. Nothing was lower than selling used cars, and he had been doing it now for a number of years. Was blackmailing a dirty-record manufacturer worse than selling used cars? It was hard to tell.

While he sat at his desk in the little house in the center of his lot, he saw an old brown Cadillac draw up to the curb. A large colored woman stepped out, wearing a cloth coat. She walked toward him, smiling, and he recognized her as Mrs. Lane.

Rising, he went outside to meet her.

"How do you do, Mr. Miller?" she said, in a pleasant and yet somehow slightly mocking voice. "How are you? Seems to me I just saw you not an hour ago, and here I am to visit." Her smile broadened.

"Come on in," he said, holding open the door of his office.

"Thank you." She entered, stood while he arranged a chair for her. "Thank you," she repeated, and sat down, crossed her legs and smoothed her skirt. "Mr. Miller," she said, when he had also seated himself, "you was in talking to me about a lot? For your used-car sales business?" Frowning, deep in thought, she said, "I have called several persons and I have come up with several locations, one of which I think has special importance possibly to you. It would be ideal for a used-car sales lot, although it never been used that way before." Her voice, soft, slurred, came over him like a cloud; he sat listening, letting it happen to him.

Outdoors a passerby stopped to examine one of his cars. But Al made no move; he did not stir from his chair.

"This lot," Mrs. Lane said, "is in downtown Oakland, around Tenth Street. In the real business district where you don't see so many lots. I mean, it isn't on no used-car lot row."

"I see," he said. And then, drawing himself up in his chair, he said, "I'll tell you; I've been considering another line of business entirely. A new business opportunity that came my way since I talked to you."

Glancing up at him doubtfully, she said, "You mean since you saw me? An hour ago, when you was in my office?"

"Yes," he said.

She eyed him for a time. "My goodness," she said.

"It's an entirely different line," he said. "I was sitting here giving it some thought."

"You haven't decided," she said. "For sure."

"No," he admitted.

She said, "Mr. Miller, of course I don't have no idea in the world what line it is you talking about. I know you could go into it however and do a bang-up job; I know that. However, I do point out to you that used-car sales is what you have been doing for some time, and in my opinion there's no doubt but what that your chosen profession." Her voice trailed off; she did not seem certain, now; she seemed to be trying to probe him, to draw him out. The notion of the new business opportunity had clearly thrown her off. She went on, "I like to drive you to the location in question, if you would be willing to permit me. For me, that's an offer always good. I always be willing to do that."

"I know," he said. "Thanks."

With what seemed almost anxiety, she gazed at him and said, "An' no obligation to you. That for sure, Mr. Miller." She opened her purse and fished around in it. "I want you to get the very right thing. So many people, they go wrong at this point. In relocating. It such a big thing. They don't know how to do it, and they get worried; they get appre-hensive." She trailed the word out.

"I guess they jump at the first thing," he heard himself say. But it was a perfunctory remark; he did not really care about this, now. He was still thinking about Harman.

Mrs. Lane said, "Your whole life depend on a decision of this kind. I tell my clients that. They don't see that, even though it they who going to be affected for years to come. I know more about them in that regard; I see it all in the almost fourteen years I been a licensed real-estate broker in the state of California. There people right now who buy a particular piece of property through me, thinking of it as a way of making money or an investment . . . and it change their lives. They not the same now. I could give you one for instance after another, but I know you a highly intelligent man, Mr. Miller, and I don't have to go into the particularities. Like look how you get to know Mr. Fergesson and it make you a different person because of." Her voice had a low, earnest quality, not like a sales voice at all; he was back once more, as he had been in her office, listening to the mother-lecture, or whatever it was that she did. Whatever it was, it had no relationship to the conventional business interchange, at least as he knew it among whites.

"I think you're right," he managed to say, feeling sleepy, almost unable to keep his eyes open.

Mrs. Lane shut her purse and held it upright on her lap with both her large oddly-light hands. What fine hands she has, Al Miller noticed. Almost like a man's. Completely competent, as if all the possible muscles and tendons had been used for every skill there was. As if the hands had been everywhere, done everything. And how wrinkled they were. The rest of her was smooth; she had the flesh, the skin of a young girl. Now she had taken off her coat. Again he paid attention to her bare arms. She did not even seem to perspire. Amazing, he thought. And, back to her hands . . . in texture, in color, in size they bore no relation to the rest of her. Hands joined on to her, he decided. The palms had an almost pinkish quality. The skin there, he thought, was quite thick, almost like leather. And very dry.

Studying him with her large smoky eyes, she said, "I see someone I know drop by here. You may have had the experience from your office like I have from mine; you can see up and down the street, and when nobody visiting you keep looking out for curiosity. Don't it was Mr. Harman who come by in his Coupé de Ville not so long ago, after you talk to me?"

At that he nodded.

"I know him," Mrs. Lane said. "Let me ask you." In a halting, preoccupied voice she said, "It is he you going into a business opportunity with?"

Al Miller made a sound that was neither yes nor no. He woke up now. So Mrs. Lane knew Harman; it made him aware and interested. And also cautious.

"I decipher from your tone," she said, "that you been in a negotiation with Mr. Harman, and you had reference to that when you say a new business possibility come your way since you saw me in my office. Well, I want to tell you something." She looked now, it seemed to him, actually a little frightened. She wet her lips, hesitated, gripped her purse with both hands and shifted about on the chair. "This a little chair," she said.

"Yes," he agreed.

"I know him," she said, "something like five year. Naturally I hear a lot of things. That my business. He come up in my business, the real-estate business, all the time. He buying and selling, like they say. He get in on things. What they call an operator."

"I see," Al said.

"He got quite a lot of—" She paused. Then, with a sudden broad smile, showing her ornamented gold front teeth, she continued, "Well, he ain't like you, Mr. Miller; I mean, he ain't worried he doing the world wrong."

Al nodded. The woman's mellow tone had altered; a flatness, a surprising harshness had come into it. She really did not like Harman, he realized. Her feelings had come out because she was not a hypocrite. It was not possible for her to pretend to like someone she did not like.

"You think," he said, "I ought to steer clear of Harman."

Her smile had become softer, now. More pensive. "Well," she said slowly, "that your business, of course. Maybe you know him better than I do."

"No," he said.

"I think you a honest man and he not." She regarded him with calmness. And yet, behind the calmness, was agitation. So difficult, he thought, for a Negro. To sit here with a white man and discuss in unflattering terms another white man; at any moment the boom can fall on her. I can cut her off, dismiss her. But it was not precisely that that she feared; it was more that she feared he would cease to pay attention to her. That he would freeze up inside his white-man's prejudice and ignore what she said.

"I know you have my interest at heart," he said, but although it was deeply meant it had a phony ring. A phrase, merely.

She nodded her head up and down.

"I'll watch my step," he said.

5

Not long thereafter, as Jim Fergesson lay on the floor of his garage, beneath a Buick, he heard a car pull up not far from him and stop. By the sound of it he guessed it to be a new car. He wheeled himself out, and found himself facing the fender of a nearly-new Cadillac. The door had already opened and a man in a business suit and black shiny shoes was stepping forth.

"Hi there, Mr. Harman," the old man said, sitting up. "I see you got back. I was out when you were by before. Not too much wrong with your car, is there? A nearly-new Cadillac like that." He laughed nervously, because he did not want to get involved with Harman's car to any extent; he had neither the tools nor the experience for this kind of car, this new expensive car with its interminable power assists and accessories.

Harman, smiling, said, "Every machine has bugs, Jim. As you're always telling me."

"That's sure true," Fergesson said.

"Nothing serious," Harman said. "Just the greasing."

"Okay," Fergesson said, with relief.

Harman said, "Jim, they tell me you're quitting business."

"I'm taking a rest," the old man said.

"For good?"

"It's sold," he said.

"I see," Harman said.

"Listen," the old man said, starting to put his hand on Harman's shoulder and then quickly changing his mind; he stood wiping his greasy hands with a rag. "There's a couple of good garages in town; you don't have to worry. I know a couple of mechanics you can trust. These days, with these God damn labor unions—"

"Yes," Harman interrupted. "The employers have to hire the men the unions send over. Whether they're competent or not."

"We're both in business," Fergesson said. "We know how it is."

"You'll get men," Harman said, "who stand around and do no work at all. And when you go to fire them—" He gestured.

"It's impossible," Fergesson said.

"Illegal."

"And that's why you got nothing but leaf-rakers, like in the W.P.A. days. It's socialism." The old man felt excitement in him, a kind of frenzy. How pleasant it was to stand here like this with this man, his well-dressed customer Mr. Harman who drove a 1958 Cadillac, talking to him on an equal basis, one businessman to another. That was what it was; they were equals. His hands jumped about madly; the rag slipped away and he gave it a kick to free it from his trouser cuff. "I been in business a long time. And look what taxes have done to me. It's part of their system to make it ridiculous for a man to devote his life to work because when he's all done, what does he have? Income tax." He spat on the floor.

"Yes," Harman said in his cultured calm voice. "The income tax definitely is part of the share-the-wealth scheme."

"They put it over on America," the old man said. "During Franklin Roosevelt's administration. Every time I think of that Roosevelt—and that son of his, that colonel."

With a mild, good-humored smile, Harman said, "That takes me back. Thinking about Eliot as a colonel."

"I'm keeping you," the old man said.

"No," Harman said.

"You got lots to do and so do I. I tell you, Harman, we both got too much to do. Only the difference between you and me is that you got the vitality and youth to do it, and I don't. I'm worn out. I tell you the truth; I'm finished."

"Hell no," Harman said.

"It's a fact."

"Why? My God, when I came in—"

"Sure, I was down under that Buick. But listen." The old man moved as close as possible to Harman—as close as he could without getting grease on him—and said in a low voice, "One day when I'm down under that; you know what? I'm going to have a heart attack and die." He stepped back. "So that's why I have to get out of here."

"And with all your skill," Harman said.

"It's a shame," the old man said. "But I have to listen to Fratt; that's his business. I go to experts. I'm not a doctor. All I know is that for years now I had indigestion and I went to Fratt and at first he didn't find anything, but then he took my blood pressure." He told Harman what his blood pressure was. It was terrible, and he saw Harman's face show the response.

"That's a shame, Jim," Harman said.

"But if I take it easy—I don't mean loaf around the house—but find something less strenuous. It's the lifting." He paused.

Harman said, "Had you ever thought of hiring someone? To do the heavy work?"

"Could never find anyone to rely on."

"Did you discuss it with your broker?"

"You mean Matt Pestevrides?"

"Your attorney," Harman said. "Or your realtor. Who do you talk over your business matters with? Who did you consult before you sold your place?"

The old man was silent.

"Didn't you discuss it with someone experienced in business matters? You could have gotten someone in to manage your shop for you, a foreman. It's done all the time. Any good business consultant could have researched it for you and come up with someone reliable; that's a matter of care and study, a matter of procedure."

The old man could think of nothing to say.

"I'm surprised at your broker," Harman said.

The old man said, "I just called him up and said I wanted to sell my garage, for health reasons."

"A distress sale. Didn't you take a loss?"

"Yes," he said.

"If you don't mind my asking, how much did you get for it?"

"Thirty-five thousand."

Harman glanced about him at the building. "That seems a fair price." He pondered, rubbing his lower lip with his knuckle. "Listen, Jim," he said. "Obviously it's crying over spilt milk to discuss any use you might have put your garage to. But you did get your price. You did cash yourself out."

"Yes," the old man said, feeling pride.

Glancing up acutely, Harman said, "I hope you didn't take paper."

"Paper?"

"Seconds. Second deeds of trust."

"Oh no," he said at once. "No paper. Ten thousand cash and the rest at two hundred a month."

"At what interest?"

The old man could not remember. "I'll show you." He led the way to his cluttered office; Harman followed with long strides. "Here." From the desk drawer he got the papers; laying them out he stepped back to permit Harman to see.

For a time Harman examined the papers. "I think you did very well," he said at last.

"Thanks," the old man said, with relief.

Standing by the desk, Harman thumped the closed papers in a deeply absorbed manner. He thumped them again and again. "I tell you what. Listen. You want some—what'll I call it? Not advice." Lifting the papers open once more he leafed through them. "Over on the other side of the Bay. In Marin County. They're doing a lot of building. They're expanding." He stared at the old man.

"Yes," the old man said. He held his breath.

"They're rebuilding parts of Highway 101 completely. A multimillion-dollar project that'll take years. Have you been over there?"

"Not for a year or so."

"There are several new shopping centers," Harman said. "One at Corte Madera. A truly magnificent job. Now listen." His voice had a harsh, brusque quality; it penetrated, and the old man went to close the office door, although Harman had not told him to do so. "Don't kid yourself," Harman said. "That's where the growth is, not here. Not in the East Bay. The master plan—" He laughed. "There's still no room. The East Bay is filled up. So is the peninsula. The only place you can grow and build is Marin County!" He stared at the old man wide-eyed.

"Yeah," the old man said, nodding.

Reaching inside his coat, Harman brought out a flat, dark gray wallet; he opened it and took a business card from it. With his fountain pen he wrote slowly and deliberately on the back of the card, then passed it to the old man.

On the back of the card Harman had written a phone number, re-inking the prefix several times. It was not an exchange that the old man knew. *Du*, he read.

"Dunlap," Harman said. "Call that."

"Why?"

Harman said, "Call him in the next twenty-four hours. Don't wait on this, Jim."

"What is it?" he demanded, wanting very badly to know; needing to know.

Seating himself on the littered desk, Harman folded his arms; he gazed at the old man silently for a long time.

"Tell me," the old man said, writhing, hearing his voice writhe with a whining tone he had never heard before in his life.

"This man," Harman said, "is Achilles Bradford. You would know him if you were anywhere involved. If you get him before he's decided, get your attorney and drive over there. He'll do business. He wants to do business. But he can't wait. He's got about one million of his own money in it now." In a calmer voice, he went on, "It's a shopping center, Jim. Up Highway 101 out of San Rafael toward Petaluma. At Novato. There's the Air Force base up there, Hamilton Field. Many tract-home subdivisions. More going constantly."

"I see," the old man said. But he did not see.

"What I hear," Harman said, "is that they're trying for an automotive center. Agency, probably Chevrolet but possibly Ford. Or even one of the hot imports, such as VW. Anyhow, they'll absolutely be putting in a garage. Those people commute, Jim. All the way down to San Francisco. They drive two hundred miles a day on that eight-lane freeway, and it's bumper to bumper at rush hour. And listen. *There is no train service.* You see what that means?

Those people have to maintain their cars. The auto center would be complete. New-car sales, parts supply, repair garage—it stands or falls on the repair. And it means a big garage, Jim. Not like you had here, a one-man operation. To keep those people on the road means a twenty-four-hour repair service. With something in the order of ten to fifteen mechanics on call all the time. Tow trucks. A jitney service to the City for parts. You begin to get the picture?"

"Yes," he said. And he did.

"It's a new idea in garage development. Oriented toward the future. The garage of tomorrow, in a sense. Capable of taking on the responsibility for tomorrow's traffic. The old-fashioned garage will be obsolete in five more years. You were right to sell out when you did; you were very smart."

Fergesson nodded.

"You could get into this," Harman said. "Can you get over there? Can you get your attorney and make your move?"

"I don't know," the old man said.

"If not, then go over without him. *But get over there.*" All at once Harman hopped down from the desk. "I have to go. I'm late." He started from the office, swinging the door wide.

Following him, Fergesson said, "But my health—the whole point is I can't do garage work."

Pausing, Harman said, "The garage investor puts up initial capital and supervises the shop. He contributes know-how and experience. The physical work will be done by union mechanics. Don't you follow?"

"Oh," the old man said.

Holding out his hand, Harman said, "So long, Jim."

Awkwardly, Jim Fergesson shook the hand.

"The rest," Harman said, "is up to you." He winked, a great, friendly, optimistic wink. "You're on your own." Waving, he strode to his Cadillac and jumped in. As he started it up he called, "Have to get the grease job tomorrow; can't wait now."

The Cadillac disappeared out into traffic.

For a long time Jim Fergesson gazed after it. Then, by degrees, he moved back toward the Buick on which he had been working.

An hour later the telephone in the office rang. When he answered it he found himself talking to Harman.

"What did he say?" Harman said.

"I haven't called," the old man said.

"You what?" Harman sounded astonished. "Well, you better get in on it, Jim; don't let this slip past you." He said a few more things of that kind, and then hung up, after asking the old man to let him know when he had talked to Bradford.

In the office, the old man sat at his desk meditating.

I'm not going to be rushed, he told himself. Nobody can stampede me. It's against my nature.

He thought to himself, I'm not going to call. Now or ever.

What I'm going to do, he decided, is go over there, to Marin County. To see that place, that shopping center. And take a look at it with my own eyes. And then if I like what I see then maybe I'll talk with the guy.

Inside him he felt a deep spurt of his own nature, his own cunning. And he laughed. "The hell with that," he said aloud. Go and call without knowing anything? With only having someone's word?

Why should I believe Harman? Why should I believe anybody? I didn't get where I am by relying on what people tell me. On rumor.

But he had to be sure he saw the right place. So, lifting the phone, he called the number next to Harman's name on his sheet of old customers.

*   *   *

That night, when he got home, he passed his wife without a word. He went directly into the bathroom, closed and locked the door, and before Lydia's voice could distract him he had turned the tub water on full.

As he lay in the water soaking, he thought, I know where it is. I can find it.

It was his plan to go up the next morning as early as possible and to be back to his garage by noon. Lying in the tub on his back, staring up at the steam-drenched ceiling, he went over each bit of the plan. Relishing it, revolving it in his mind, he made of it the most he could; he filled it in so that nothing was left unthought.

A new one, he thought. It would be new, every aspect of the place. No grease, no stale smell; the dampness, the sense of age, the discarded parts heaped in the corner . . . all gone. Swept away. Piles and pools, the dust. None of that.

The hell with them, he thought. I'll have an office with all glass and soundproofing; I can see down at the mechanics. I'll be overlooking. With several intercoms. Maybe the kind without wires. Fluorescent lights everywhere, like in the new factories. Lots of automatic stuff. All organized; no wasted time costing money.

It'll be science throughout, he told himself. Atomic, like in the labs. Like Livermore where they invented the Bomb.

He saw himself a part of the new world, along with Harman, along with all other enterprising men. This is America, he thought. Vision. What you do with capital and imagination. And I have both.

Boldness, he thought. You have to be bold. Even ruthless. Or otherwise they'll get you. They're always in wait, trying to pull you down to their level; naturally when you get up there they resent it.

They envy. You ignore that, however. Like Nixon does; he stands and sneers when they insult him, throw rocks, even spit. Risks his life.

His eyes half-shut, submerged in the hot water, with new water roaring, the old man thought of himself that way, not lost in the dirty, unimportant San Pablo Avenue of drive-ins; he saw himself with the big people who mattered. I'm in industry, he thought. Not politics; that's not my game. This country is founded on business. It's the backbone.

Investment! I'm investing, in the future of America. Not for my own good—hell, not for profit—but to expand the economy. *And it will count. What I do will count.*

6

The early-morning street was damp, and over all the houses was a fog, wet enough to start drops slipping across the upright surfaces. Nobody was out, but occasional yellow rectangles were kitchens in which, Jim Fergesson imagined, men stood before open ovens with their rumps to the heat.

He shaved, and fried some mush left over from the day before, drank gritty dark coffee that had been standing in the pot, and then with his overcoat around him he descended the stairs to the basement garage in which his Pontiac was parked. Lydia was asleep. No one heard him; no one saw him go.

Moisture had gotten into the engine and it died twice as he backed the car from the garage. Its hollow coughing continued as he drove down Grove Street, and he could not help thinking that had he the time he would take the car entirely apart. Almost everything in it was worn; nothing engaged. He did not shift into high gear but remained in second until he reached a stop light;

there he looked carefully and without stopping turned right. Soon he was driving at thirty-five miles an hour through Oakland. By the time he had gone a mile the engine had warmed and was working a little better. He put on the radio and listened to a program of the Sons of the Pioneers.

Most of the drivers along Eastshore Freeway had in mind the idea of going to San Francisco. Traffic was heavy facing him but his own lanes were open as he continued toward Richmond. The windows of the Pontiac were up and the heater was on. He felt comfortable and sleepy, and the cowboy music lulled him. Gradually he let the car slide from its lane, and then, as a car behind him honked, he drew himself up on the seat and concentrated. The time was six-thirty.

Along the flat shoreline of the East Bay, on his right, ran the Aquatic Park. He had by this time reached a speed of sixty miles an hour, and that seemed to him plenty. Apparently he had not been this way in more time than he realized; there were changes in the freeway, new overhead ramps being built, detours and cut-offs which confused him. And already, he noticed, the freeway was twelve lanes wide. Did they have to make it even wider? The pavement was white cement and there were no stops. The flatness of the pavement pleased him. He held the wheel with both hands and gazed at the houses and hills to his right.

Now the problem came of finding Hoffman Boulevard; he had to get over to the right or he would not be able to leave the freeway. So he drifted gradually, thinking that this was the best way. Cars on his right, however, did not think so; a chorus of horns jolted him. Gunning the car forward, he shot into an open space in the right-hand lane, almost the asphalt shoulder. A moment later his car coasted along the narrow, bumpy temporary start of Hoffman; he shot past a green light at an intersection and under an ominous black-iron overpass with huge warning signs and winking yellow lights; the lights alternated in a pattern that made him feel, as he drove beneath them, that something terrible was going to happen. The passage under the overpass was so narrow that for a moment he thought the car would not make it. He had the illusion that he would scrape on both sides, and it was all he could do to keep his hands on the steering wheel. But already he had come out on the far side; there, once more, was the Bay to his left.

Several miles later Hoffman entered a strip of cut-rate gasoline stations and truck drivers' cafés, and then the worst section of run-down Negro shacks that he could recall. Traffic moved very slowly, with huge diesel trucks interspersed among the cars. This, he understood, was Richmond. Trash littered the broken sidewalks.

To his left he saw factories and wharves. Near the water, he realized. Train tracks, one after another. And then, ahead, a steep hill with houses. The street turned sharply. He saw an open place, and then the immense Standard Oil refinery. All at once the street became a freeway again, climbing, with the cars picking up speed on all sides of him. He whizzed along a broad curve, above the refinery, and now he saw the Bay once more, and the bridge that connected the East Bay to Marin County. It was the ugliest bridge he had ever seen, but it did not depress him; instead, it made him laugh.

He slowed at the toll plaza of the bridge, paid his seventy-five cents, and then found himself on the bridge. They had built it so that the driver could see nothing, no water, none of the islands, not even his destination; all he could pick out were the heavy metal rails.

What genius, he said to himself. What planning. Again he laughed.

At last one sight became obvious; he fastened his gaze on it, far ahead. San Quentin Prison, clay-colored buildings like some old Mexican fort, spread out at the water's edge, all in very good shape. The bridge passed to the right of the prison and let him off on a wide freeway which led into one cut-off after another. Again he was confused. But a sign told him which cut-off to take to get onto US 101 North. And so he took that.

He sped across a flat plain at enormous speed, a car behind him and another ahead. Wind whipped at his Pontiac. There was San Rafael and US 101; he had almost arrived, and it had not taken very long. He was well ahead of schedule, and his spirits rose even further.

When he saw a gas station on a little side cut-off road he made a signal and coasted from the freeway. After several turns he found himself at the gas station. Leaving the road he brought the car to the nearest island of pumps. The morning air, as he opened the car door, was warm. Wind riffled the stalks of weeds growing in the surrounding fields.

He lifted the hood and with a page of newspaper took an oil reading. The oil level was down, so he picked up a quart of 30 weight from the rack by the pumps. The boyish attendant in his white uniform was hurrying over as the old man emptied the oil into the pouring-can that had been put nearby.

"Hey," the boy said indignantly. "None of that."

"Sorry," Fergesson said, remembering, now, that he was not in his own garage. "Give me five of the regular." He had already begun to reach for the gas hose, but he pretended that he had been reading the price. Ethyl was thirty-nine cents a gallon. He showed amazement at the amount as the boy lifted down the hose.

The boy was still upset. As he walked to the rear of the car and removed the gas cap, he watched the old man as if expecting him to tinker again with the company's property. Self-consciously, the old man got back inside the car and remained there until the boy came around to wash the windshield. "No, no," he said to the boy, wanting to leave, pushing several one-dollar bills at him.

The boy gave him change and retrieved the pouring-can. The hood slammed down and the old man drove from the station back onto the road. There a milk truck honked at him as he pulled in front of it.

As he drove, his eagerness increased. Now, at any time, he might see the sign leading to Marin Country Gardens. But he had left the freeway; the little road did not lead back to it but brought him out on a residential street. A huge wire cyclone fence separated him from the freeway, and beyond the fence cars shot along at enormous speed. However, he continued on with no diminution of spirits, disconnected from the freeway as he was. Evidently he had entered San Rafael, a town to which he rarely, if ever, came.

Between silent houses he drove at twenty-five miles an hour. The blocks were short. A number of men could be seen on their way to work, walking rapidly, some wearing suits, others in work clothes. They all had a speeded-up motion, as in an old film. That amused him, too.

For a time he drove through the town, still keeping in sight of the freeway, wondering where he was but enjoying himself. And then at last he sighted something heartening. The broken-up expanse of new dirt which, he realized, was construction beyond the freeway. Great culverts lying in rows, the ceramic drainage system which would go down first, before anything else. And parked machinery. Big ones. The major equipment which the Federal Government used in its work; he had seen them when Highway 40 had been rebuilt, the Eastshore Freeway.

He came, then, to the very edge of the construction zone, and halted his car; he had no choice but to halt—the pavement ended in a series of jagged projections that had already cracked. The road on which he drove had been scooped away by the digging equipment. He saw down, into a drop-off. Dirt only. The underneath part which they usually never got to see. It frightened him, and he pulled on the handbrake. Machines, he thought, had carried away everything here; had left nothing at all. What power to remove! Nothing could stand . . . he looked to the right and left. Furrow for a long way, and so God damn wide. Did cars go across? Could one go and rejoin the freeway on the far side? He saw, high up, tiny swift dots. Cars on the freeway.

Parallel to the freeway ran a double track. Tread marks in the dirt, imprinted by pressure. Some vehicles. So he started up the car and drove down, off the asphalt; the car bumped, creaked, lifted on first one side and then the other. He drove carefully along the rutted tracks. The car shuddered as stones broke beneath the wheels. He gripped the steering wheel and eased the car into holes and out again.

Once he passed workmen who gaped at him. Then he passed mounds of machines. And, at last, he saw a metallic bulk approaching him head-on.

He stopped the car as the object became a bulldozer. The driver, perched high up in his seat, shook his fist and shouted; he, too, stopped, and the two vehicles faced each other. Fergesson did not get out. He remained behind the wheel.

The driver of the bulldozer jumped down and walked over. "Who the hell are you? Get this heap out of here."

To Fergesson the bulldozer and the angry driver were unreal. He heard the man panting and saw his red face moon up at the window, but still he did not stir. He did not know what to do.

"Get back!" the man shouted. "Get back to the road! Come on, fellow!"

Fergesson said, "You know Mr. Bradford?"

Other workmen arrived and with them was a man in a business suit. They pointed at Fergesson's Pontiac and waved more workmen to follow. A line of figures grew along the rise of equipment and dirt: onlookers.

The man in the business suit came to the window and said, "I'll have to ask you to back your car the way you came. This is a private road for use by the State."

Fergesson could think of nothing to say. He had come almost a mile along the rutted tracks in low gear. The idea of backing bewildered him. He felt confused and he could not speak.

"What's the matter with him?" the driver was yelling. "Christ, I have to get by—I can't fart around here."

A workman said, "Maybe he doesn't speak English."

"Let me see your driver's license," the man in the business suit said.

"No," Fergesson said.

A workman said, "He don't know how to back out."

"Move over," the man in the business suit said. He opened the car door. "I'll back it. Move over, buddy. Look, we can give you a citation; you're on State property. You're a trespasser. You have no legal right to be on this road; it isn't a road, it's a construction project."

He pushed Fergesson over, slammed the door, and, putting the Pontiac into reverse and peering over his shoulder, began to back. The driver returned to his bulldozer and followed. It took a long time to reach the point at which the genuine road had ceased. Fergesson gazed at the floorboards and said nothing.

"Okay," the man said, tugging on the parking brake and stepping out. "It's all yours."

"How do I go?" Fergesson said.

"Back, up the rise, the way you came."

Fergesson pointed across the expanse of dirt, at the freeway on the far side.

"Go back," the man repeated. "Back to San Rafael and find a

street to cross there." He walked rapidly off and Fergesson was alone. He could hear the rumble of the bulldozer and the sounds of the workmen; they were starting their day. Shifting into gear—the teeth clashed—he drove clumsily back along the road and once again found himself in the residential section of San Rafael, among the houses and lawns.

When he saw a man walking along the sidewalk, Fergesson leaned out the window and called, "How do I get across?"

The man glanced at him and went on without speaking. Fergesson rolled up the window again. He felt shaken and depressed and he did not pursue the man. The time was now nine o'clock and the sky was warming. Yellow sunlight hung over the trees and sidewalks; the lawns sparkled. A mailman walked slowly along and Fergesson brought the car to the curb beside him.

"How do I get across 101?" he said.

"Where do you want to go?"

"Marin Country Gardens," he said, resting a little as he sat behind the steering wheel.

The mailman consulted with himself. "No," he said, "I never heard of it. Go down to the city hall and ask them. Ask somebody down there; they'll know." He continued on.

From then on the old man drove aimlessly, not knowing where to go or whom to talk to. He seemed to be getting farther and farther away from the main part of town; the streets became steeper and the houses older. At last he came out into what seemed to be a housing tract, but an old one; the houses were decayed and the weeds high in the yards.

Once he saw a policeman, but the policeman looked tough and unsympathetic so he did not stop there either. The time was now a quarter past ten. This is a hell of a thing, he thought to himself. Where am I? Still in San Rafael? He saw, past the tract, what appeared to be a glimpse of open country. Fields, hills far off.

At ten-thirty he came to an intersection at which was a small imitation-stone building with a sign over it: DOWLAND REAL ESTATE NOTARY PUBLIC RENTALS. So he parked the car and went inside.

Behind one of the three desks sat a middle-aged woman in a print dress, wearing a hat and talking on the phone. She smiled at him, concluded her conversation, and then came over to the counter. "Good morning," she said.

Fergesson said, "I want to go to Marin Country Gardens."

The woman pondered. She seemed well groomed with gray hair pulled back and waved; her clothes looked expensive and she smelled of powder and perfume. "That's not ours," she said. "That's one of the new subdevelopments on the far side of 101." Hesitating, she said, "I frankly don't even know if they're showing, yet."

"I want to see Mr. Bradford," he said.

The woman leaned against the counter and tapped at her teeth with a yellow lead pencil. "You can double back for a mile or so and then get across. Or you can go on. Your subdevelopment is up the highway toward Petaluma, so you might as well go that way. They're working all around there; you really should be careful. It's easy to get lost."

By bringing a map to the counter she was able to give him directions that he could make out. He thanked her and returned to his car, feeling new confidence. Maybe now, he thought. At least it did exist; she had recognized the name.

Once more he was in motion, and again in the area of construction work. The road became a tangle of dirt and asphalt, broken down, he decided, by heavy equipment; but it did cross the highway and he reached the far side, flagged by an old man in blue jeans, along with a group of other cars. There he was sent left along a pitted old blacktop road that followed the course of the freeway, but perhaps a mile to its left. On each side of him were orchards of dead fruit trees. He could not tell what sort they had been.

To his ears came the racket of machinery. Now he saw them, far off, like toiling insects. But he thought now, really thought, that he could see Marin Country Gardens; at least there was some sort of new housing development going up the side of a broad, brown hill. He could make out where the ground had been cleared, new narrow roads put in, foundations begun. Feeling buoyed up, he rolled the car windows down and let the warm summer air into the car, the dry country air, so different from the city's. The smell of drying grass seemed satisfying and the sight of the flat fields gave him the absolute conviction that he had finally found it; the view which he now saw through his dust-and-bug-spattered windshield exactly fitted his expectations.

Now, to his delight, the sign itself appeared. As he passed he made out only the larger words; the information, painted on the wood in blazing green and red, dwindled row by row into facts about down-payments, floor-plans, number of bricks in the fire-place, colors. He read:

MARIN COUNTRY GARDENS
ONLY ¼ MILE AHEAD
OPEN FOR PUBLIC INSPECTION

This no longer was a State or Federal construction project, this area of dirt and machines ahead; this was a private business enterprise. And yet it fit in. It was part of the general stirring, the activity. All joined, and here his part entered; here he fit in. His wrists and hands burned with perspiration; he blinked and felt a new kind of feeling, or rather an old one, left over from his childhood. He yearned to spill from the car and get his feet onto the ground; he wanted to run and leap and grab up things to throw.

The road led to a small building with tar-paper roof and parking lot before it. A single dingy black Ford was parked there. The ground was muddy and trampled; he saw several rolls of roofing paper stacked up beside the small building. And a half-empty cement sack.

When he had parked and put on the handbrake—he made himself act methodically—he walked to the building with slow, easy steps. The door was open to an office in which a man sat behind a desk with his feet up and crossed. He was reading a paperback book. The office smelled of varnish. On the desk were a telephone and wire baskets of papers, and on one wall was a glossy calendar, new and crisp, with a print of a girl in a long flowered skirt.

"Greetings," the man said. He turned the pages of his book as if discarding the unread part. Then he tossed it down on the desk, loudly, and folded his hands. He was young, with a long horse-face and thick hair. His suit was informal, single-breasted; his teeth projected and the skin of his neck was red and rough. Surprisingly, his socks hung in folds around his ankles. "You read these things?" he said, pointing with his thumb at the closed paperback book.

"No," Fergesson said, panting with exertion and excitement.

The man picked up the book and regarded it. "*Brain Wave*," he said. "By Poul Anderson. Science fiction. I read all these science fiction books. I must have read fifty the last month or so. The desk's full of them. People give them to me; I don't have to buy them."

Fergesson, with his urgency, had arrived at this little closed spot of timelessness. The gigantic public works, protracted over decades, were unfolding close to this office and man; he had taken on their viewpoint. At his desk, with his heap of books, he was an Egyptian officer. Emotionless, cut off, he greeted Fergesson ponderously.

"No," Fergesson said, wanting to bring the man back into motion, back into time. "Say, you know Mr. Bradford?"

The man nodded.

"Is he here?"

"Bradford isn't here," the man said. He rose to his feet and extended his hand, which Fergesson found heavy and dry. The man stooped from the low ceiling of the office and his height had gone into his shoulders. "My name is Carmichael. What is your name?" He asked it with a rising inflection, as if he had known it and forgotten it and expected to recognize it once he heard it repeated again.

"Jim Fergesson."

"Hello, Jim," Carmichael said, twisting his head on an angle and squinting. "Is that an Irish name?"

"I guess so," Fergesson said. He was calming now, feeling his blood pressure wane.

"Sit down, Jim." Carmichael pushed a chair out and returned to his own chair facing across the desk. His two flinty hands rubbed together, upright, forming a vertical surface. Then, with his thumbnail, he tugged down his lip and pried at his gum. "Well, Jim," he said. "What can I do for you? Can I sell you a house?"

"No," Fergesson said, "I want to talk to Mr. Bradford. I have something to discuss. When is he here?"

"You do not want to buy a house," Carmichael said. "I didn't think you wanted to buy a house, actually. Mr. Bradford came out here once that I know of. Actually Bradford is part of the financial bunch that backs this place. The work is done by Gross and Duncan . . . contractors." His voice slowed. "I represent the company. So you can talk to me."

Fergesson had decided that he would not give himself away, that he would pretend to be something else and not what he really was. He really was here to see what had been accomplished; he was passing judgment on Marin Country Gardens and the work and schemes of its backers. In him was the capacity to decide, not merely about himself but about them all. And Carmichael was in on it because he was being decided about; he was part of the subdivision and the new shopping center, as were the workmen with the bulldozer and the man in the business suit who had backed the Pontiac, and, in a way, the policeman and the mailman and the real-estate woman and all the rest of them.

"I want to see what they're doing," Fergesson said. "Can we look?"

"Why not?" Carmichael said, making no move to get up. He seemed resigned and pleasant, but not particularly involved. "What line of work are you in, Jim?"

"Mechanics," Fergusson said.

"What do you do, design or invent or make machines? You work with machines?"

"Cars," Fergusson said.

"Do you?" Carmichael seemed interested. "I used to have a souped-up buggy I worked on. During the war I was in the C.B.s. I had some engine designs I worked up . . . mostly carburetor changes. Feed for each cylinder. That's why I read this stuff." He picked up his science fiction book and dropped it flat to the desk again. "You know, these guys who write these things . . . these rocket ships and time-travel machines and faster-than-light drives, all that stuff. If you want the hero to be on Mars you say something like—'he turned on the automatic high-gain propulsion tubes.' This one isn't so bad but some of them are. They go barreling around the universe. It must be easy to write this stuff; they must bat it out."

"I see," Fergesson said, not following the man's talk.

"I'd like to meet one of these science fiction boys. I'd hire myself out as a technical consultant." Carmichael's great horse-teeth showed in irony. "Ten or fifteen percent of the price he gets. This stuff is just fake. They fake it as they go along. This one here," he said, lifting the book around so that Fergesson could see it. "This is about the I.Q. of everybody going up overnight." He laughed suddenly, a loud startling noise. "Animals become as smart as people. You ever read this stuff?"

"No," Fergesson said. He was impatient to go on; he walked to the door of the office and looked out at the half-completed houses.

"What do you do with cars?" Carmichael asked from the desk.

"Fix them. I have a garage. In Oakland."

"What part of Oakland?"

"San Pablo Avenue," he said, and opened the door to go outside.

Carmichael pushed back his chair and followed after him. His hand descended on Fergesson's shoulder. "You say you want to go look around?" He started down the gravel path beside Fergesson. "Well, I'll show you around."

"Thanks," Fergesson said. Straining, he saw the flat tract at the bottom of the hill; a muddy path went down and across a deep ditch, past heaps of pipe and piled lumber. Separate crews worked laying foundations. A cement mixer churned and the echoing racket of a hammer stirred the midday air. The air smelled of fresh-cut wood.

"Pretty nice," Carmichael said, stopping to light a cigarette. He tossed the match a long distance off. "Don't you think, so, Jim?"

"Yes," Fergesson said.

They worked their way down the path. Under their feet clumps of dirt rolled and Fergesson tottered as his heels slid in the ooze. "Watch your step," Carmichael said from behind him. He himself descended with calm. "No, Bradford doesn't come out here. You see, Jim, I'll tell you how this thing works. Bradford has nothing to do with the building. They put up the money and Gross and Duncan do the work. The selling is handled by two or three agents. Now the deal I have is, I live here on the tract. I get one of the houses rent-free for the first year or until the tract fills up. For each house I sell I get a flat five hundred dollars. Other than that I get no salary. But all I have to do is sell two houses a month. You can see my house. It's a show house. Full of department-store furniture and an electric kitchen completely equipped. My wife's there." He pointed and Fergesson could see curtains in the windows of the house. It was a one-story California ranch-style house with a garage and a picket fence and a lawn bordered by flowers. The cement walk led to the mire of dirt that was the street. All the other houses were unfinished, unpainted and empty. Their skeletons were identical. He saw no variation along the rows.

"There's four different styles," Carmichael said. "But right now you can't see the difference. It's in the color and the lattice work and the number of bedrooms."

"I see," Fergesson said.

"Over there will be the shopping center." Carmichael gestured. "That's a separate enterprise. They think it's too much of a gamble. They want it operated on its own. They're sure the houses will go, but the shopping center is something else."

"Why?" Fergesson said. "People have to buy, and they live out here."

"They live here," Carmichael agreed, "but did you ever see a woman that wanted to buy near home? The ladies want to go into town. They won't buy here; they'll drive to San Francisco. It'll give them an excuse to go to the big downtown department stores.

Maybe a food market here. A market and a gas pump and a lunch counter. But they're talking in terms of—" He spread his arms. "Bakeries, and pottery shops, and circulating library, and shoe repair."

"A town," Fergesson said.

Carmichael glanced at him. "The works, yes."

"You don't think it'll pay?"

"Well, they don't need it."

"They're not risking anything."

"No," Carmichael agreed, "they'll leave it on its own. If it sinks they'll be free."

"The garage," Fergesson said. "I was thinking about buying into that."

Carmichael was still looking at him and Fergesson knew that he had been figured out from the start. The man had appraised him; that was his job. Fergesson walked across the flat ground. When he reached a group of workmen he halted. They were setting frames for concrete to be poured, for the foundations of the house.

"Well," Carmichael said, beside him. "It would cost you forty or fifty."

"Yes," Fergesson said.

"What about this garage in Oakland?"

"I sold it. I'm selling it."

"Why?"

Fergesson did not answer. He felt tense and disturbed and he walked away from Carmichael with his hands in his pockets.

After a while Carmichael followed him. "Let's go back to the office," he said. "We can talk."

Fergesson said, "What do you get for these?" He meant the houses.

"Twelve or fourteen. They're good. Nothing special but they're well built. Gross and Duncan know their business. Nobody's getting swindled." Carmichael ground his cigarette out in the mushy soil. "At one time I was thinking about the auto thing. The supply shop; me, I mean. But they want people to buy in to get in on that. I couldn't raise that. When they talk that kind of money, I'm out. They're sound enough on this auto business. The people who live this far out won't be getting into town for their auto parts and work; they'll have it done here because when they need it they'll need it right away."

"That's what I figured," Fergesson said, and he thought then of something else. "The women won't be going to the garage. The men bring in the car."

"How long have you been in the garage business?"

"Most of my life."

"How do you like it?"

"It's okay." He felt impatient. "A lot of hard work crawling under cars."

"You like what you see here?"

"Yes," he said.

"It's a damn funny thing," Carmichael said. "Come on, let's go back." He guided Fergesson with his arm and the two men walked toward the ditch and the rise. "People come out here, drive all the way from the City . . . they know it isn't finished; they know the freeway isn't done and the houses aren't either, and when they get out here they look around and bellyache—like— hell. What do they want, for Christ's sake? I can see this place; all you have to do is look. In two or three years this'll be lawns and wives out watering and kids crawling everywhere. What do they need? These places look alike—so what; they won't look alike when people get in them. It's the people that makes them look different. You take any six blocks of empty houses; it's scary. The people bring in the personal furniture and hangings."

"How many houses have you sold?" Fergesson said.

"Six. Seven. There's other salesmen, back in the City." They crossed the ditch and halted so that Fergesson could get his breath. "Would you bring anybody else in with you?" Carmichael asked.

"No." He was panting again with the exertion of climbing. To excuse himself, he looked back at the houses to see them once more before they took the rise. "I could run it alone, the financial part."

"But you'd hire mechanics."

"Yes," Fergesson said.

"You're married? You have a family?"

"Yes," he said.

Carmichael started leisurely up the hillside and Fergesson followed. The old man's shoes disappeared into the yellow clay, and the grass, as he clutched for support, slid through his fingers. Carmichael climbed upright, with ease and sureness, talking slowly.

"It would be up to you. There's no reason why it wouldn't work out. They have a mint tied up in this place and it's all geared in with the freeway. They know approximately when they should have most of the houses sold. You'd start getting a return on your investment right from the start anyhow, because there're a lot of other tracts around here, a lot of them filled, and people coming down from Petaluma. And on weekends this is busy with traffic going up to the Russian River. You saw the number of cars on 101. This is a busy area, and getting more busy all the time. What else can it do but grow?"

Jim Fergesson climbed with effort. Ahead of him Carmichael talked on and he listened as best he could. His hands were wet and they stung from the edges of the grass. At one point he stumbled and fell against the dirt; his fingers dug and floundered and he shut his eyes. Carmichael was at the top and going on, slowing because he saw that the old man was not keeping up with him. Fergesson stood up and stepped widely, to finish in three last strides. At the top was a collection of steel support bars and as he reached them his toe caught in the dragging weeds that had grown across them. He stepped forward and his body collapsed. The air rushed out of him and he fell into darkness, fell so suddenly that he could say nothing. It was as if the ground had magnetized him. He went over on his face like metal, with his arms out; he did not feel the ground come up and he did not hear himself fall. One moment he was laboriously climbing behind Carmichael and then he lay face down in the ooze.

Carmichael, still talking, walked a few paces. He said, "Oh hell," and came back, bending, with his placid horse-face dipping toward Fergesson. The old man felt his presence and grunted, wanting to lift himself. But he couldn't. He had no strength. A distant humming was all he could hear and although he could remember Carmichael's voice, he could not really catch the sound of it.

Taking hold of the old man's arm Carmichael tried to lift him. He lifted with both hands but Fergesson did not budge; Carmichael could not budge him and Fergesson felt his own weight, heavy and dead, snapped tight by the magnetic ground. He had been snared and he could do and say nothing; he could only wait. He hoped that Carmichael would have an answer.

"Hey," Carmichael said to some workmen along the hillside. "Give me a hand."

The workmen walked over. Fergesson did not feel foolish or frightened; he felt a little sick at his stomach and now his chest was beginning to hurt. He could, with his mind, trace the outline of the steel support bars. They were under him. The pressure became pain and he winced.

"What happened?" a workman said.

"He fell," Carmichael said. They lifted the old man to his feet; they tipped him back to a standing position. Fergesson found himself upright, dripping mud and crushed weeds. The pressure remained on his chest, however; he lifted his hand and brushed reflexively. His face seemed puffy and leaking, as if it were drizzling blood.

"Thanks," Carmichael said; the workmen went off. "Hey," he said to Fergesson. "You really took a spill."

Fergesson nodded. The pain in his chest numbed him. He touched himself with his stiff fingers but he felt nothing at all. He could not talk, either. Now he was frightened.

"Let's go into the office," Carmichael said. With his hand on Fergesson's shoulder he walked him toward the tar-paper-roofed shack. "How about a cup of coffee?"

"No," Fergesson said. His voice sounded a long way from him and discordant. As if he were hearing it through a wire. "I have to get back."

"You want to get into your car?"

Fergesson nodded, and Carmichael walked with him to the parked Pontiac. Carmichael opened the door and the old man got in behind the wheel. He leaned back against the upholstery and sucked in huge gusts of air. The air hurt his throat, as if it too were skinned by the fall. He held his hand against his chest and pushed in.

"How do you feel?" Carmichael said.

He nodded.

"You have to watch that wet dirt; it's tricky."

"Yes," Fergesson said. His head was beginning to clear and he could see. But he felt so sick that he knew he had broken something inside; he was trembling and scared and he wished Carmichael would leave. He wanted to go back to Oakland.

Carmichael, leaning by the car door, was talking at great

length, continuing his discussion as if nothing had happened. His infinite calm had not been broken; the old man had fallen and Carmichael had arranged to get him back on his feet. The old man perspired as he lay against the upholstery of his car, and he thought about driving back. He was sure he could do it; he could, if necessary, pull off the road. He wanted to leave right now and he opened his eyes and interrupted: "Thanks, Mr. Carmichael. I'll see you." With his right hand he put on the ignition and with his foot he pushed down on the gas. The motor started.

"Wait," Carmichael said. "I'll give you my card."

Fergesson accepted the card and put it in his pocket. He let the car go forward a yard and Carmichael walked along beside it. Staring through the windshield Fergesson blinked as sweat got into his eyebrows and down into his eyes. The pain was more intense, less dull; he felt it locate itself in his heart and suddenly he understood that he had had a heart attack; not much of one, a small one, from the climbing and the excitement.

"Goodbye," he said. Nodding with the motion of the car he drove down the road.

"I'll see you, Jim," Carmichael said. He was lost to Fergesson's sight. The sound of his voice dwindled. Fergesson drove with both hands clutching the wheel. When he had gone a mile or so he slowed and lay back again, trying to make himself comfortable. The pain seemed to be fading. He was glad of that.

By the time he had found his way back onto the highway he was able to sit up entirely. The cramp, or pain, was fading. Trembling, he shifted for the first time into high gear. The roar of the engine subsided.

He was still frightened and as he drove he sang to himself, "Bom, bom. Bom, bom." It meant nothing and he had never made sounds like that before; with his lips he repeated the sounds again and again, as if they were important. "Bom, bom." He was relieved to see San Rafael on both sides of the highway, because that meant he would soon be on the bridge and going back across to the East Bay. "Bom, bom," he said to himself, hearing his own voice. He gained strength and said it louder. The midday sun was hot and it made perspiration steam down his cheeks and into his collar. His coat stuck against him and when he moved he felt the sticky plucking of fabric. Perhaps, he thought, his chest had been laid open by the steel beams.

7

The garage had not been opened for the day; its wooden doors were shut. The old man parked his Pontiac in the entrance and got clumsily out to unlock the padlock that held the doors together. As he dragged them up a rush of dank, dismal air billowed past him.

When he had brought the Pontiac inside he went into his office and unfastened his coat. He dug down to his flesh, under his shirt and undershirt, and found the cloth soggy with blood. A deep indentation crossed his ribs. It was still bleeding. Presently he went to the washroom, and, with the bar of Lava soap, sponged away the blood. The indentation was white and the flesh was not as much cut as dented away.

So, he thought, back at his desk in the office, the pain had come from the impact, from the blow; steel had hit him across the chest and there was no reason to suppose anything more serious. The pain was gone. He felt weak and sick. Leaning, he opened the bottom desk drawer and groped for the half-pint of Christian Brothers Brandy. A paper dixie-cup, filled with paper clips, was the only glass he could find. After he had drunk some of the brandy he sat pushing the clips across the desk surface. Then at last he looked up Harman's telephone number and dialed.

"Look," he said. "Harman? Mr. Harman?"

"Just a moment," the girl said. "I'll connect you with Mr. Harman." A series of clicks, a wait. Then a man's voice.

"Yes, this is Harman."

"This is Fergesson," he said. "I'm interested in that place but I can't get hold of Mr. Bradford."

"Oh yes," Harman said, sounding puzzled for a moment.

"I went up there but he wasn't there."

After a pause Harman's voice said, "My friend, I've been thinking about you and this business. I think what you better do—have you got an attorney or not?"

"No," Fergesson said.

"Well, who drew up the papers on your garage?"

"Matt Pestevrides. Real-estate broker."

Harman said, "It seems to me if you're going to deal with Bradford you should deal through somebody. There's no offense intended in my saying this. I think, though, Jim, you'd really be a lot better off if you could deal through a representative who's used to operators like Bradford. Who can—do you know what I mean?—talk their language."

"I want that place," Fergesson said.

"The auto repair?"

"I want to buy it!" he said loudly in Harman's ear. The racket of his voice jangled back.

"Well, look," Harman said. "Get a lawyer. Have him approach Bradford. Have him tell them he's got an interested party who wants to know more. He'll know how to approach them.

Probably Bradford and his associates already have a prospectus drawn up; you know what that is, it's a financial statement giving all the particulars. Have your lawyer go over it and see what he thinks. Or get hold of an investment broker. Somebody who's used to this sort of thing. Or bring it to me, if you want."

"I'll take it to Tsarnas." That was the Bulgarian property attorney who had handled the papers on his garage when he had first bought it. "Thanks."

"If you want I'll give you the name of my own attorney," Harman said. "He's very good."

"No." His chest was beginning to hurt again. "Thanks." He hung up the phone.

Why, he thought, couldn't he see Bradford? Why did he have to work through somebody else? Bradford was like God, up in the sky, unseen; known only by his works. The big men, the financiers, would hear of Jim Fergesson indirectly and by degrees; the awareness of Fergesson would creep up gradually if it crept up at all. And how important would that be to them? How much would it count? But he had made up his mind to go ahead.

Dialing, he called Tsarnas's office. Tsarnas's daughter answered. "Let me talk to Boris," he said. "This is Fergesson."

He told Tsarnas to find out about Marin Country Gardens and then, when he had hung up, he opened the desk drawer and found a Dutch Masters cigar still wrapped in cellophane. The cigar tasted good and he was able to relax. Down in his chest the pain was an ache, dull and uniform, going on like a pulse.

Outside the office were cars to be worked on, cars with metallic dust on their hoods from the valve-grinding of the past days. One Plymouth was up on its end, suspended by the hydraulic hoist; he had not remembered to let it down. The Plymouth had been upright for three days. It was a wonder the air had not leaked out of the hoist. After he had smoked the cigar he left the office and took tools from the workbench. He kicked the wooden flat-cart out and lowered himself onto it.

Once again he was beneath a car, down in the cold darkness, among the indistinct shapes. He found the protected electric bulb on its cord and dragged it beside him; the yellow area spread out over the transmission and flywheel of the car.

When he rolled to pick up a socket wrench his chest cracked. At it his mouth flew open and he let the wrench go. The pain, as it had been, hopped back and was there again, as before. The pain settled on him and he could not breathe. Through his mouth he swallowed air, wheezing as if his throat were clogged.

"Fuck," he said, when he could speak, and rolled back onto his shoulders. He lay face up, his arms at his sides, seeing the blaze of the electric bulb. Something was wrong inside him. A permanent thing had broken. He had not recovered.

For a time he lay under the car and then he slid the cart out. He threw his tools on the bench and walked to the office. For an hour he sat doing nothing. The time was three-thirty and he had not eaten since six. In the white sunlit entrance of the garage the outlines of people passed. He wondered if anybody would come in. If so, maybe they could get him a sandwich at the café down the street.

Late in the afternoon, after the heat had left the sun's rays, Al Miller got out the gallon jug of polish and began polishing a 1954 Oldsmobile which he had picked up from a wholesaler. While he waited for the polish to dry he turned on the hose and began washing off his other cars; he slung the hose here and there. The glare this time of day was intense, and he had put on his dark glasses. Because of the glare he kept his back to the street and sidewalk.

As he moved behind a car he turned and caught sight of

someone coming toward him, a figure that had already gotten onto the lot without him noticing. Walking very fast, the woman approached him in a straight line. She bore down on him as he stood with the drizzling hose in his hands; shading his eyes he tried to make out who it was, if it was someone he knew. Often women who wanted parking-meter change came that way, so rapidly and purposeful.

The woman, broad, middle-aged, suddenly began to yell at him in a high voice, "Oh, you terrible person, you standing here. You doing nothing like always." She repeated her words several times, jumbling them together; he stared at her open-mouthed, taken completely aback.

The woman, he saw now, was Lydia Fergesson.

"Just stand there!" she yelled at him, her face elongated, drawn out, made over from inside. "Never do anything in the wide world except for yourself, you selfish dreadful man."

"What?" he said, moving to shut off the hose.

Lydia pointed at the garage.

"He isn't there," Al said. "He's been gone all day. I looked in around two."

Her mouth opened and she said, "He lay in there sick."

Oh my God, Al thought. The thing did happen. "What kind of sick?" he said. "Will you tell me?" His own voice rose, almost as shrill now as hers. "You hysterical foreign nut!" he yelled at her, standing so close to her that he could see every pore of her skin, every wrinkle and line and hair. She backed away a step, showing fear. "Get out of here," he yelled. "Get off my lot." As she retreated he ran after her. "What happened to him?" he yelled, dropping the hose and grabbing hold of the sleeve of her coat. "Tell me!"

She said, "He had an attack."

"Where is he?"

"At home." Her voice was lower, without the accusation. "A good customer who has fondness and care for him happened to come and find him sitting in the office; he could not even call. And he was driven to the doctor who took X-rays and taped him."

Some of Al's fear vanished. "You made it sound like he was dead. Like he croaked." He was shaking and his voice wavered.

"Good-bye," Lydia said. "I came down here by cab in order to tell you what your attitude might have done."

"What attitude?" He followed her to the edge of the lot. There, in a parking slot, was the cab, new, yellow and shiny; the driver sat reading the newspaper. "I'll drive you back to the house," he said. "Is it okay to see him? Can I see him and see how he is?"

Lydia said, "Will you drive with care?"

"Sure," he said, already going to his best car, the Chevrolet, opening the door and starting up the motor, racing the motor by pushing down on the foot pedal. Then he strode over to the parked cab and paid the driver. Returning, he found that Lydia had already gotten into the Chevrolet, in the back seat. She sat staring ahead, her face expressionless . . . on purpose, he decided as he got in front, behind the wheel. Came down here to make me feel bad because I didn't find him.

He drove through traffic. Neither of them spoke.

When he got to the house on Grove Street he went on ahead of Lydia, up the steps and onto the porch. The front door, how-ever, was locked, and so he had to wait for her. As soon as she had unlocked the door he went inside.

There in the living room he found the old man, looking about the same as always except that he had on a blue wool bathrobe and slippers, instead of his cotton work suit and shoes. He sat in the center of the couch, his feet up on a hassock, watch-ing the television set. The room was filled with the din of the set.

Al stopped and stood looking at the old man, who did not seem aware of him.

At last Al went over to the set and turned the sound down. Now the old man turned his head and noticed him.

"What's the matter?" Al said.

The old man said, "I got a cut on my chest."

"Nothing more?"

"Maybe a cracked rib. The doctor took X-rays. It's taped up."

"How'd it happen?"

"I fell," the old man said.

"Slipped on grease?"

"No."

Al waited. "How, then?" he said finally.

"On some wet grass," the old man said.

"Where the hell'd you find any wet grass?"

From behind him Lydia said, "He was in Marin County."

"Taking a vacation?" Al said.

"On business," the old man said. He sat silently for a time, with a look on his face of grimness. He said nothing more. Al could not think of anything to say; he stood around, getting his breath, calming down. It did not seem so bad after all. Obviously the woman had gone off the deep end.

"Do you need or require anything?" Lydia said, approaching the old man.

"Maybe some coffee," the old man said, "Cup of coffee?" he asked Al.

"Okay," Al said.

Lydia disappeared into the kitchen. The two men remained together, both of them silent.

"She sure had me worried," Al said.

The old man said nothing, nor did he show any expression.

"You're feeling pretty good, aren't you?" Al said. "How soon can you go back to work? What'd the doctor say?"

"He'll call me. When he gets the X-rays."

Al nodded. "Anything I can do?" he said presently.

"No," the old man said. "Thanks."

"Call some of your customers for you?"

"No."

"Okay," Al said. "You let me know."

The old man nodded.

From the kitchen, Lydia called in a clear voice, "Mr. Miller, please come in here a moment."

He went down the hall and into the kitchen.

At the sideboard, fixing the coffee, Lydia Fergesson said with her back to him, "Please get out of the house now that you have seen him long enough."

Al said, "Listen, I've worked with this guy for years." His anger, his dislike for her, filled him.

"Long enough," she said in a brisk, bright, commanding voice, almost a merry voice, as she went about getting coffee cups.

"What did I ever do?" he said.

Turning in his direction, Lydia said, "Despite what he says he is ill. He is an ill man."

"Okay," he said.

"Allow him to remain at home where he belongs and recuperate. Make no demands."

"What like?" he demanded. "What demands? What do you mean? What do you think I do to him or get out of him? You think I'm always having him fix up my cars for me? Maybe that's it." He felt both hate toward her and gloom, his old usual gloom. Certainly it was so; he did make use of the old man. And she had never liked him. She used the old man, too, and so she could easily see what went on. "Consider that I give him a hand," he said. "With the heavy stuff. Did you consider that? You better consider that, too."

She said nothing. She went on bustling about in her kitchen, paying no attention to him, smiling in her fixed fashion. Waiting for him to leave, now that she had said her piece.

For a time he stood there. He tried to think of something to say, but no idea came. Only his feeling. At last he turned and walked back to the living room. He found the old man again watching the TV set, with the sound still turned down; the old man faced the set and kept his attention on it, on the watery gray shapes.

"So long," Al said. "I have to be going."

Presently the old man nodded. Al waited, but the old man did not speak. So he stuck his hands in his pockets and walked through the house to the front door.

A moment later he was outside on the sidewalk, getting back into his Chevrolet.

Driving away, he thought, I shouldn't have left. I should have stuck around and saved him from that witch. That old harpy.

But he could not think of any excuse for going back, any way to put it that would make his return seem justified.

I really don't amount to a good God damn, he said to himself. I'm a bum, nothing but a bum. No wonder I don't get anywhere. I have no drive, no ambition. I'm doomed and I know it. There's no place for me. I don't have the guts to carve any place out.

He did not go back to the lot; instead, seeing that the time was nearly five, he drove on home to his own apartment in the old gray three-story wooden building.

When he opened the door he heard sounds and smelled smells; Julie was home ahead of him, in the kitchen cooking chops on the stove for dinner. He came in and greeted her.

"Hi," she said. She had on jeans and sandals, and that recalled to him that this was one of her non-working days. "Dinner won't be ready for another half-hour. You're early."

He went to the cooler and got out a bottle of sherry.

"Somebody called for you," Julie said. "A woman."

"What's her name?"

"Mrs. Lane. She left her number. She had something worthwhile to tell you, she said. You're supposed to be sure and call."

"A realtor," he said. He seated himself at the table. "The old man had an accident today. A fall. They took him home."

"That's a shame," Julie said, with no reaction at all in her voice, no surprise or regret or concern.

"Don't you care?" he said.

"I don't see why I should," she said.

"I'm thinking of going back there," he said. "To the house."

"Don't forget about dinner," she said.

"You mean I better not. I better be here."

Julie said, "I'm not going to fix it for you if you're going over there. Why should I?"

To that he had no answer. He sat fooling with the sherry bottle.

"Are you going to call that realtor?" she said. "That Mrs. Lane?"

"No," he said. "She's a pest."

"She sounded very nice."

He said, "Tell her I'm out, if she calls again."

While his wife fixed dinner he sat at the table drinking sherry. Presently he began to think over the idea he had for blackmailing the big businessman, Chris Harman. He had decided that the best way was to be absolutely direct about it, to call Harman's number on the phone, either his business number or home phone, and when he got hold of him say simply, "Listen, I know you used to make dirty records, and that's against the law. Pay me a lot of money or I'm going to the police about it." Although he had tried he could not think of any improvement on that approach.

Maybe I ought to go do it now, he thought. While I'm in the mood. So he put down his glass and made his way into the living room, where the phone was. Seated at it, he turned the pages until he came to the Hs. At last he had the number of a Christian Harman, who lived in Piedmont. The address seemed right, and, taking the receiver off the hook, he began to dial.

But after he had dialed the prefix he changed his mind; he put the receiver back down and returned to pondering. Probably there were well-known better techniques for doing it, known to anyone who had ever gone into the matter. Who would know? Somebody like Tootie Dolittle, perhaps. He had done a lot of various things.

"Who are you calling?" Julie said, from the kitchen. "That realtor woman?"

"No," he said. Getting up, he shut the door so she could not hear. It occurred to him, too, that Harman would recognize his voice.

When he dialed Tootie's number a woman answered.

"Let me speak to Tootie," he said.

"He not home yet," the woman said. "Who is this, please?"

He told her to have Tootie call him, giving his name.

"He just come home," the woman said. "He just walk in the door. Just a moment, please." The phone banged in his ear; there were shufflings and murmurings, and then Tootie came on.

"Hello, Al."

Al said, "Listen, I got something I can't do that you can do for me. It'll only take a second. It's a phone call." This was not the first time they had exchanged favors of this kind.

"Who to?" Tootie said.

"I'll just give you the number," Al said. "You ask for Chris. When he comes on, you tell him you know about the 'Little Eva' record."

"Okay," Tootie said. "I tell him I know about the 'Little Eva' record. What he say?"

Al said, "He should get upset."

"He get upset."

"Then you say, 'But I could forget I know about the "Little Eva" record,' or something like that. Something suggesting you want to do business with him."

"I forget about the 'Little Eva' record," Tootie repeated.

"Then get right off the phone. But say you'll call again. Then get off. Don't hang around."

Tootie said, "I call from a booth. That the way I work those kind of thing."

"Fine," he said.

"From in front of the liquor store," Tootie said.

"Fine."

"Then I call you and say what he say."

"Fine," Al said.

"What he number? You give me that like you say."

He gave Tootie Harman's phone number. Ringing off, he sat back to wait.

Half an hour later the phone rang, and when he answered it he found himself again talking to Tootie.

"I call him," Tootie said. "I say, 'Look here, man, I know about them "Little Eva." What you going to do?' That right?"

"Fine," Al said.

"He say, 'What.' I say what I said again."

"Did he sound nervous?"

Tootie said, "No, he not."

"How did he sound?"

"He not sound at all. He ask me how many I want."

"What?" Al said, puzzled.

"He say, 'How many "Little Eva" you want?' He intend to sell me some 'Little Eva' record; he in the record business. I got the name written down." A pause. "It called Teach Records."

"For Christ's sake," Al said. "He thought you were a record dealer trying to order."

Tootie said, "He say he sell only in boxes of twenty-five at forty percent off. An' he say, 'How many joke folder you want? They come free.'"

"What did you say?"

"I say I call back, an' hung up. Okay?"

"Okay," Al said. "Thanks a lot."

"Listen," Tootie said. "That 'Little Eva' have to do with colored people and their problems?"

"No," he said. "It's a song. A record."

"My wife say," Tootie said, "'Little Eva' a colored person."

He thanked Tootie again and rang off.

Well, that had not worked out at all.

From the kitchen, Julie appeared. "I can't hold dinner any longer," she said.

"Okay," Al said, preoccupied. As he walked into the kitchen and drew up a chair to the table, he thought, The guy certainly isn't very nervous about his dirty records. And they aren't a skeleton from his past; he's still able to supply them in boxes of twenty-five.

As he sat eating dinner he mentioned to his wife how Lydia Fergesson had thrown him out of the house. Julie's face became inflamed.

"God damn her," she said, in a frenzy. "She did that? If I'd been there I'd have settled her hash. I would have." She stared at him, so deeply gripped by her emotions that she could not speak.

"Maybe he'll die and leave me something," Al said. "Maybe he'll leave it all to me. He's got no children."

"I don't care about that!" Julie shouted. "I care about their treatment of you. First he conceals what he's doing from you, even though your whole economic existence is bound up in that lot, and then they walk over you. God, I wish I'd been there. And she got you to drive her home. Like a chauffeur!"

"It was my idea," he said. "To drive her back home, so I could see how he was."

"It's a closed part of your life," she said. "Never think about that old man again; forget you ever saw him or knew him—think about the future. Don't ever go to their house. I'm not ever going back, not after the way they patronized me."

"Frankly," Al said, "I was thinking of going back tonight."

"Why?" She snapped out the word, quivering.

"I don't like to get thrown out. I think I owe it to my sense of honor and pride to go back."

"Go back and do what? She'll just insult you; you can't hold your own with either of them; you're too weak to deal with either of them. Not weak. But—" She gestured; she had ceased eating entirely. "Unable to face the harsh realities."

Al said, "Now I have to go back. After you saying that." At least that was the way he saw it. There was no other honorable way. Even my wife, he thought, looks down on me.

"Then you better take one of those pills," Julie said. "Those Dexymil pills you have. When you take one of those you show a little more fight."

"That's a good idea," Al said. "I will."

"You're serious?" Julie said. "You want to keep batting your brains out against those people, for no gainful purpose?"

Al said, "I'll go over and ask what the hell he was doing in Marin County in the middle of a weekday. It makes me curious."

But it was really to retackle Lydia Fergesson; he felt that he had to vindicate himself. His wife had made him come to that conclusion, or at least she had speeded up the process. In a day or so, he decided, I would have gotten around to it anyhow.

8

Hearing a car parking at the curb outside the house, Lydia Fergesson went to the window and looked down. She said, "There is that
disgusting, nauseating man again. That Al."

"Good," the old man said. Propped up on the couch in the
living room, he had been thinking to himself that it would be nice
to have company. He was still depressed. He did not feel strong,
nor able to get dressed; he had on his bathrobe, and Lydia had
served him his dinner there instead of at the table.

"I won't let him in," Lydia said.

"Let him in," he said. He could hear Al coming up the front
steps. "We can have a beer. Go get out some beer. He had to go
right away before."

The doorbell sounded.

Lydia said, "I will not open or unlock the door. Did you
know I have it locked? I have the chain in place."

It did not surprise him. Getting heavily to his feet he made his way step by step across the living room; she watched him as he got closer and closer to the front door. It took him a long time, but at last he made it; he unlatched the chain and turned the doorknob.

"Hi," Al said. "Glad to see you up."

"We heard you park," the old man said, holding the door open. "Excuse me if I go sit down again."

Al entered the house and followed him back across the living room. Now there was no sign of Lydia; she had disappeared. The old man heard a door close somewhere, probably her bedroom door. It was just as well, seeing how she felt about Al.

"It's nice in here," Al said. He seemed more tense than usual; he stood with his hands stuck in the pockets of his cloth jacket, grinning in the harsh, humorless manner that the old man knew so well. Behind his glasses his eyes gleamed.

"Sit down," Fergesson said. "Your wife didn't come along. I guess she's still sore at me."

Al seated himself across from him.

"I'm buying a new garage," the old man said.

After a moment Al began to laugh.

"I mean it," the old man said.

"I know you mean it," Al said.

"You surprised? You are."

"Sure," Al said. "When did this happen? Today?"

"I went up and looked at it today," the old man said. "It's over in Marin County. I got a hot tip so I went over there. There's a lot of big financiers involved in it. You ever heard of Achilles Bradford? He's the big gun behind it all. They have millions involved."

Al said, "Involved in what? I don't get it." He had lost his grin; he seemed to be bewildered.

"In a shopping center," the old man said. "It's called Gardens." For the life of him he could not remember the name; it had escaped him. "Marin Gardens," he said. "One of those tracts. Along the highway." He ceased. The talking had made him pant; he sat getting back his wind, rubbing his chest with his hand. Al saw the motion, the care with which he explored and touched himself. The old man moved his hand away and laid it down on the arm of the couch.

"I'll be darned," Al said, in a slow voice.

"I don't do any work," the old man said. "Any physical work. Only supervising."

Al nodded.

"What do you think?" the old man said.

"Sounds fine," Al said.

"It's just what I've been looking for," the old man said. "It's as new as tomorrow." That was how he thought of it; he had come across that expression, and it fitted perfectly. "It's part of the atomic world," he said. "You know. Modern. Everything modern." Again he ceased talking and merely sat.

"Fine," Al said.

"I'm really on the in," the old man said. "This is the inside. I have people working for me, in contacts. This is something nobody knows about. This opportunity. I didn't even tell Lydia."

"I see," Al said.

"You ought to get something like this," the old man said.

"It takes money."

"Sure," the old man said. "I have to put up something like forty-five thousand dollars."

Al's face showed deep reaction; he was impressed.

"A lot," the old man said, smiling. "Plenty of dough. I got thirty-five thousand from the garage. Then ten I have already. In stocks and bonds. Savings account."

Al said, "You're putting up everything on this? You better watch your step."

"I'm watching my step," he said.

"You have legal advice?"

"Sure," the old man said. "Listen, you know who's going to deal with Bradford for me?" He had been thinking it over, and he had made up his mind. "Boris doesn't know anything about this kind of stuff," he said. "It takes an expert."

"Boris is your lawyer."

"That's right." Breathing heavily, the old man said, "Harman is going to represent me and deal with the big boys."

Al said, "Chris Harman? The dirty-record man?"

"Yes," the old man said. "He drives the '58 Cadillac; he owns that record place, Teach Records. I told you about him."

"The motherfucker is a crook," Al said.

"No," the old man said. "The hell."

"He is."

"What do you know? How do you know?" He felt his pulse labor. His body labored. "Listen, you don't know him. I know him for almost six years. We're both businessmen."

"He put you onto this?" Al said. "He wants your money."

"You don't know," the old man said. "What do you know? How much have you amassed? Nothing." His voice escaped him; it shook and faded. Clearing his throat, he said, "A bunch of old wrecks."

"Listen," Al said in a low voice. "That guy is a crook. I know he is. He probably owns this place, this Gardens. Everybody knows it, that he's a crook."

"Who?"

"Mrs. Lane. The realtor."

The old man sat up, saying, "That colored realtor?"

Al nodded.

"A colored pal of yours? That's how you know?"

"That's right," Al said. "You talk to her. Call her."

The old man said, "When do I call a colored and ask advice."

"Now," Al said. By degrees his face flushed.

"I don't listen to colored," the old man said.

"You listen to that fancy-dressed crook, because he's got a Cadillac."

They were both silent, facing each other, both breathing through their mouths.

"I don't need your advice," the old man said.

"You sure do. You're getting senile."

The old man could think of nothing to say.

"You must have fallen on your head," Al said. "On your God damn head. Call your lawyer and tell him you're being swindled by a crook. Call the district attorney. I'll call the district attorney, the first thing tomorrow."

"You keep out of it," the old man said as loudly as he could. "Mind your own business."

Suddenly there was Lydia in the room. Neither of them had noticed her come in; they both turned their heads at the same moment.

Lydia said, "What's this about a crook swindling you out of your money?" She moved toward the old man, her eyes black and shining. "What does Mr. Miller mean? Why didn't you say you invested your money from the garage in this place, which you don't even know the name of?"

"It's my business," the old man said. He did not look at either of them; he stared down at the floor.

No one spoke.

To Lydia, Al said, "This guy's a con man. I know he is."

Going to the telephone, Lydia reached down and lifted up the receiver; holding it to Al she said, "You call this man, whatever his name is, and tell him there is no intention by my husband; he does not want to go into this."

"Sure," Al said. He started toward the phone. "But it wouldn't mean anything," he said. "What I say."

"Then you say," Lydia said to the old man. "You call him and tell him now. You have nothing in writing, do you? You did not go and sign anything, did you? I know not. I know in my heart that God did not permit you to go ahead; I have that faith."

At last he said, "No. I didn't."

"Thank God in the heavens above us," Lydia said. "As Schiller says, it is an ode to the joy of the heavenly father beyond the band of stars." Her eyes sparkled with relief and happiness.

The old man said, "I'm going to see him tomorrow."

"No, you are not," she said.

Al said, "There's no problem; all you have to do is get hold of the district attorney and show your husband that this Harman is involved in this real-estate venture, this shopping center he wants Jim to invest in."

The old man said, "Of course he's involved in it. Otherwise how would he know about it?"

"I mean there's a connection between him and Bradford," Al said. "The guy who you're going to have Harman represent you with."

"If there wasn't a connection," the old man said, "how would Harman have known about it?" Excitedly, he said, "That's the whole point. I know he's connected; that's the point."

Al said, "I mean financially connected. This shopping center is financially his."

"Then he really believes in it," the old man said. "If he's willing to put up his own money. That proves he thinks it's reliable. He let me in on a good investment and he invested in it himself.

Of course he did; you don't know anything. You know nothing about this thing. You keep out of it—" He waved his hands at both Al Miller and Lydia. "You keep out of it, you women and boys. This is for me. What I say goes!"

Neither of them were smiling at him now; Al's bitter grin was gone, and Lydia's glassy fixed Greek smile was gone, too. Al had begun to look depressed. He scraped his shoe against the floor and fingered the edge of his jacket; he began zipping and unzipping his jacket. It seemed to the old man that Lydia had begun to draw away. Her face was blank. As if she could no longer bear the situation; it was too much for her. And, seeing that, he felt triumph; he felt the victory.

"Listen," he said, "neither of you ever even seen it. So what do you know about it? Did you go over to Marin County?" They did not answer. "Just me," he said. "You're talking about something you never even saw." To Lydia he shouted, "And you never met Mr. Harman either, so you don't know anything at all."

They gazed back, without answering. He had the floor.

"You better come take a look at it," the old man said to Al. "You drive over there and take a look."

"Hell," Al said, "I don't want to see it. I'm just giving you advice. My advice."

"Sure," the old man said. "Just advice. You won't go look; you know if you see it you'll admit you're wrong." He wheezed with exultation; he had them, both of them. "I been in business a long time, a lot longer than you. You're just a bum. A bum who sits around. You know what you do? You—" He broke off.

"I sell used cars," Al said in a wooden tone.

"To colored," the old man said.

Al was silent.

"And that's all you'll ever be," the old man said.

"I got a couple of irons in the fire," Al said.

"At least you're not crazy," the old man said, laughing. "Isn't that right?"

Al glanced up at him.

"Like me," the old man said.

Al shrugged.

"You can come and visit me while I'm sitting up there," the old man said. "In my new auto garage with the mechanics. Everything spic and span."

"Okay," Al said. He seemed to have no energy now. No more willingness to fight.

Lydia slipped from the room. Back, probably, to the kitchen or her bedroom; anyhow she was gone. Only the two of them remained.

"Off to a seminar," the old man said.

"What?" Al murmured.

"Off to class."

Al said, "Well, I better get going."

"See you," the old man said.

His hands in his pockets, Al moved off toward the hall and the front door.

"Don't look so depressed," the old man called after him. "Cheer up."

"Sure," Al said, turning. "Lots of luck," he said.

"Same to you," the old man said.

Al opened the front door. He hestitated, started to speak, and then shut the door after him. Presently the old man heard the front door open again, stealthily. She's going after him, he said to himself. At that, he laughed with delight. Sitting on his couch in his bathrobe he laughed to himself, thinking of Lydia and Al conferring in secret outside on the front porch, trying to figure out how to do something. Find some way to stop him.

* * *

As Al Miller opened the door of his car he heard a voice behind him. Lydia Fergesson came hurrying down the steps and across the sidewalk. "Listen, Mr. Miller," she said. "Just a moment so that I can talk to you."

He seated himself behind the wheel and waited.

"I depend on you," she said, her black eyes fixed on him.

"Hell," he said, "I can't do anything." He felt anger and futility. "Do it yourself."

"He would never have told me anything," she said. "He never said a word, only about his fall; he would go on and give his money away to the crook with no word to me ever, and leave me with nothing. That is how he feels about me."

Al closed the car door, started up the motor, and drove away.

Why the hell did I go over there? he asked himself. Why didn't I stay home?

They're both nuts, he said to himself.

How'm I going to get out of it? I have my own problems. Let them take care of theirs. I don't have the time. I can't even solve my own problems; I can't even get anywhere with them, and they're really simple. All I need to do is find another location for Al's Motor Sales.

And then another thought came up from deep inside him; he had not been aware of it, but it had been there nevertheless. I hope he does get swindled, he thought. I hope Harman takes him for everything he has. It's exactly what he deserves, what the two of them, him and that crazy Greek wife, deserve.

What I ought to do is find some way to swindle him myself. That was it; that was really it.

He had worked with Jim Fergesson for years, and surely if anyone deserved to get the money it was he, Al Miller, not some well-to-do customer driving a Cadillac who knew the old man only as the guy who greased his cars. I know him better than anyone, Al said to himself; I'm his best friend. Why does it go to Harman and not me?

He thought, But if I tried to swindle the money from the old man, I'd foul it up and land in jail. There's no use even trying to; I can't swindle the old man or blackmail Harman. I just don't have the talent.

Why can't I be like him? he asked himself. I'm a failure, and Chris Harman is what I ought to be; he's everything I'm not.

But, he wondered, how do you get to be like that?

There was no easy way. As he drove along the street, Al Miller sorted through every possible way; how did a person like himself become a person like Chris Harman? It was a complete mystery to him. A riddle.

No wonder everyone looks down on me, he thought.

What I'll do, he decided, is go by Harman's house, and when he comes to the door I'll tell him I want to go to work for him. I'd like to be a dirty-record salesman. I'll tell him that. He can find something for me; if not that, then something else. I can repair the pressers that make records. Or I can work at his house, on his cars; he doesn't have a mechanic now. I can devote all my time to his Cadillac and his Mercedes-Benz, polishing them and greasing them and aligning the front ends.

What I ought to do, he thought, is show some real ambition and make up something really good; I could tell him, for instance, that I have a mystical ability, that I can heal sick cars, or sick record-pressers. It's done by a laying-on of hands. Or by singing. Something that'll really attract his attention. Isn't that how the great Americans in the past made it? They all had a flair. When they were, say, nineteen years old they got into Andrew Carnegie's office for *one minute* and they told him they never saved string, or that they charged twenty-five dollars an hour for their time. That did the trick.

I have to get it exactly right, he told himself. I have to think until I come up with the really terrific new idea that will swing it. Anything less and I am doomed; I'll go on like I am, and never be anything more than I am.

This is my chance to break out and be something.

My whole life, he told himself, my whole future, depends on it. Can I do it? I have to. I owe it to Julie, and to myself; in fact, to my family. I can't wait any longer; I can't go on drifting like this. This is opportunity knocking, this guy Chris Harman; this is the way it's been set up and if I ignore it I'll never be given another chance. That's the way it always is.

And then something else occurred to him. I think I'm out of my mind, he thought. That whole business in there, that argument with the old man, drove me crazy. I'm out of my skull.

And yet there was something in the idea. What would I be like, after working around Chris Harman for a while? he asked himself. He might give me something really good. Probably he's got his hands into so many enterprises that he's got plenty of jobs to dole out; he probably employs hundreds of people.

In fact, he thought, Harman's probably hiring and firing all day long.

Should I call the district attorney and report Harman as a crook? Or should I try to blackmail him for trying to swindle the old man? Or should I show up at his house or his place of business and try to talk him into hiring me? Or should I just go home and go to bed with my wife and get up the next morning and go to work at Al's Motor Sales?

It was a hard question to answer. He could not make it out, try as he might.

What I need is a drink, he said to himself. Ahead the green and yellow lights of a bar could be seen, a bar he had never been to, but still a real bar, one that had a permit to sell wine and beer. So he parked the car and got out and crossed over to the other side of the street and went into the bar.

That whole argument really shook me, he said to himself as he pushed past people and up to the bartender to order his drink. Finding out about Harman swindling the old man, and then having him laugh at me and insult me because I told him the truth. Too much. That's what I get for trying to wise him up, he realized. That's my reward for breaking the news to him; he doesn't want to hear it, so I get the blame.

"Hamm's beer," he said to the bartender.

Poor sick old nut, he thought. Wrapped up in his bathrobe and his slippers on his feet, watching TV for all he's worth. What's going to become of him? Maybe he'll have a heart attack and die, or another heart attack. Maybe he's dying now. Maybe he had a stroke and part of his brain isn't functioning; it certainly could be that.

But he's always been that way, Al realized. He's no different, only more determined. The stupid old fart.

And then a terrible thought came to him, worse than any of the others. Suppose Mrs. Lane was just trying to keep me in the market, he thought. Trying to keep me from going into business with someone who already has all the real estate he can use; suppose what she said about Harman was just a sales pitch to keep me on the ropes.

That's a really smart woman, he realized. She can wind me around her finger; it's like having my mother after me, back in St. Helena. Maybe I'm wrong about Harman; maybe he isn't trying to swindle the old man after all. My God, maybe I told the old man wrong. Maybe he's right about me, me and my colored friends, and all the rest.

He drank his Hamm's beer and ordered another. He stayed at the bar far into the late evening, drinking by himself, thinking it all over, admitting to himself again and again—it always seemed to be there—that he absolutely lacked the ability to see how things really stood. It seemed to be a major defect in him, and it continued to stare him in the face the more he thought about it. The defect did not go away; it was real. It was ruining his life.

And what could he do about it?

Several hours later he thought he had the answer. As best he could, he made his way across the bar to the phone booth. There he looked up Mrs. Lane's home phone number, put in a dime and dialed.

When she answered, he said, "Hello, there. This is Mr. Chris Harman. Why are you telling lies about me? What do you have against me?" There was a lot more he had intended to say, but at that point Mrs. Lane interrupted him, more with a giggle than with her sentence.

"What you doing, Mr. Miller?" She went on giggling. "I know your voice; you can't fool me. Sound like you out somewhere celebrating."

"I wouldn't swindle that old man," he said. "He's kept my cars running for years. You must be out of your mind. I ought to hire a lawyer and sue you. How'm I going to keep my cars running now that he's selling his garage? You ought to feel sorry for me instead of persecuting me."

"You mean Mr. Fergesson?" Mrs. Lane said. "You talking about him?"

"You're against me," Al said.

Mrs. Lane said, "I never heard anybody carry on so. Where you at?"

"I'm at the Forty-One Club," he said, holding up the package of matches the bartender had given him. "On Grove Street. They cater to only the best of trade."

Giggling, Mrs. Lane said, "You better go home, Mr. Miller. And let your wife put you to bed."

"Why don't you come down here and I'll buy you a beer?" he said to Mrs. Lane. "Bring your husband if you have one. If you don't, bring him anyhow."

"You really crazy," Mrs. Lane said. "You go home; you hear me? You go home."

"I hear you," he said. He hung up the phone, left the bar, looked around until he had found his car, got into it and went home.

9

The next day Jim Fergesson felt well enough and rested enough to dress and go down to the garage. He did not plan to do any heavy work; he intended to do only light stuff, and to be there to answer the phone when his customers called. He wanted to explain to them what had happened, his accident and what he intended to do.

The mailman appeared at nine o'clock, shortly after the old man had unlocked the big wooden doors. Among the usual ads and bills he found an odd-looking letter. It was in a personal stationery envelope; it did not look like a business letter. The name and address—his—had been written by means of an old typewriter; the letters were out of alignment, and partly red, and dirt-filled.

At his desk he opened the envelope. The letter inside had been written on the same old machine.

Dear Mr. Fergesson,

    I understand you are thinking of going into a business situation with Mr. Christian Harman, the man who owns that record business up on the corner of 25th Street. Seeing as I am in a position to know about matters of that sort, I advise you that you better be careful as Mr. Harman is not reputable. I would sign my name to this only Mr. Harman is smart enough that he would sue me. However I do know about what I speak. Also, I am sorry that you have sold your garage.

There was no signature on the letter.

Did Al write this? the old man asked himself. He began to chuckle to himself as he reread the letter. It was the kind of gag that Al would think up; he could imagine Al tracking down an old typewriter, the older the better, the dirtier the keys the better, and then boning up in his mind as to how to phrase it, making it sound as unlike his usual style as possible. Making it sound like some ignorant Okie or possibly coon; yes, he thought—like some colored person.

On the other hand, he thought, maybe it wasn't from Al; maybe all sorts of people knew about his going over to Marin County and having a look at Marin Country Gardens. The word had gotten around to the other merchants along San Pablo Avenue.

Thinking that, the old man felt angry. What business of theirs was it? Maybe they were jealous, he thought. Resentful that he was about to break away from this run-down district. Maybe it was Betty at the health food store. The more he thought about it, the more it seemed to him that this was exactly the sort of letter that old Betty, with her worries and fads, would write. I think I'll go over there, he decided. And show it to her and get her to admit she wrote it.

Are they all talking about me? he wondered. Getting together and discussing me? God damn them, he thought. He felt anger at all of them, the whole bunch.

But suppose Betty hadn't written it. If he showed it to her then, he would appear foolish. Better not to show it to anybody, even Al, just in case Al hadn't written it either.

But then a new sensation came to him; it entered him so gradually that at first he did not notice it.

It pleased him to think that they were talking about him.

Sure they are, he decided. Word's got around. Al spread the word. This letter proves it.

Things always got around fast along the street, from one store to the next. Rumor and gossip, about everybody's business.

Leaving the office, he walked out of the garage and down the sidewalk. A moment later he was opening the door of the health food store, greeting Betty at the same time.

"Hi, Jim," she said, rising and going to get the Silex coffeemaker. "How are you, today?"

"I'm okay," he said, seating himself at the counter. There were a couple of other customers, middle-aged women whom he did not know. He glanced around, but there was no one whom he recognized, except of course Betty.

"Anything with your coffee?" Betty asked. "A roll?"

"Okay," he said, turning the stool so that he could watch the entrance of the garage. "Listen," he said, "you heard about me, did you? About what I did?"

At the shelf of rolls, Betty halted. "You told me about selling your garage," she said.

The old man said, "Listen, I bought another garage."

The wrinkled, elderly face showed pleasure. "I'm glad," she said. "Where is it?"

"In Marin County," he said. "A new one. I'm putting up a great deal of money, more than I got for the old garage. I got an inside tip. I can't tell you exactly where it is, naturally. You'll find out in due time. These things take time."

"I'm really pleased," Betty said. "I'm so glad."

Accepting his cup of coffee from her, the old man said, "I guess you know this guy Chris Harman. He always brings his cars to me; he drives a '58 Cadillac. Very well-dressed man."

"I may have seen him," Betty said.

The old man said, "I'll tell you; I'm taking a real risk. A real risk. Here's the risk." He felt more and more excitement; his words came out almost faster then he could speak them. "I have to keep my eye on this guy Harman. A lot of people wouldn't take the chance." He winked at Betty, but she gazed back without comprehension. "He's got a reputation," he said.

"What kind of reputation do you mean?"

"A lot of people think he's a big-time crook," the old man said.

Her face showed dismay. "Jim," she said. "Be careful."

"I'm being careful," he said, chuckling. "Don't worry about me. He's really a well-known crook. He's skinned a lot of people. He may skin me. I wouldn't be surprised. It could happen." He laughed out loud; now her face showed both worry and agitation. "Maybe I'll wind up with no garage and no money," he said. "Wouldn't that be a hell of a thing? Things like that do happen; you read about them in the paper every day."

"Jim, you be careful," Betty said. "You watch your step. You spent years acquiring the money that you have."

"Oh, he might get me," the old man said. "He's smart." He drank down more of the coffee, then set the cup back down. "I have to get back," he said. "I just came over to break the news to you." Getting carefully to his feet, avoiding any too-sudden move-ment, he started to the door. "If you see me going by with a tin cup," he said, pausing at the door, "you'll know why."

"Make sure you think everything out," Betty was saying to

him as he shut the door of the health food store after him and started down the sidewalk, back to the garage.

They're all talking, he thought to himself. They know I'm possibly going to get swindled out of everything I have. That'll give them something to talk about for a long time. They know Harman is a big-time swindler, a real professional; you can tell by the way they dress, by the expensive clothes. The tailoring and the car; look at the car he drives, a '58 Cadillac. There's nothing small-time there, he realized. And the house he owns, and his business connections and enterprises; he has his hand in just about every kind of thing. He's really a big man. An important businessman.

They know he's made a lot of money. He's really rich; he might even have a couple of hundred thousand dollars. Maybe he owns the whole of Marin Gardens outright. Maybe there isn't even somebody named Bradford, or if there is, he's just a front. Somebody Harman hired to represent him, like he hired Carmichael.

But there's one thing to be sure about, he said to himself as he re-entered his garage. There's nobody over Harman; there's nobody he's taking orders from. He's the real boss of the whole thing. I've known him for years, and he's nobody's servant. He's in charge.

I wonder who else I can tell, he thought. Maybe the barber across the street. He could go over for a haircut later on.

The exhilaration which had come over him after reading the anonymous letter continued to grow; it had gotten into every part of him. It made his hands and feet twitch with the need to do something, to be active. This is really something I'm involved in, he said to himself.

For a moment he stood in the doorway of his garage, listening to see if the phone were ringing; at the same time he peered into the gloom to see if any customers had entered and were waiting around. He heard no one and saw no one, so, after a moment, he went on down the sidewalk to Al's Motor Sales. I'll drop in on old Al, he said to himself, and see what he has to say.

However, to his surprise, he found that Al's Motor Sales was closed up; the chain that linked the corner posts of the lot was still in place from the night, and the door of the little building had its lock on it. Also, he saw, a few items of mail stuck from beneath the door; Al had not shown up at all today. He had never arrived to open his lot, and here it was almost ten-thirty now.

Standing there, the old man felt disappointment. God damn him, he said to himself. His previous anger returned. The hell with him, he thought as he turned and started back to his garage.

I don't know why I should be talking to him anyhow, he decided. What did he do, but cast aspersion on everything I'm involved in? Some of Al's words of the night before returned to him, and he felt his ears and neck become hot. Let him go his way and I'll go mine, he told himself. He'll sink down and I'll rise, because we're different; we're at opposite ends of the spectrum.

There's no way we can talk to each other, he thought as he entered the garage once more. We've got nothing to say. Not if he's going to take the line he does, begrudging, as he always does, another person's success because he's so bitter about his own failure to amount to anything. It's the same old story; if you get anywhere in the world, all you incur is envy and malice. Everybody hates you because they wish they were you, and they know they never will be. That's why they all hate Chris Harman, and that's why they hate me.

As he re-entered his office, he thought, Al's probably home sleeping off a morning-after. When he left my house he probably went directly to a bar; it would be typical of him. And now he can't make it to open up his lot. He's probably still in bed. And his wife is out at her job, supporting the two of them; supporting that bum.

And he'll never change, the old man thought. He'll never grab opportunity and rise; he'll always be the bum he is now, until the day he dies.

That morning, at ten o'clock, Al Miller sat in his car parked at the corner of 25th Street and Pershing Avenue. Across from him the three-story Teach Records, Inc. building dominated the neighborhood, making much more of a showing than the medical-dental building next to it, or the accounting offices of a chain of supermarkets.

For half an hour he had been sitting in his car, with the motor off, watching Teach Records, smoking, noticing the people going in and out and along the sidewalk and the trucks pulling up and leaving.

Should I go in? he asked himself.

If I do, he thought, it'll change my life. I have to be sure I want to; I have to decide now, because once I'm in there, it'll be too late. The thing only works one way; it only goes in, not out.

To assist—but not guide—himself he had brought along an Anacin tin filled with pills. Now was the time. Opening the tin, he took out a flat green pill that looked like a candy heart; this one was a Dexymil, and he swallowed the whole pill, washing it down with Coke from a bottle he had brought along. Taking the Dexy made him feel better almost at once; it gave him a feeling of anticipation, because he knew, from experience, that before long a good mood would settle over him, and that out of this mood good things would come. But there was also the problem that, when he had taken a Dexy, he tended to talk too fast and too much. So to balance the little flat green candy-heart-shaped pill, he now swallowed down a round red shiny-coated pill, a Sparine, which looked like nothing so much as a ladybug with its feet drawn in. The Sparine was not a stimulant but a tranquilizer. He hoped that together the two pills would bring about the state he wanted, the state appropriate for what he was about to do.

For good measure he also took two Anacin tablets. And that was it; he closed the tin and put it away in this pocket.

The next he knew, he was crossing the street. Then he stood in a fluorescent-lit office, facing a girl at a desk and switchboard. The girl, pretty, young, with earrings, looked up and said, "Yes, sir."

He said, "I want to see Mr. Teach."

"Mr. Teach isn't here," the girl said. "He's dead."

"Dead!" Al Miller said, amazed. "What happened? I didn't know him, but what the hell happened?"

"He was shot down in North Carolina," the girl said. "By someone; I think his name was Mayhard or Maynard." She waited, but he could think of nothing to say; he stood mutely in front of her desk. "You could see Mr. Knight," she said. "He's the manager. What was it about?"

"Okay," he said, but then he remembered that it was not Mr. Teach that he wanted to see at all; he had gotten the name from the sign over the building. It was Chris Harman that he wanted to see. "I want to see Mr. Harman," he said.

"Mr. Harman is tied up right now," the girl said. "If you will give me your name and sit down, I'll notify his secretary and find out for you if he has time to see you today."

He gave the girl his name and then went to sit down on one of the modern office chairs.

In what seemed to him to be no time at all the girl began to beckon to him. He put down his *Life* and walked over.

"Mr. Harman has a few minutes to see you now," the girl said. "He can squeeze you in, if it doesn't take too long." She pointed to a hallway. "The first office on the right."

It was like a plastic and glass doctors' office, with side cubicles. He found the office, and there sat Chris Harman.

"Good day, Mr. Miller," Mr. Harman said pleasantly, indicating a chair. "What can I do for you?"

Seating himself, Al said, "I'm sorry to hear about Mr. Teach. As I told the girl, I didn't know him, but I know the Teach catalog, and—"

"It happened a long time ago," Harman said, smiling. "In 1718."

"Beg pardon?" Al said. "Oh, I think I see." He laughed. It was a gag or something. He could not follow it, so he let the subject go. "You're in charge?" he said. "You own this place?"

Mr. Harman, smiling slightly, nodded.

"Listen," Al said, "do you remember me?"

"I think I do," Harman said. "I know I've seen you before." He glanced down, and Al knew that Mr. Harman was inspecting his clothing, his cloth jacket, slacks, shoes, sports shirt. Sizing him up by what he wore.

"I'm a used-car salesman," Al said.

Mr. Harman nodded. "Ah, I see," he said.

"You remember, now?"

"I think so."

"I'm a no-good crook," Al said. "One of the worst used-car salesmen there is."

Mr. Harman ceased smiling, and his eyes became larger. His mouth fell open slightly. "Oh, indeed?" he murmured.

"I feel I came here to be frank," Al said.

"Please be," Harman said.

"I do all the things I can to get a sale," Al said. "It doesn't matter one bit to me what condition the car is in, just so long as I sell it. Let's face facts. The cars I have on my lot—"

"Yes," Harman interrupted. "You have a used-car lot. Al's Motor Sales. I remember now."

"They're turkeys," Al said. "Dogs. They ought to be junked. Let me give you an example. Do you have the time?"

Harman nodded.

"I got in an ex-taxi cab the other day. The way you can tell is a cab always has four doors, and usually it's either a Plymouth or a Studebaker. It's got no accessories except a heater, and the cheapest car in the line. And they paint out the company name on the doors. And on the top there's holes where they mounted the name-plate. So I knew this was a cab. It was a real wreck. It must have had three hundred thousand miles on it. I got it for a hundred bucks. I repainted it, cleaned it up, got it looking good, and then I made up a story to go with it."

"You set the speedometer back?" Harman said.

"The odometer," Al said. "Yes, back to eleven thousand miles. It was last year's car."

Harman lit a Benson and Hedges cigarette with a gold-inlayed cigarette lighter; he offered the box to Al, but he declined. He was too involved in what he was saying to want to smoke.

"What I said," Al said, "is that it was my wife's car."

Harman gray eyes sparkled.

"I said she's been driving it to school," Al said. "She has a phobia about buses; she can't stand to be shut in. I got it for her new from the Plymouth dealer up on Broadway; I got it wholesale, because I know the guy. So I can pass on the savings. I got it for her but we really didn't need two cars. All she did was take it up to school once a day, and maybe shopping. And I had to wash and polish it: It just took up space in the garage on weekends, because when we went anywhere we took our Chrysler."

"I see," Harman said.

"So I finally told her we couldn't keep it. I'd sell it and she could use the money for a vacation to Hawaii. So I wasn't interested in making a profit. I'd let it go for thirteen hundred."

"Did you sell it?" Harman said.

"Not the first time," Al said. "Some guy came in, and I told him that. But he noticed that the car had been repainted, and that bothered him. I told him she picked the original color, elephant gray with pink, and she got tired of that right away and got the Plymouth people to repaint it during the original guarantee. But he noticed that the shock absorbers were no good, so he knew the car had been used a lot. Anyhow, I finally unloaded it." He paused. "To a ubangi."

"Pardon?" Harman said, cupping his ear.

"To a Negro."

"Ah," Harman said. "Ubangi." He smiled.

"Naturally, he didn't have cash. He put four hundred down. I financed it through my loan company across the street."

Harman laughed.

"All I do is walk across San Pablo," Al said, "to the West Oakland Guarantee Savings. I got twelve percent compound interest on the unpaid balance, including loan charges and other fees. And if we have to repossess the car, the ubangi is still liable for the entire unpaid balance. It's a thirty-six-month contract. Actually, in all, the interest comes to a realistic twenty-four percent, because it's what we call discounted."

"I think I understand that type of interest," Harman said. "I believe I've run across it."

"So in all, I got almost two thousand dollars for the ex-taxi cab," Al said. "Originally, it cost only about sixteen hundred, new. All I had to do was paint it and clean it. And when I painted it, I didn't even have the rust sanded off, or the dents banged out; I had the dents filled with compound and painted over."

Again Mr. Harman laughed. He seemed quite interested; he showed no sign of impatience, or wanting Al to hurry up and get to his point, or to leave; he seemed quite happy to go on listening.

"I mean," Al said, "I'll do anything to sell a car. I always re-groove tires."

"What is that?"

"Taking smooth tires—with no tread—and cutting right into the fabric with a hot needle. Putting fake tread on, and then paint-ing the tire black, so it looks new."

"Isn't that dangerous?"

"Sure," Al said. "If the guy so much as backs over a hot match, the tires'll blow. But he thinks he's getting a set of good tires, so he goes ahead and buys the car when he otherwise might not. It's part of the business; everybody, or nearly everybody, does it. You have to move your stock. The main thing is to have a story that'll explain everything. If you can't get a car started, you always say it's out of gas. If a window won't roll up or down, you say the car came in just this morning and your boy hasn't had a chance to go over it yet. You have to be able to come back. If the customer notices that the floor mat is worn from wear, you say the car was driven by a woman who wore high-heeled shoes. If the seat covers are torn up from wear, maybe from kids, you say the owner had a pet dog he took with him, and in a week the dog's nails did it. You always give a story."

"I see," Harman said, paying attention.

"If the engine makes a lot of noise because of bad bearings, you say it's just a tappet adjustment."

Harman nodded.

"If the car won't go into gear, you say it's because you just had a new clutch put in, and it isn't adjusted yet."

Harman, considering, said, "Suppose the brakes don't work? Suppose you allow a customer to drive one of your cars, and when he tries to stop it, the car simply won't stop? What can you say?"

"You say some delinquent kids siphoned out the fluid," Al said, "during the night. And you sound off about kids stealing cigar lighters and light bulbs and spare tires; you sound really angry."

Harman nodded. "I see."

"I've done a good business," Al said. "I enjoy it, matching my wits against theirs. It's exciting; it's stimulating. I wouldn't go into any other business. It's my life-blood. I was born to it. I know all the tricks."

"Apparently you do," Harman said.

"But I have to get out of it."

"Why?"

Al said, "It's not big enough to hold me."

"Ah," Harman said.

"Listen," Al said. "I'm live-wire. I have go. I can't be held back by something small-time. For me, selling used cars has been a training ground. It's taught me about the world. Now I'm ready for something worthwhile. Something that really tries my mettle. It used to be a challenge, but now it isn't. Because—" He made his voice low and sharp. "I know I can win. Every time. They're no match for me. I take them one and all. Once they step onto my lot—" He made a swiping motion. "I have them. No contest."

Harman was silent.

"This is an expanding economy," Al said. "A growing country with destiny. A man either gets bigger or smaller; he either goes up with the economy, or he goes down. He becomes nothing. I refuse to become nothing. I intend to tie myself in with the American system that has room for a man with drive and sincerity."

Harman regarded him.

"That's why I can do it," Al said. "That's why I can take them every time. *Because I believe in what I'm doing.*"

Harman nodded slowly.

"It's no job," Al said. "No mere making a buck. Money means nothing to me in itself; it's what money represents. Money is proof—proof that a man has ambition and determination, and that he isn't afraid of opportunity when it knocks in his face. Money shows that he isn't afraid to be himself. And he knows others like himself. He recognizes them because they have the same drive, the same unwillingness to be turned down or set back by defeat."

Harman said, "What made you come by here, to Teach?"

"I met you," Al said. "That's the answer." He made a gesture, showing that he would add nothing more.

There was silence.

"Well," Harman said. "What do you want here? So far all you've done is detail your history."

"I want to work for Christian Harman. It's as simple as that."

Harman raised his eyebrows. "There's nothing open, that I know of."

Al said nothing.

"What did you have in mind? You have no experience in the record business."

"Shall I be frank?" Al said.

"Please." Harman smiled once more.

"I don't know records," Al said. "Let's be realistic. But a salesman doesn't sell his product. *He sells himself.* And that's what I know, Mr. Harman. I know myself. And with that I can sell anything."

Harman considered. "You would take any job with us? By what you say, I gather you're willing to—"

Interrupting, Al said, "Let me clarify. I intend to work for someone who can make use of me. I don't intend to rot. I need to be used, and used properly. A man doesn't grind valves with a hoe. A man doesn't use a beautiful pistol, made by hand, by the finest European craftsmen, to shoot tin cans." He paused. "But it's you, Mr. Harman, who knows who goes where. It's you who knows the organization and what it needs, and as far as I'm concerned, it's the organization that comes first. Do I make myself clear?"

"I think so," Harman said. "In other words, you'll be willing to leave it up to me."

"Precisely," Al said.

"Well," Harman said, scratching his nose, "I'll suggest this. You can give the girl your name, and where we can reach you. I'll talk it over with Mr. Knight and Mr. Gam, and we'll see. Generally I let Gam do the hiring."

At once, Al rose to his feet. "Thanks, Mr. Harman," he said. "I'll do that. And I won't take any more of your time." Holding his hand out to Harman, he waited. Mr. Harman reached up and took his hand; they shook, and then Al strode from his office.

Outside, he halted at the secretary's desk. "Mr. Harman instructed me to give you certain information," he said briskly.

The girl gave him a pad of paper and a pencil; however, he whipped out his ballpoint pen and wrote down his name and his address, and their apartment phone, which was listed under his wife's maiden name. Then he smiled at the secretary and left the building.

As he came out on the street the bright sunlight smote him, and at once his head began to ache. The Anacin, he realized, was beginning to wear off. And so, too, were the Sparine and the Dexymil. Now he felt tired and let down; he walked slowly to his car, tugged the door open, and got in behind the wheel.

I wonder if I'll hear from him, he thought.

Anyhow, I made my pitch. I did everything I could.

After a time he started up the car and drove away, in the direction of Al's Motor Sales.

On Friday, when he had fairly well given up hoping, a car pulled over to the curb at Al's Motor Sales, and a young man in tie and shirtsleeves got out.

"Mr. Miller?" he said.

Coming out of his little building, Al said, "Speaking."

"I'm from Teach Records," the young man said. "Mr. Gam has been trying to get hold of you. He'd like you to call him as soon as you can."

"All right," Al said. "Thanks."

The young man got back in his car and drove off.

This is it, Al said. He walked across the street to the coffee shop and entered the pay-phone booth. A moment later he was connected with the switchboard girl at Teach Records.

"This is Mr. Miller," he said. "Mr. Gam asked me to call."

"Oh yes, Mr. Miller," the girl said. "We just sent a man down to your place of business. Did he succeed in finding you?"

"Yes," Al said.

"Just a moment and I'll connect you with Mr. Gam."

Presently a deep middle-aged man's voice came on the phone. "Mr. Miller," the man said, "I'm Fred Gam. You were in discussing a spot with us, with Mr. Harman. If you're still interested, we've batted the idea around among us and come up with something. It would probably be worth your while to drop by sometime early next week."

"I could make it today," Al said. "I'll cancel all down the line."

"Fine," Mr. Gam said. "I'll look forward to seeing you, say, around four."

At four, Al closed up his lot and drove over to Teach Records. He found Mr. Gam to be a good-natured heavy-set man with gray hair, using an office that seemed the same size as Mr. Harman's.

"Glad to meet you," Gam said, shaking hands with him. On his desk he had a number of papers, through which he now glanced. "Well, Mr. Miller," he said, "you want to join the organization, it seems."

"Right," Al said.

"Come along then." Gam rose, beckoning, and Al followed him down a corridor, past one door after another.

They came out in a huge area in which men were working. The air was heavy with smells of machinery. Noise beat at Al's ears, a constant mechanical din.

"This is the operation," Mr. Gam said. "Where we do the actual pressing."

It looked to Al like a tire-retreading outfit; he saw the same round machines, a man at each, the tops opening and shutting.

"You won't be involved with this end," Mr. Gam said. He led Al from the area and down another hallway.

Al said, "I consider Chris Harman the most inspiring human being I've ever had the privilege to meet. And in my business I see a good slice of mankind."

"Yes, Chris said he ran into you at your car lot. You were obviously quite open with Chris, so we'll be equally open with you. You came to us at exactly the right moment. You couldn't have picked it better if you'd had some buddy planted in the organization." He halted and eyed Al. "This job didn't exist three days ago, and it has to be filled right now. It's a good job, Miller. It's ring-ding."

"Fine," Al said.

"Want to know what it was, Miller?"

"Yes," Al said.

"Your sincerity," Gam said. "Don't ever lose that. It's so God damn rare in this society of ours."

"I could never lose it," Al said. "Because I got it in a moment of supreme courage and danger. I got it in Korea. When the Commies had me pinned down. I got it when I faced death at the hands of a bayonet and the frenzied slant-eyes of a gook. I learned to know myself, Mr. Gam. I took a good look at myself, all I am, all my maker meant me to be. And that's not something a man loses."

After a moment Gam said, "I wish it could be shared. I wish it could be passed on to every man. I'll never have what you have."

"Afraid not," Al said.

"You told Chris it wasn't money. That reached him. For Chris, it isn't money either. It never was and it never will be. Why did he go into the record business? Because he wanted to ameliorate the condition of the average man through the one thing that can ameliorate—not bigger cars or better TV sets, but through art, through music." Mr. Gam pushed open a heavy door that led to a parking lot; he and Al slowly crossed the lot. "Naturally, there have had to be compromises. A business has to pay. We know that. It's the harsh reality. That's why there's been Glee Records and—let's face it—the Teach Catalog itself. You know the catalog, of course. It's mostly trash. It's supposed to be, because it serves the commercial market. Rock-and-roll, Negro jazz combinations, what they call race. Country, that is, Okie steel guitar. And pops. We've had a few hits. Teach has made the top ten, and made it often. Frank Fritch has been on Teach for years."

"I'm familiar," Al said.

"Frank Fritch's piano meanderings has been one of our best sellers. And Georgia O'Hare and her Merrymen of Song. Our best-selling item in the catalog right now is 'Pride.' You've heard it in a thousand lunch counters all over America."

They had entered another building now.

"Your concern," Mr. Gam said, "will be the new label, the one that Chris Harman has always wanted to bring out but never could before. Its called Antiqua. The long-playing record has made it possible. You'll be in charge of promotion. You'll receive a salary of seven hundred and fifty a month, plus traveling expenses—the usual expense account system, which we'll work out gradually, as we get to know you better. And your base salary will go up, in due time."

"I see," Al said.

"We've bought this building here," Mr. Gam said, as they walked down a newly painted hall. "We're making it over. It's not quite finished. Your office will be here." He took out a key and unlocked a door; Al found himself looking into an office which smelled of paint.

"What will be on the Antiqua label?" he asked.

"Mr. Harman's great project," Mr. Gam said. "The medieval and early-Renaissance masses and choral works. Palestrina, Des Pres, Orlando Lassus. Polyphonic and monody. Gregorian, if possible; if there's a market."

It was a long way from a used-car lot, Al thought to himself as he gazed at the barren, newly painted and decorated office. Is this what I got for my pitch to Chris Harman? Is this what he saw in me, and in what I said?

Is this the man that is trying to swindle Jim Fergesson? The man who peddles the dirty version of "Little Eva on the Ice"?

He felt ill and discouraged. The whole thing made no sense to him, and unfortunately he had no pills with him, no Dexymil or Sparine, to help him out. All he could do was go on listening to Mr. Gam. He had gotten too far in, too deep into Teach Records and Chris Harman's organization, to back out.

10

That night, as Al Miller sat across the dinner table from his wife, the terrible thought came to him again and again that Chris Harman was a completely reputable man, not a swindler at all.

He offered me that job, Al thought, to rehabilitate me.

"I've got some news," he said to Julie at last, breaking his mood of introspection. "I got offered a job."

At once she said alertly, "What job?"

"For seven-fifty a month," he said. "Plus expense account. And that's just starting salary."

"Seven hundred and fifty dollars?" she said, her eyes wide. "Tell me about it. What do you have to do? Who is it?"

"A phonograph record outfit," he said. "It would be public relations." His tone was so gloomy, so resigned, that her face fell. "It's just a fluke," he said. "I'm not qualified for it. I'd last about two weeks. Or two days." He continued eating.

"But why not take it?" Julie said. "Maybe you're wrong; you

know you're always so pessimistic, and you just sit around and let things happen—this job falls in your lap and you just sit there. You don't exert yourself."

"I exerted myself," Al said. "I went out and got it."

"Then you must think you can do it," Julie said. "Isn't that logical? You're just having doubts, your usual doubts. I know you can handle it."

Al said. "He just offered me the job because he felt sorry for me." He could not rid his mind of the idea; it had been there ever since he had left Teach Records.

"What did you tell them? You didn't turn it down, did you?"

"I said I'd consider it," he answered. "I said I'd tell them by Monday morning." That gave him three days.

"All right," Julie said in a brisk, practical voice. "Suppose they do just feel sorry for you. What does that matter?" Her voice rose. "It's still a good job; it still pays well. What do you care about their motives? That's paranoiac!" She gestured excitedly with her fork. "What's the name of the place? I'll go down and talk to them; I'll phone—that's what I'll do. And say I'm your secretary and you've decided after long consideration to accept the position."

The whole world's mad, Al thought. It's all sham.

"If you have the gumption to go out and rustle up a high-paying job opportunity," Julie said, "you have the gumption to take the job and do good at it. They wouldn't offer it to you if they didn't have faith that you could do it. Take it, or Al—I'm not exaggerating—if you turn it down, I know myself and I know I'll react by considering that you won't have been loyal to me. We took marriage vows. You're supposed to honor and obey me."

"It's hard to obey in this case," he said.

"Not obey, here," she said. "But honor and respect. By taking a decent job so that we can have children, and do all the other things we want to do and deserve to do." Her voice had become harsh with anxiety; he recognized the tone. "Don't let me down again, Al; please don't give way to your neurotic anxieties. Promise me."

"We'll see," he said. It seemed to him that he had suffered some crushing defeat by being offered a straightforward, worthy job at a good salary, and now this reaction, this sense of things having gone wrong, began to worry him. On the surface, his reactions did seem odd, to say the least. Maybe Julie was right; maybe now that at last someone had decided to have confidence in him, to take a chance on him, his own inner sense of worthlessness had begun to emerge. He was as neurotic as Julie said; it was true.

Defeat or success; it's all the same to me, he decided. It's all a grind. A snare and a delusion. Who wants it? Either one.

"You're afraid," Julie said, "to stick your neck out. If you fail, then you'll sink even deeper into apathy; you're conscious of that. You have that much insight. You'd prefer to stay as you are, because the risk of failure is so great; it has such dreadful consequences to you. Isn't that so?"

"I guess so," he said.

"So you'll just go on like you are forever. Drifting. Getting nowhere. Al—" She faced him with a stony expression. "I really don't know if I can go on. I just don't know. I want to, but I can't; I really think I can't. If you let me down again, here."

He grunted a meaningless response.

After dinner he dropped over to Tootie Dolittle's apartment. Both Tootie and his wife were home; they were cleaning the burners of the kitchen stove. Newspapers had been spread out everywhere. The sink was filled with soapy, gray-gritty water.

Seating himself out of the way, Al discussed his job prospect with Tootie, who listened carefully to all the details.

"Maybe it's a front," Tootie said, when Al had finished.

That idea had not occurred to him, and it cheered him up; it put an entirely new interpretation on the situation, on the job offer and on Harman. "Maybe so," Al said. "You mean they still don't want to give me the real dope. They're still holding up a smoke-screen."

"Sure, they're going to break it to you after you've worked there awhile. After they know you real well. That's natural." He went on to recount to Al the details of a job he had had driving a woman around who ran an abortion mill. It had been months before he had out that it was not a Swedish massage place; they had kept it from him as long as possible.

He then took Al off into the other room, so that the two of them could talk in private.

"There's one thing you may be missing," Tootie said. "I happen to know about Teach Records, because of my interest in music. They got a good catalog, but you know why they call themselves that name. They are a pirate label."

"What's that?" Al said.

"They stole their master discs. I mean they pirated the original records and dubbed from them. They got no legal right to the masters they press from, but they always pick something where the company is out of business and the artist dead and so on. Or some foreign label. Anyhow, Teach was a pirate. That was Black-beard; his name was Edward Teach."

"I see," Al said, pleased. "I didn't make the connection."

"So there's no doubt they're up to that," Tootie said. "So maybe this one fact enough to make you more cheerful. You obviously feel only somebody doing something crooked is going to pay you almost eight hundred dollars a month. If they honest, they're not going to pay you anything hardly at all. That's because you know perfectly well down inside you, and I say this from being a friend of yours and knowing you pretty well, you know you not worth anything."

"You want your block knocked loose?" Al said.

"I knock your block loose right back," Tootie said. "Now

listen to me. You not worth anything because you got nothing to sell. You like a lot of colored boys who come up North, to cities, from the farmland in the South. You come from a farm town, up in Napa County. You more like those boys than you know. I know, though. I see a lot of the same things in you as in them, but you too ignorant to recognize that; I mean ignorant of what I happen to know, although you plenty smart in other ways. Here all they got to sell when they come to town. *Their work.* Laboring somewhere, like in the Chrysler plant or driving a truck or putting on tires at Monkey Ward. *Why* anybody pay them anything? Why *you* pay them? You hire them to wash your cars on your lot for you, if you had any money; other lots do that—other lots have a colored boy. You so poor you your own colored boy."

"So what?" Al said.

"So other people not going to go on like that," Tootsie said. "They want to rise and be well-to-do, so they figure out something they can sell; they find something they can do somebody else want enough to pay for. But you too dumb. You not learn nothing to do. In that respect you different from most people, white and colored. You got to learn to do something other people want. Like my dog Doctor Mudd. He learn to bat balloons with his nose, so everybody pay to watch; he a lot smarter than you. Nobody pay you to do nothing, because you dull. You miss out. You go on being what you are, instead of being what other people pay to watch. Maybe when you get old you realize this, but then it too late. You got to assume a vivid personality. Live like you a dangerous, terrific person, like a spy or something. You got to go around create mystery. Nobody know when you come or go or what you do. Listen. That exactly what Mr. Harman do. He make everybody tell tall tales about him, and they not really know what he do or what he is. But they know what Al Miller; it written all over him."

Al was silent.

"You not got glamour," Tootie said. "That it in one word. You nothing but ditch-water walking around on two feet."

"Maybe so," Al said.

"Life like Ed Sullivan's program," Tootie said. "I watch that every week on the TV. That the best TV show there is, now that Milton Berle retire. I watch these show people come up; they got no talent. That the truth. What they got is personality. Who got talent these days? Al Jolson; he never had no talent. Nat Cole; he can't sing. Frank Sinatra never could sing. Fats Waller couldn't sing; he croak like a frog. Johnny Ray terrible singer. Sammy Davis Jr. nothing but a big ham-bone, but he very popular. Kingston Trio; bunch of college kids. But they got personality. You have to learn how to do that."

"I can't."

"You did for one minute, when you walked into that man's office. Or he not have decided to hire you. You done it once, so you can do it again, and not for a second but all the time. You live like you some French foreign agent in Tangiers; you make up stories to keep yourself interested, and pretty soon they get interested in you. If by popping a couple of those goofballs you can do it, then you don't need them; you throw away that little tin you carry and you make it alone, on your own. I know you can. And by God, you worth eight hundred a month starting salary; he right to pay you."

Al was silent, thinking about what Tootie was saying.

"I be frank," Tootie said. "I give my right arm to be where you are now. Getting an offer like that. But I never will. Partly because nobody hire colored for any big dough except in the entertainment industry, and partly because I am no-talent. That why I have to earn my living as clerk in the County Department of Health, writing up reports on outdoor toilets. I just a clerk. But you basically a big bullshitter; basically, you got a line already. All you need is to get it out."

"I was taught it was good to tell the truth," Al said.

"Sure, you get to heaven by being a truth-teller. Is that where you going to go? Is that your destination? Or you determined to live a happy life here? If the latter, you learn to give out with your line, and never stop; never let down. Not till you dead. Then you can tell the truth; you not actually a big butter-and-egg man from Boise, who own six oil wells and be president of local chamber of commerce."

Al felt thoroughly crushed.

"The truth vastly overrated anyhow," Tootie said, half to himself. "Actual truth is, everybody stink. Life a drag. Everything that live going to die. Truth is, nothing worth doing; all end badly anyhow. You tell that, you doing nobody a service."

"That's not the only side of reality," Al said.

"Okay, maybe not. Other side is what? You tell me."

Al considered, but he could not express it. However, he knew that Tootie was wrong. Tootie was embittered. Possibly rightly so. But his outlook had been poisoned years ago by his clerical job in fact and his dreams of glory in fantasy. No wonder he hung around bars with Doctor Mudd, attracting attention as best he could, living it up when he could; he was right to do that, but surely there were other ways, better ways out.

"You're basically a bitter man," Al said. "I have a feeling you hate people. You hate me."

"Hell you say," Tootie said.

"You'd be pleased if I debased myself by becoming what Chris Harman wants."

"What does he want?" Tootie said mockingly. "You don't even know. Evidently you hit on it by accident for a minute. Maybe you could keep hitting on it, maybe not."

"I'm not going to try," Al said.

"Oh, I think finally you come around," Tootie said. "If you

can get your wits going and manage to figure it out. It take time, and you do a lot of talking, but you come around. Your fear is because you afraid you can't hit on it; you afraid you try and fail. What's so virtuous about that?"

Al could not give an answer to the question. Perhaps Tootie was right; perhaps he simply lacked the courage to try to tailor himself along the lines that Chris Harman sought. The courage and the talent.

"You jerk," Al said. "You're eaten up with envy because I got this good job offer. You're just trying to make me feel bad. You're getting back at me."

"Listen, Daddy," Tootie said. "You better be careful."

"I'm careful," Al said. "Careful enough not to bring any more good news to you."

Tootie said, "So it is good news." He grinned. "You really tickled pink down inside about this job; you secretly gloating away about it—couldn't wait to get over here and tell me. Some cracker offers you eight hundred a month—you hardly able to sit still in your pants, thinking about all that bread. You really live good—you buy Old Forrester all the time, pretty soon, instead of that stuff the liquor store have on sale, that Colonel St. Masterson bourbon that taste like it come down a drainpipe from the roof."

The door from the kitchen opened. Mary Ellen Dolittle put her head in. "Listen, you boys getting a little too much carried away. Better calm down."

"Okay," Al said. Tootie nodded woodenly.

"I surprised at you," she said in her small, delicate voice. "Both of you always quarreling; and tonight both of you sober, an' still quarreling. It not do you either any good to stay sober, it look like." She remained, while they stared down at the floor. "I tell you what ail you, Al Miller," she said. "I listen to everything you say through the door while I clean the stove. What you not got is, you not got faith in God, like you ought to. I know you two sneak out of the kitchen because you know I start talking God-talk to you, but it too bad, because I talk it to you anyhow, whether you like it or not. Not any grown man any good to he fellow man unless he spend time in he church at least once a week meditating on the value of the word come down to earth. You know, Al Miller, the world going to pass away and there be an Armageddon one of these day soon. And the sky roll up like a scroll, an' the lion lie down with the lamb."

Tootie said, "Mary Ellen, you a nut. You go clean the stove and leave us alone. You worse than being married to some old grandma."

"I tell you perfect truth," Mary Ellen said. "It all written down in the weekly five-cent magazine, *The Watchtower,* which we Witnesses put out and distribute. Mr. Miller, you not leaving here until you fork over five cents for a *Watchtower*, which carry the word of God in ninety languages—I think it is—throughout the world."

Tootie said, "She just come out of the jungle, I think sometimes. Like being married to a savage or something." His face was contorted with shame and fury.

"I go home," Mary Ellen said softly, bending down. "One day. Back to my home."

Al said, "You mean Missouri?" He knew that she had been born there; had been in California only three years.

"No," she said. "I mean Africa." The door shut then; she had gone back to cleaning the stove.

"Christ," Tootie said. "She calls Africa 'home,' and she's never been east of Missouri. It's that religious stuff, that Jehovah's Witnesses. She never even met anyone from Africa, except at their meetings they have speakers from Africa who lecture."

They grinned at each other.

"How about a drink?" Tootie said, rising. "Some Colonel St. Masterson, age one year."

"Okay," Al said. "With water."

Tootie went into the kitchen to get glasses.

By the next morning, Saturday morning, Al Miller had decided to take the job.

As he unlocked the chain at Al's Motor Sales and bent to pick up his mail, he realized that the first person to tell was not Julie, nor even Chris Harman, but the old man.

The doors of the garage had been opened; Jim Fergesson, as usual, was at work for at least the early part of Saturday. He would probably work until noon or one, depending on how much work had to be done.

And now, Al realized, is the time to tell him. As soon as possible, now that I've decided. In view of what I said to him about Chris Harman.

Accordingly, he left his lot and entered the garage by the side door. The old man had opened it to get more ventilation and light.

He found the old man in the office. Fergesson sat opening his mail; he glanced up at Al, his eyes red-rimmed, watery. In a hoarse voice, he said, "Long time no see." His attention returned to the letter which he was reading. So Al sat waiting.

"Any news from your doctor?" Al said, when Fergesson had finished reading the letter.

Fergesson said, "He said I had a mild heart attack."

"Hell," Al said, with dismay.

"He's making more tests." The old man began to tear open another letter; Al saw that his hands were shaking. "Excuse me," the old man said. "I have to read my mail."

Taking a deep breath, Al said, "Listen. That guy Chris

Harman. We were talking about him. Maybe I was wrong; maybe he's not a crook at all."

The old man raised his head; he stared at Al, blinking rapidly. But he said nothing.

"I'm no judge of people like that," Al said, "that far up. I have no experience. I was relying on secondhand advice anyhow. He could be a crook. The point is, I don't know. I can't prove it either way; it's a mystery to me." He paused. "I was over there."

The old man nodded.

"I had a long talk with him," Al said.

"Oh yeah," the old man murmured, as if preoccupied.

"Are you still sore at me?" Al said.

"No," the old man said.

"I thought it'd make you feel better," Al said, "if I came and honestly admitted that I don't know one way or another about Chris Harman. You'll have to make up your own mind."

He had meant to go on then, to the part about his asking Harman for a job. But he did not get the chance.

"Listen," the old man said, "get out of here."

Oh God, Al thought.

"I'm not speaking to you," the old man said.

"I thought this would make you feel better," Al said, unable to grasp what was happening. "Now it makes you sore," he said, "to have me say I don't think he's a crook." It was the most incredible thing he had ever seen. "Okay," he said. "I'll get out, you old nut." He got quickly to his feet. "You want him to be a crook?" he said. "You want to be swindled? Is that it?"

The old man said nothing. He continued to read his mail.

"Okay," Al said. "I'll leave. The hell with you. You're not speaking to me—I'm not speaking to you." He started out of the office. "I don't get it," he said.

The old man did not look up.

"You're really addled," Al said, at the door of the office. "Your brains are scrambled. That heart attack must have done it. I read an article about that once. Eisenhower is the same way, a lot of people think. So long. I'll see you." He unsteadily made his way to the entrance of the garage and out onto his lot.

That's the craziest thing I ever heard of, he thought. He really ought to be put away; his wife is right. She ought to get an attorney and have him put away.

I can understand a man getting sore when somebody tells him he's getting swindled, he thought. But not a man getting sore when somebody tells him he's not getting swindled. That's not human. I ought to send away for one of those Mental Health pamphlets and drop it into his mailbox. It's going to be hell staying around here with him, he said to himself. Working around a madman.

What a crazy world, he thought. The old man sells his garage without telling me—he ruins my life, puts me out of business—and then he winds up mad at me. Not speaking to me.

Going across the street to the coffee shop, he closed himself in the pay-phone booth and dropped a dime into the slot. He dialed his home phone number and presently Julie answered.

"I'm going to go ahead and accept that job," Al said.

"Fine," she said. "What a relief. I was so afraid you wouldn't and it really does look good, doesn't it?"

"It pays well," he said. "And it looks as if it would be interesting. Anyhow, I have to do something. I can't stick around here."

"It took you so long to see that," Julie said.

"Well," he said, "I'm stuck here with a senile lunatic. Naturally I see it; there's nothing else to see." He rang off, paused, and then, putting in another dime, dialed the number of the Harman organization. The receptionist answered. "Teach Records."

I never did get to tell him, Al thought. The old man. I went over there, and he didn't give me a chance. "Let me talk to the man I was talking to before," he said to the receptionist. "Mr. Gam, I think his name was."

The girl said, "I'm sorry, sir. Mr. Gam is no longer with us."

Floored by that, Al said, "I was just talking to him. The other day."

"Who would you like to talk to, sir?" the girl said. "Since I can't connect you with Mr. Gam."

"I don't know," he said, completely at a loss. "They offered me a job. Mr. Gam had it all worked out."

"Is this Mr. Miller?"

"Yes," he said.

"Mr. Knight will talk to you," the girl said. "Mr. Gam and Mr. Harman turned your name over to him. He's familiar with the situation. Just a moment, Mr. Miller." There came a series of clicks, then a long silence. Then, at last, a hearty man's voice loudly in his ear.

"Mr. Miller!"

"Yes," Al murmured.

"This is Pat Knight. Glad to meet you, Al."

"Same to you," Al murmured.

"Mr. Gam is no longer with us. A position came up he'd been waiting for, and he flew. He made his move. That's the way it has to be. He'll be in the office from time to time. Well, you're going to join us?"

"Yes," Al said.

Knight said, "Well, now, listen, Al. There're a couple of things I'd better discuss with you. When Mr. Gam talked to you he was a little confused; he had a lot on his mind, this new spot he was after. He got you mixed up with another fellow that Harman was sending around, a Joe Mason or Marston—he never came in. He—that is, this Marston—used to be a retail dealer up in Spokane. We wanted him to handle our esoteric classical for us, and Gam got you involved in that. He got you picked out for that spot. He had the idea that was what Harman wanted." Knight laughed.

"I see," Al said, feeling parts of his mind fade out into numbness. They ceased to function; he merely stood at the phone nodding his head up and down, listening.

"We do have a spot for you," Pat Knight said, more slowly and soberly. "Listen, I'll level with you, Al. Right here and now on the phone. What we need is an aggressive, hard-working young man who isn't afraid of rising above his fellows and making something of his life. Is that you?"

"Sure," Al murmured.

"The profits are big," Knight said. "So's the responsibility. You'll have to be able to meet the public. You can do that. I see by your file that you're an automobile salesman."

It occurred to Al that he should say he was not; it was not right. It had to do with a big new-car agency, with glass windows, new shiny cars, salesmen in striped suits standing around by potted palms . . . that's not me, he wanted to say.

"I'm a dealer," he said.

"What's that?" Knight said.

"I have my own place," he said.

"I'll be darned," Knight said. "Well you're no doubt what we've been looking for. I can see why Mr. Harman told us to keep our eyes open for you. Well, I suggest you drop over and we'll settle this. There's been some confusion, here, but we can iron it out to everybody's satisfaction. The spot we have is right up your alley, Al. I know you'll really go for it."

"What is it?" he said loudly.

"Now listen," Knight said, in a slightly frigid voice. "I want to meet you face to face, Al. I have to see what kind of man I'm dealing with. I can't just hand out jobs over the phone, like greetings cards." He sounded huffy now. "When can I expect you?" he said in a brisk formal voice. "In about an hour? I can squeeze you in at exactly one-thirty, for about fifteen minutes."

"Okay," Al said. He nodded. "I'll be over." He hung up the phone and left the booth.

I'm helpless, he realized. They've got me like a bug in a mayonnaise jar. As soon as I said I wanted the job, they stabbed me.

They highballed me, he said to himself. The old trade-in trick. Every car dealer uses it. Quotes the customer such a high trade-in for his car that he has to come back; he can't turn it down. And when he comes back he discovers that the offer has been withdrawn in the meantime; a new shipment has come in, or the salesman who made the offer isn't with the firm anymore . . . and by this time the guy is hooked. He's already made up his mind to wheel and deal.

Like me, Al thought. I've decided to join the Harman organization, even though I don't know what the job is or what it pays. I know nothing, except that I've decided to make my move. It's a Mutt and Jeff act, he realized. Between Harman, Gam, and Knight. And I fell for it; I fell so completely that I'm going over there and taking the job they have, the job they had for me from the start, no matter what it is. And I think I know what it is, he thought. It's a salesman job. Selling records. That's what they mean: a flunky with a bow tie, a crew cut, a briefcase and a glad-hand stuck out. They mean me; what I'm going to be in a little while. My destiny.

They saw me coming, he thought to himself as he recrossed the street to the lot. The boy from the country. The farm boy from St. Helena who has no chance, no hope, in the big city of Oakland, California.

Getting into one of the lot cars he drove home in order to change his clothes. In order to get a clean shirt and tie and suit, so that he could impress Mr. Knight.

This is how they break you, he realized. This is how they break your spirit bit by bit. They don't come right out and make the offer; they don't look you straight in the eye and say, We've got a salesman's job for you; take it or leave it. No. They do a snow job on you; they sell you. And why not? They're better salesman than you are. Look where they are; look who they are. And then look who you are.

I should have known, he thought. If Harman was smart enough to build up that organization, to have the kind of house and cars he has, to dress like he does, he's smart enough to make mincemeat out of me. I should never have tried to take a confidence man, he said to himself. Harman knows a million tricks I never heard of. I'm an amateur. We all are, compared to him.

And they know I'm hooked, he thought. They know it's too late for me to back out; I'll take the job, whatever it is. They're masters of manipulation, of using psychology.

I'm their white rat, he thought. And I'm deep in the maze by now. Far too deep to get out. And the cleverer I am, the smarter I act, the deeper I go. It's fixed that way; that's part of the system by which it works.

I've told my wife and my friends I'm getting a big-time job; they knew I'd say it, pass the word around. Now I have to pretend. I have to start living a lie; I have to keep telling them—and telling myself—that I've got a nifty job at nifty pay for a nifty outfit, that I'm going somewhere. But in fact I'm not going somewhere. However, I have to keep that quiet; I have to keep that to myself.

And the proof of how well they have me is that I will keep it to myself. I'll be smiling all the time. I'll have to be; from now on there's no choice.

11

For over an hour, Al Miller had been sitting in Mr. Knight's small, modern waiting room. He wore his best suit, his best tie and shirt, his best shiny black shoes. So far there had been no sign of Mr. Knight; his office door remained shut, although now and then sounds could be heard.

My mind knows what my body doesn't, Al thought. My mind knows that this is all a plot, a hoax. But my body is geared along another line; it thinks this is a grand climax. This is success. All its hormones were released—on purpose, by those who know how to do it. They have control of my body, he realized. Only this one tiny part of my mind looks down and sees. Sees the lies and the mechanism.

Even this long wait. It's to make you more and more helpless. More dependent. Praying they'll see you. When the girl says that Mr. Knight will see me, I'll be glad to go in. And I'll be so glad to take the job; I really will be. It won't be simulated. Because by now there is an even worse possibility. That I'll have done all this in vain, for nothing.

"Mr. Knight will see you now," the girl said, from her desk.

At once, like a machine, he was on his feet. He wheeled smartly and strode through the open door, into Knight's office.

There sat a man only slightly older than himself, but with a round, smooth, pink, shaved, double-chinned face. A man with plenty of flesh on him, well-dressed, with beautifully manicured nails; a good-looking man in an easy-going mood. A relaxed man who had nothing to worry about or be gloomy about.

"Sit down," Knight said, indicating a chair.

Al sat down.

"How are you today?" Knight said.

"Fine, thanks," Al said.

"Sorry to keep you waiting," Knight said.

"That's okay," Al said.

"You've never had any experience with the record business," Knight said, tapping his pencil reflectively.

"No," Al said.

Knight pondered. All at once he raised his eyes and scrutinized Al with silent ferocity. The man's light-colored eyes took on such power that Al felt paralyzed; he could only gaze helplessly back.

"Okay," Knight said. "We'll go along with you, boy." He rose from his chair. "It's a deal. We're not looking for experience. We're looking for the right man." It all came out in a rush now. "We have an idea that the next big thing in the record business—hell, in popular music on TV or whatever else you find it—is going to be barbershop."

"I see," Al said.

"Barbershop," Knight said. "But not the old harmonizing; the old sentimental crooning in unison. This will be barbershop with the new sound, electronic barbershop. With plenty of presence. It'll sweep the nation. Modern science will supply what barbershop has always lacked, a modern quality to which modern people, like teenagers, could relate. We're starting a new line. It'll be called Harman-E. It'll be barbershop, and it'll carry everything else inside six months." Seating himself on his desk, Knight scrutinized Al again. "Do you know," he said, "where the great artists in this medium are going to come from?"

"No," Al said.

"From small towns," Knight said. "Right here in California. From towns like Modesto, Tracy, Vallejo. Not quite the country and not quite the city. The real backbone of America, where we all came from and where we all want to go back."

"I was born in St. Helena," Al said.

"I know," Knight said. "That's why you were picked. Do you sing?"

"No," Al said.

"I do," Knight said. "I sing barbershop. In fact I just got back from a barbershop balladeers' convention in El Paso, Texas. Here." He reached into his desk and brought out a glossy print, which he handed to Al.

The print showed Knight wearing a striped old-fashioned vest, along with three other men, all dressed exactly the same way. Each man held a derby hat in his hand.

"My group," Knight said. "We sing three nights a week, for veterans' organizations, hospitals, private parties, kids' groups. And my wife—" Again he held out a print for Al to see. This one showed four young women wearing taffeta gowns, holding tiny parasols. "The one on the end is Nora," Knight said. "The ear is an oscilloscope. Did you know that? It can detect sounds only two cycles a second apart. Yes, that's a fact. Our music is tempered.

Bach did that. What barbershop does is go back to the untempered music of Renaissance polyphony. You read barbershop from bottom to top, you know. Not from left to right. What we strive to do is get the chords to ring. That takes about five years of practice. A chord rings when the voices blend at no more than two cycles apart. The sounds reinforce. Here, I'll show you." He walked over to a large console phonograph in the corner of the office. "This group," he said, as he picked up a long playing record and put it on the turntable, "won the International Barbershop Championship in 1959. The Aristotelians."

He put the record on. It was "When You Wore a Tulip."

As he listened, Al tried to tell why it sounded so bad. At first he thought that it was because it was so loud. Knight had turned the volume all the way up, and the office rattled and vibrated. But that was not the reason, because Al had often sat in bars listening to loud jukeboxes, and he had never felt this before; he had never been physically sickened by sound in this fashion. At last he realized that it was the piercing quality of the voices. It did something to the fluid of his ears; it made him dizzy and unsteady. Even after the piece ended, the disorder in his system remained; he had to sit gazing down, keeping himself immobile.

The sound had penetrated as pure vibration, as pure disturbance of the air. It was sound reduced to—as Knight had said—cycles per second, reinforced sound emanating from four vocalizing simps who had managed to tune themselves to the exact same pitch, intervals apart, and then this sound had been reinforced by all the modern electronic gadgets, sound chambers and all the rest, so that in the end it bore no relation to what the performers had done, bad as it was. The original sound could have been escaped; but this final product, he realized, would get a person through concrete and sandbags and steel. It would follow him into the bomb-shelter and even the grave. It was, as Knight said, the natural next success for the popular music media; perhaps it would prove to be the final success, the ultimate success. The tune itself had no merit to start with; the singers were amateurs, probably men like Knight himself, well-fed, optimistic, with three evenings a week to devote to barbershop singing after their dinners, after their regular jobs were over. And all, of course, lived in small towns.

"The overtones," Knight was saying. "The harmonics. That's what the Budapest String Quartet once in a while achieves. They're working with fretted instruments." Standing at the phonograph, he shut the turntable off. "Ever heard anything like it?"

"No," Al said.

"Not like the old barbershop, is it? Not the Mills Brothers all over again." Putting the record away, Knight turned toward Al. "What do you think of it?" He eyed Al seriously.

Al said, "It's the worst crap I ever heard in my entire life."

The serious expression on Knight's face did not change in the slightest. "You're right," he said. "You put it exactly right. But you're missing a point. It's good because it's so bad. There's a lot of time and a lot of talent and ingenuity involved in what you heard. A lot of heartbreak and sweat went into producing that sound. It's there in the sound, too; you can hear it. This stuff wasn't arrived at by chance; it wasn't just tossed out for want of something better. It's not mediocre, Al. This sound is something you'll remember. You won't be able to get it out of your mind. Six, ten weeks from now that sound'll still be there inside your head. It made an impression. A mediocre thing makes no impression; it's forgotten as soon as it's done. You think you can forget the Aristotelians singing 'When You Wore a Tulip'? Don't kid yourself. You won't forget it. And that's given this item something that insures it being a best seller, something without which there is no popularity on the market today. Identity. This sound has identity. When the Aristotelians sing 'When You Wore a Tulip,' you know what it is; you couldn't mistake it for anything else. Yes, it's bad. It's so bad that it's an achievement that ranks with—well, say, with Al Jolson or Johnny Ray or any other of the greats. With the Andrews Sisters."

"I see," Al said.

"Do you see?" Knight said. "You use the term 'bad.' You call something 'bad' that's going to enter the hearts of Americans everywhere and become a part of their lives. Is that your idea of bad? Something that'll give pleasure and a moment of relief from the worries and fears of this H-bomb age of ours? That's a funny idea of what 'bad' is, Al. What do you call 'good'? Something that adds to the fears? Something that makes our lives a little bit harder to bear?"

There was silence.

"These guys," Knight said, "the Aristotelians—I know them personally; they're all good friends of mine—got a lot of pleasure out of making this record. They're not intellectuals. They didn't go to school; they didn't read Kant. They're just good, simple, nice guys who love to get together in the evenings and sing. And we're going to pass their pleasure around and share it, by pressing their harmonizing. That's our business. That's what we're here for. That's what you'll be here for, if you see fit to join us. We're not trying to change the world. We're not educators or reformers. We're supplying pleasure, not instruction. Is that bad?"

Al said, "No. That's good."

"Yes, that's good," Knight said. "What these boys have done is good, good for people. That's the only good we know. When professional musicians hear this, they flip. They do. You should see their expressions. It's worth watching. They know they're hearing sounds that disappeared hundreds of years ago. Sounds

they thought they'd never live to hear. Now, here's what we're going to do with you, Al, here at Teach. We're going to send you up
into the small towns that you know so well, and you're going to sit
in on the different barbershop groups until you find us the ones
who amount. Then you're going to get in touch with our A. and
R. man, and we'll get a team up there with an Ampex tape-
recorder and some kind of a piece of paper, and we'll get them
down on tape."

Al said, "You think I have the background for that?"

"For something new," Knight said, "really new, there's no
such thing as background."

"I'm no musician," Al said. "Why don't you hire a musician?"

"This has nothing to do with musicianship. We're recording
sound. Like sports-car exhausts, which has been one of our best-
selling items, incidentally. Sounds Out of Sebring. You know, it's
been proved that beans grow fastest when a record of sports-car
exhaust sound is played as a background."

"What comes next?"

"Symphonic," Knight said. "They grow well to that, too."

"I think you've got the wrong person," Al said. "All I know is
the used-car business."

"The job pays five-fifty a month," Knight said. "Plus gas and
oil for the car, naturally. After ninety days, if all works out, the
base pay goes up to six, then after six months up to six-fifty. Do
you want it, or do you not want it? If not, I've got a lot to do."
Knight returned to his desk and reseated himself; he at once
placed papers in front of him and began to go over them.

"I'll take it," Al said.

It was a better job than he had expected. And at better pay. It
was not a salesman's job after all.

And then he realized that he had been lowballed. Another au-
todealer's trick had been worked on him; they had made him

think it would be worse than it was, so that when they had broken the actual news to him he had been so happily surprised that he had taken their offer.

Nor was that all. Why had they hired him? Why did they want him? Because he had come from St. Helena. That was the extent of it. He had nothing else to offer that interested them, no talent or experience; only his rural background.

"Suppose it turns out I lied," he said suddenly. "Suppose I wasn't born in St. Helena; suppose I was actually born in Chicago."

Knight said, "We checked up."

"Is that all you see in me?" Al said. "Isn't there anything else?" It seemed terribly important.

"You know those little towns," Knight said. "Point Reyes, Tracy, Los Gatos, Soledad. That's your element." He riffled through papers. "And you know those back roads. You won't get lost. Those county roads are murder. Nothing but gravel and pot-holes. That's the kind of roads you grew up on." He fixed his intent gaze on Al. "Tracking down these barbershop groups in these little towns means a lot of driving. Days of nothing but driving." Returning to his papers he added, half to himself, "And if your car gets stuck or breaks down you can fix it yourself. You know how to do that."

After a time, Al said. "When should I start?"

"Monday," Knight murmured. "We'll see you then. Check in here at nine in the morning. Ask for Bob Ross. He'll be in charge of the project. Ross is Harman's son-in-law. This is Harman's great project, the one he's giving his entire backing to."

"I thought he was backing the early-classical project," Al said.

"The Antiqua label? The public isn't ready for it. Maybe next year." It was obvious that Knight was through talking to him; he had become involved with his paperwork. There was nothing to do but leave, and so presently Al shut the office door after himself.

* * *

Although it seemed to Al a calamity that he had been given a job because he had been born in St. Helena, his wife took a different attitude. She considered it a stroke of luck.

"Suppose you hadn't been born in St. Helena," Julie said, when he discussed it with her that night. "You wouldn't have gotten the job. Or suppose they weren't interested in a project of recording music in small towns." She went on, with rapture; the job appealed to her because it meant that he would be able to get out of the Bay Area. "Maybe we can settle up around Sonoma," she said. "I always wanted to live up there. Or up around the Russian River. I like to be near the water."

"They humiliated me," Al said.

"No that's all in your mind. You project your own motives onto the whole world; just because you're in the used-car business you see everyone in terms of used-car sales tricks. They had one job for you, and then that project didn't go through, so they were good enough to dig into your background and find another faculty that you possessed that they could make use of. I think it bodes good. It sounds as if they're resourceful, intelligent people. I'm very anxious to meet Mr. Harman."

Al said, "Maybe I'll be able to strike it rich in Arroyo del Seco." That was as small a town as he could think of, offhand.

"And you'll be working directly with the boss's son-in-law," Julie said. "That means you might be able to rise right up to the top. It sounds as if the road will be open to you."

"By killing him?" he said. "And taking his place?" It sounded like something out of *Macbeth*.

"By immediately making yourself indispensable," Julie said. "That's the key to success. I read that in an article in some women's magazine; wait—I'll go get it." She began to rummage about the apartment.

There is no success, Al Miller thought, in a job that requires a man to search through one small town after another, searching for the worst possible singing groups that exist on the face of the earth. And then, when the worst possible singing groups have been turned up, they will be recorded with the worst possible modern sound techniques. He saw himself wandering farther and farther, in ever expanding circles, until at last he was not even in California; his search for the worst possible singing groups would extend into Oregon and then into Idaho and finally into Wyoming and New Mexico and Nebraska and Mississippi, and at last over the whole United States. He would uncover, at last, in a final triumph, the worst of the worst; he would be responsible for unearthing the singing group so bad that no worse one could ever be found, no matter how long the search went on. And then he could retire. He would have done his job for his country and race.

"Poor Doctor Mudd," he said aloud.

"What?" Julie said, pausing in her search.

"Tootie Dolittle's dog," Al said. "He missed out. What he does isn't audible. It can't be recorded." In neither new sound nor old, he thought. A balloon-bunting dog could no longer become part of the American way of life because he could not make it with hi-fi.

If Doctor Mudd could hum spirituals while he bunts the balloon, Al thought, he might have a chance. But that's asking the impossible. For even the electronics industry there has to be a limit.

And poor Tootie Dolittle, he thought. Imagining that the key to success lay in having a mess of glamour. No wonder Tootie had missed out. Those days were gone. The exotic, the striking, was no longer wanted. Now it was all down home. It was all just folks. Success lay in the hands of the plump, smiling amateur girl-trios, who wore first-prom gowns and who swayed back and forth as they sang "Down By the Old Mill Stream." Tootie's mistake had been to not be born in St. Helena or Montpellier, Idaho, or some such place. He had been doomed from the start.

And as for me, Al thought, I almost missed out. But now I've been shown the way.

On Monday morning Al Miller put in his appearance at the Harman organization. A receptionist sent him on in to an office on the second floor, where he found himself facing two men, one of which was a recording engineer, the other of which was Harman's son-in-law, Bob Ross. They had between them an Ampex tape-recorder, battery powered, and aluminum fifteen-inch reels of tapes, mikes, and playback amplifiers and portable speakers.

Ross wore a woolly brown suit with a vest, a narrow tie, and massive glasses. He greeted Al in a deep voice, almost an announcer's voice, which struck Al as quite a contrast to his chubby, almost babyish face. Certainly he was neatly dressed, but he was so badly proportioned that he looked to Al like an overgrown adolescent. He had, too, a scholarly, overserious, boyish manner.

"You're the driver?" Ross said.

"I guess so," Al said. "I was just hired."

"Milton," Ross said.

"No," he said. "Miller."

"Can you handle a four-speed truck box?"

"Sure," Al said.

"Let's go," Ross said. "Let's get the stuff in the truck and take off; there's no point in hanging around here."

Al began picking up equipment; the recording engineer did so, too, while Ross examined a clipboard of papers. The recording engineer led the way downstairs and out onto the parking lot, where a ton-and-a-half GM truck, several years old, was parked.

"Where to?" Ross said to Al, as the last of the stuff was being put into the truck.

Without hesitation, Al said, "Fort Bragg."

"That's where we'll find it?" Ross said.

"Right," Al said. He had picked the town at random. He had never been there. It would take all day to get up there and back, and he looked forward to the trip.

"Shouldn't we start closer to home?" Ross said. "There're a lot of towns between here and Fort Bragg."

"They've been picked over," Al said.

"Hell," the recording engineer said. "If we go all the way up there we might not get back for a couple of days."

"Let's be realistic," Al said. "We have to get out of the good TV reception area. TV has ruined the natural folk-culture for a radius of a hundred miles around here."

Ross said, "You sound pretty confident of your judgment."

"I've been in this business a long time," Al said.

"If we're going that far I better call my wife," the recording engineer said. He excused himself to go and phone.

Getting out a pipe and a self-sealing plastic pouch of tobacco, Ross said to Al as he lit up, "Frankly, going out of the metropolitan Bay Area doesn't appeal to me. So far we've done most of our taping in clubs in San Francisco. Most folk singers are willing to come down here, and we get plenty of pop and jazz personalities at places like Fack's Number Two and the Blackhawk and the Hungry I."

"Okay," Al said. "You wait around Fack's Number Two and see how long it takes for a truly authentic barbershop quartet to show up. One that isn't already signed up."

Soon they were on the road, with Al behind the wheel of the truck. Bob Ross puffed on his pipe and read a trade journal. The recording engineer propped himself against the door of the cab on his side and soon fell asleep.

"I admire your courage," Ross said, glancing up from his magazine. "In speaking up and defending your point of view."

"Thanks," Al said.

"We'll get along," Ross said. "However, I think we'll stop off at my father-in-law's house for a moment and check with him. Before we go that far."

He directed Al up into the Piedmont hills, along streets of tall trees and large terraced gardens with stone walls overgrown with ivy. Presently they were parking before a house set well back from the street, behind a row of poplars.

"We'll both go in," Ross said, as he slid past the sleeping recording engineer and stepped from the cab onto the sidewalk. "He's taking the day off. Attack of hay fever."

Together, they climbed a path of flagstones, past beds of old roses and gladioli. Ross led the way around the side of the house, to the patio in the rear. They found Chris Harman stretched out on a terry-cloth towel, wearing bathing trunks, listening to a portable FM radio and sunbathing. He had a tall glass of iced tea beside him and a pile of *U.S. News & World Reports*. As they approached, he turned his head.

"Hello," he said genially.

Ross said, "We won't bother you for more than a minute."

"Not at all," Harman said, resting his chin on his folded arms in order to see them.

"We're heading for Fort Bragg," Ross said, "to track down some unsigned barbershop quartet groups."

At once Harman said, "Oh no."

"Why not?" Al said.

"That's not the area at all. Fort Bragg is too close to the water. It's cold and foggy up there along the coastline. That's lumber country. Where you'll find barbershop is in the farm towns. In the Sacramento Valley, or the Sonoma Valley. Where it's hot and dry and flat. I'll tell you." He scrambled to a sitting position. "This is not to deride your judgment, Miller, but you go over to Sonoma County and have a look around Petaluma."

"You're familiar with Petaluma?" Al said.

"Oh certainly," Harman said, smiling. "I'm over there all the time. The chicken and egg capital of the world."

"We'll go there," Ross said. "That's only about two hours at the most."

"And remember," Harman said, with his cultured, affable smile, "there are other towns nearby. Sebastopol, Santa Rosa, Novato. That's a well-settled farm area, and very hot. A very dull area. Just right for barbershop." He rose to his feet and began putting a blue and white robe around him, which he tied with a cord sash. "You'll have plenty of opportunity to exercise your judgment as time goes on, Miller," he said. "Sorry to have to overrule you, but as Ross well knows, I have a good sense about this sort of thing."

"That's been my experience," Ross said.

"I'm glad to learn something," Al said. "I consider myself as being reasonably good in this particular field, but I can always learn. A man is never finished in the school of life."

Harman said, "How about something to drink? Before you take off on that long hot trip?"

"That would be terrific," Ross said.

"Thanks," Al said. "It really would be appreciated."

"Excuse me then," Harman said. He disappeared through a French door, into the house, leaving the two men alone on the patio. The FM radio continued to play music.

"You'll learn a lot more," Ross said, presently, "working in the Harman organization. Chris is truly an astonishing man, a real giant. You've probably got the idea, for instance, that Chris is mainly involved in the record business. Nothing could be farther from the truth. Basically, he's an investor."

"I see," Al said.

"He's worth about two million dollars," Ross said. "All told. And yet he's one of the major contributors to the A.D.A. in Oakland. He's supported all manner of liberal causes, over the years. He's a kindly, educated man, with a great deal of background in the humanities. For one thing, I know he's read Plato in the original Greek. One of his hobbies is stamps. He's got as good a collection of early British as anyone on the West Coast."

"For Christ's sake," Al said.

"He'll be having you over to the house," Ross said, "now that you're a part of the group. Everyone comes over. Chris has absolutely no sense of snobbery; he wouldn't even know what it meant. When he goes into a store to buy something, the morning paper for instance, he's as gracious and polite to the clerk—" Ross gestured "—as he is to his family and friends. He makes no distinction. To him a man is a man. I'm not kidding."

"I'll be darned," Al said.

"That's the mark of a real aristocrat," Ross said.

"I guess so," Al said.

"Even those who can't stand him say that," Ross said.

"Who can't stand him?" Al said. "How can that be?"

"A lot of people can't stand him," Ross said. "You'd be surprised. He's got a lot of enemies who wish him the worst luck in the world and don't mind putting in a bad word for him, about him—not to his face, generally—any chance they get."

"Why?" Al said.

"I've puzzled over it for a long time. It's because of his luck.

They could forgive him his breeding, his education, his talents along business lines and cultural lines. But not his luck. They could even forgive his wealth. But luck—" Ross gestured, spilling tobacco from his pipe. A burning fragment landed on the ground and he carefully wet his fingers and put it out.

"They think they ought to have luck, too," Al said.

"Right," Ross said. "It ought to be evenly distributed throughout the civilized world. Of course, if that was true, there wouldn't be any such thing as luck anymore; nobody would even know what the word meant. I mean, let's consider what luck is."

Al said, "Luck is when things are breaking for you."

"Luck is being able to make use of chance," Ross said. "It means that when something goes wrong you can turn it to your own advantage. It doesn't mean, say, always drawing a good hand. It doesn't mean getting three aces and two kings every time." Turning to face Al, he said, "It means that when you draw a nothing hand you can still win, because in some way that eludes the rest of us you can make that nothing hand a winning hand. Do you follow me?"

"Yes," Al said. "And it's a really fascinating new concept."

"Then maybe you'll explain it to me," Ross said. "I've watched him for six years now, and frankly I can't make it out. Say he buys into a watch-repair outfit. The next day an automatic watch-repairing machine is invented, and some guy sticks one out on the sidewalk directly across the street; all you have to do is drop your busted watch in, and in five seconds out it comes again, fixed. For, say, six bits. That would put any other man out of business."

"Absolutely," Al said.

"But not Chris."

"Why not?"

"I don't know."

"Maybe he has enough capital to write it off."

"No. He turns it to his advantage somehow. He benefits. He profits, in the long run anyhow. That machine, that five-second watch-fixing machine across the street from him, actually causes him to make more in the long run than he would have if the operator hadn't set up the machine there, or there had been no such machine."

"It's amazing," Al said.

"I've seen him drop into somebody's business office," Ross said, "to give them a present, like a record sample or a bottle of whiskey, and because he happens to be there at that moment, some big golden opportunity falls his way. If he walked across the street to personally hand you a free hundred dollars, he'd happen to notice a 'for lease' sign on some place near you, and he'd immediately rent it and in six months he'd have made a killing in whatever he used the place for. It would turn out to be just what he needed, or what the public needed. Take this barbershop stuff. That was his idea, you know."

"Yes," Al said.

"He's never wrong. If he goes into barbershop in a big way, you can bet it'll be the next trend. Maybe it becomes a trend because he goes into it. I don't know. And this relationship he has with reality spreads out to some extent through the whole organization. I swear my own luck has been substantially better since I met Chris Harman eight years ago. It's good luck to meet him, even; you can date the process as starting there. Your good luck, Miller, has already begun. Don't you feel that?"

"And how," Al said.

"I mean, now you're going somewhere. You're not just standing still. You've been noticed."

The French door opened and Chris Harman reappeared, in his blue and white robe, carrying a tray on which stood a silver Martini shaker and three frosty-looking Martini glasses, an olive in each.

"Here we are," Chris said.

12

Jim Fergesson, on his first errand that morning, left his house and drove to the Bank of America. There, he transferred his money, except for ten dollars, from his savings account to his checking account. As he left the bank, he looked into his commercial passbook and read with satisfaction the sum $41,475.00.

Should he go back home? He wanted to be dressed right. I guess maybe I'll stop and get a new tie, he told himself. One of those narrow ties. So he drove along San Pablo until he saw a clothing store; parking, he got out, taking care to move slowly and not to exert himself too much. Soon he was inside the store, examining the ties in the rack by the coats.

A plump young Chinese man in shirtsleeves came toward him, smiling. "Good day," he said to Fergesson. He had on a good-looking tie: gray with bits of red. The old man, searching, found a tie exactly like it in the group. It cost four-fifty, which seemed to him a lot for a tie. "That's a nice one," the Chinese man said.

"That's handmade by a fellow over in Sausalito. He's got a patent on it."

Fergesson bought several ties and left the store, feeling pleased.

But he still did not want to go home. Lydia was there, and he felt nervous at the idea of running into her. Seated in his car he opened the paper bag of ties; by use of the rearview mirror he began to fasten one of the new ties around the collar of his shirt. While he worked at it—he wore ties so seldom that his fingers got in the way and he could not make out the length to let the small end fall—he realized that the Chinese man had come out of his store onto the sidewalk and was nodding to him sympathetically. So he got out of his car and let the Chinese man fix the tie. The man did a good job, and his fingers felt deft and friendly.

"Thanks," Fergesson said, a little embarrassed but at the same time gratified. "I have this big business appointment I have to get to." He looked at his pocket watch to show how much pressure there was on him.

The Chinese smiled at him, and watched him get back into the car and start up. He wishes me luck, Fergesson thought as he drove away into traffic. It's a good sign.

Now he felt better than he had in months. This is really an occasion, he said to himself.

He had bought over twenty-five dollars' worth of ties, he realized. Wow! That was something; that proved something.

That's a service they do, he thought, those Chinese. That's how they make those little businesses pay; they add something extra for nothing; that a white man won't do. I wouldn't mind going in there for all my clothes. I know I'd get real individual attention.

He made a note of the location. So I can find it again, he thought.

I'll bet that Chinese guy has made a lot of money, he thought as he made a left turn at an intersection.

This is really a nice day, he said to himself as he noticed the sky and the sun; he rolled down the car window and sniffed the air. I hope that damn smog doesn't show up, he thought. That really slays people; it causes lung cancer as much as cigarettes.

I can't feel this good all day, he said to himself. Already he was beginning to feel tired; the driving was hard on him, the having to watch other cars, the stops and starts. That's what makes the smog, he thought. The car exhausts, all these buses and trucks; too many people moving into Oakland—too overcrowded.

Now he felt the weight of an enormous flu come onto him. It was like the time he had been laid up with the Asiatic virus; he had had it a week before he had realized that he was sick, because the symptoms of the thing did not so much make him feel different as just worse. It had made his fatigue greater, his irritability greater, his gloom, his sense of defeat, more overwhelming. He had gone around snapping at everyone, and been unable to do his work; he had stayed on his feet, and then one morning he had been too tired to get up from the breakfast table. So Lydia had kept him home.

Like that again, he thought, slowing his car. Heavy all over, his arms in particular; his hands flopped like cement gloves on the wheel. His head wobbled. Even my eye muscles, he thought; his view of the traffic ahead became disfigured. Objects merged and then separated. My God damn left eye is swimming off on its own, he reasoned. Walleyed. Muscles must be pooped.

Well, he thought, what I need is vitamin B-one. That's that nerve vitamin. Keeping his car in motion he continued on until he could turn back on San Pablo; he made a left turn against a red light and swung over to the far lane. That's what took care of me before, he said to himself. That and a couple of good steam baths. But he could not go get into a steam bath this time, because of his being taped up. He had to stay out of the water; the doctor had warned him. The vitamin would have to do.

There was a yellow zone in front of the drive-in, and he parked there. Getting out, he carefully made his way up the sidewalk to the health food store. His feet, he discovered, seemed to sink down into the sidewalk, as if the pavement had become ooze. Sinking down a full six inches, he said to himself, lifting his right foot back up and out, setting it down again, lifting his left; left, right, left, and so on, to the screen door of the health food store. Stuck there, for a moment he rested, grinned to himself with anger, and then opened the door with the side of his hand.

"Morning, Jim," Betty said.

He sat down, dropping abruptly and grunting, on the first stool. He folded his arms on the counter and rested his head for a moment; he had done that, years ago, in school; he felt his forehead pressing his wrist. Like in the third grade, he thought. Midday nap. He beckoned to Betty and she came over.

"Listen," he said. "How about a bottle of those health vitamins again. Those therapy vitamins."

"Oh, now what did you have?" Betty murmured. "Was it the theragrams?" She moved away to the shelf. "Big red pills?"

He saw the bottle he wanted, pointed to it; she got it down.

"I remember," she said. "The B-complex. The niacinamide and panthenol group. This is very good, Jim. This has the liver fraction in it; they use it with anemic people. But it doesn't have B-twelve in it; that's the only drawback." She reached for another bottle. "This has your B-twelve, but it's a little more expensive. They're both hematinic formulas." She eyed him, holding up both bottles.

"I just want the nerve one," he said. "B-one." He reached out for the familiar bottle and she handed it to him. "Can I have some water?" he said.

"Yes," she said, going to fill a glass.

He took two of the vitamin pills there at the counter, and then, carrying the bottle, started from the store.

"We'll put it on your bill," Betty said, following after him. "I hope that does what you want, Jim. You do look very tired today. You know, you could take it as an elixir; you might find that handier." She came out on the sidewalk with him.

"Right," he said, making his way to his car and getting into it. As soon as he had sat down again he felt better; some of the weight left him.

That God damn smog, he thought as he started up the car. It really is hard to breathe anymore. And the smog, he saw, had begun to blot out the colors of the buildings. San Pablo did not go on nearly as far now; it cut off in the haze and he could not see downtown Oakland as he had been able to just a few minutes before. But who cares? he asked himself as he drove out into traffic. I've seen downtown Oakland.

Up in the Oakland hills there would not be so much smog anyhow. That's why they live up there, he told himself as he drove along a main street, in an eastwardly direction. He did not know the street, but it had a bus line running along it, so it had to go through to Broadway. I'll turn left on Broadway, he decided, and that'll take me clear out to Piedmont. Then I won't have any trouble after that.

Sure enough, the street at last came out on Broadway. And now, as he drove toward the intersection with McArthur, he noticed that the smog had fallen behind. They wouldn't let it get up here, he told himself with pleasure. There's probably a zoning law against it. At that, he laughed to himself, feeling better once more. The vitamins had helped already. The clean air gave him back his ability to breathe, and the vitamins his strength. He patted his coat pocket, the bankbook and checkbook. Hot dog, he said to himself. This is going to be something.

At McArthur he turned right, then left onto a long tree-lined residential street. Now there was almost no traffic. The noise fell away behind him and he slowed, aware of the peacefulness of the neighborhood. Piles of leaves in the gutters, waiting to be burned. A parked milk truck. Gardener at work, old jeans and sweatshirt, clipping the edge of a lawn. Fergesson drove in second gear up the hill, past larger houses. Iron fences, ivy . . . he searched for the house. This street, wasn't it? He craned his neck to see back. High stone wall, the poplar trees. Had he passed it?

He made out a street sign. Wrong street; not there yet. Picking up speed, he turned right.

Warm, he thought. Sun streamed down on him, on the sidewalk. The tie, too, made him hot; his neck had become slippery within the tight collar. With his left thumb he loosened it by stretching it still buttoned. And the car heater; it was on. He bent to switch it off . . .

A crash threw him forward and against the steering wheel. His head banged and his hands went out, hitting the windshield. He bounced back and lay hunched down, openmouthed. The car had stopped. The motor was dead.

Ahead of him a great heavy white Chrysler was stalled with its front fender locked into his. And out of the Chrysler the driver, stepping rapidly, was shaking his fist and yelling with no sound. A woman, the old man realized. A thin woman in a long brown coat, angry, scared, hurrying toward him.

"Do you see what you did?" Her face, shaking, broke into being at his window, an inch from his own. He rolled the window down. "Look what you did; my God, what'll my husband say?" She dropped away, falling to see the fender. "Oh my God, look at it."

Numbly he managed to get out onto the street. Other cars had stopped. The street, now, was blocked. His car and the woman's car blocked it completely, because of the solid row of parked cars on each side.

"Look." Her whole body was shaking. "And I have to pick him up at one-thirty. It's your fault; you were driving in the middle of the street; you didn't even see me. Did you hear me honk my horn? You didn't look up; you were looking *down*—you weren't looking at all, or paying any attention."

"No," he said.

"Don't just stand there," she said, staring at him. "Do something. Get them apart." She walked off and then got back into her car. Then, all at once, she was out again. He could not keep track of her; she was already back beside him. "Will you do something? Or are you just going to stand there?"

He squatted down and peered sightlessly at the two fenders. His mind was empty; he had no plan or notion of what to do.

Behind him the woman said, "I could just kill you. Don't you know how to drive? In ten minutes I have to be at the Claremont Hotel; I'll never make it now. Will you call a tow truck? I want your license number." She ran back to her car to find something to write on. Fergesson groped at the fenders. One of the cars would have to be jacked up.

"Are you insured?" the woman said, returning. "I suppose not; they never are. I'm going over to that house and phone for a cab. I have your license number now." She left; he saw her hurry up the path to the front porch of the house and begin ringing the bell. After a moment he returned his attention to the two fenders.

A man, coming up beside him, said, "Need a hand?"

"No," Fergesson said. "Thanks."

"Want me to call a tow truck?"

"No," he said. Going to the trunk of his car he got out the jack. Then he opened the trunk of the Chrysler and lifted out the larger Chrysler jack. With the two he raised the front end of the Chrysler. The fenders were still interlocked. Kneeling, he let the air out of the front tires of his Pontiac. With a sigh, the Pontiac gradually settled. The old man took hold of the bent green fender of the Pontiac and tore at it. The metal gave at last and the two cars were free.

He threw the jacks back into the cars and made his way down the path to the house where the woman had gone. The front door was open: he could see the woman at a telephone in the hallway. The owner of the house, another woman, appeared. "Tell her she can drive," the old man gasped. Turning, he walked back up the path, away from the house.

The woman driver appeared, still pale and shaking. "Thanks very much," she said icily.

"I got them apart." He fumbled in his wallet; his fingers were so stiff that they seemed about to crack open. "I'm giving you my business card."

She snatched the card away from him and hopped into her Chrysler. Its engine started and she drove off, the car swerving from side to side and then disappearing at a corner.

The other cars that had stopped began to go again. The man who had offered to help him remained, however. His small foreign car was parked in a driveway. "What about your car?" he said. "You have two flats."

"I can make it," the old man said. "I run a garage. That's the card I gave that lady. My garage card."

"I see," the man said. "Well, good luck." He got awkwardly back into his foreign car. "So long."

By himself, Fergesson pushed his Pontiac from the street, over to the curb. It blocked two driveways, but now traffic could get past. They actually could get by anyhow, he told himself.

They just stopped to rubberneck. The bastards. It doesn't matter to them if I get a ticket for leaving my car like it is. But there was nothing else he could do.

He was not far from Mr. Harman's house, and so he began to walk along the sidewalk, not even stopping to get back his breath. Red specks dipped in front of his eyes, and his throat burned. As he walked he breathed through his mouth, great windy gasps that startled two people passing him. He grinned at them and continued on. I only got about a block to go, he said to himself. Already he thought he could see the house, and he could get onto the grounds from this end; he could cut across and save walking.

Yes, he thought; there it was. A truck was parked in front of it, Harman's truck; it had the name of the record business on it. So he knew he was right. This was the place at last. Going from the sidewalk onto the grass he climbed toward a terrace of roses; he did not try to find the flagstone path. He did not have the time. I have to go right in there, he told himself. I have this big business deal to conclude with them; I can't afford to wait. Now he scrambled up between trees. Not with something like this. He clutched at his coat to be sure his checkbook and passbook were safe.

Crossing the rose garden he slipped and fell backward, sitting down suddenly and wheezing; he got up almost at once, staggering and brushing at himself. His coat was dirty. He went on three more steps and then he slipped again. This time he slid; his feet went in different directions and he floundered forward, reaching with both hands to touch the soil for support. Running a few steps, balancing himself with his fingers, he reached the concrete front porch. Bits of dirt and fertilizer trailed after him, bouncing from the concrete. Trembling with pain he wiped his hands together, standing on the porch by the front door. He wiped his feet. And then, after he had stood for a time and had gotten his breath back, when he felt that he could talk—he would have to be able to talk; he had to wait until he could do that—he reached out and began to knock.

Inside the house someone stirred.

I knocked too soon, he thought. I won't be able to talk. He could not even get his breath, yet, so how could he talk? He felt panic. It's too soon, he said to himself. The person was coming to the door. Don't come yet, he said to himself. If I don't knock any more you won't come; okay? He stood without knocking, making no sound except for his breathing. But they were still coming anyhow.

You bastards, he said to himself. You caught me at the wrong time; I'm not ready. But there was nothing he could do. He could not stop them now. The door began to open.

Hello, he said. Hello, can I come in? Is Mr. Harman here? He practiced faster and faster, flying along as the door opened, flying with it. Say, I came to see Mr. Harman, if he isn't busy. This is really important. He patted his coat, patted the checkbook, patted the pain. We have business, he said. He wheezed on faster to himself, like a thing. His head, like a cuckoo, went back and forth in rhythm with the door. Hello, hello.

Hello, he said. Hello.

The door all the way open. A woman, well-dressed, elegant. Smiling sideways with her hand—ring, fingers—on the door, pale red nails. Carpet in the hall and table; curved arch. Seeing in, seeing past. Fireplace.

Hello, he babbled. I'm sorry. Sorry it happened. Hot around my neck where the new tie is. Reached for heater. The sun came down on him, cracking him, splitting his head wide open. I'll get it out of there. But I can't back. Maybe you can back it. Sorry, sorry, he said to the woman. He backed away from her; retreating.

"Yes?" she said.

"Hot," he said. "Can I sit for a minute?" Have my bottle of

pills. Hemo-titic. He laughed; they both laughed and she held the door for him, so he could pass on into the cool dim hallway, with no sound at all; lost in the carpet. White Spanish walls, a thousand years old. He did not even dare to breathe.

"My husband's here," she said from ahead of him as she walked. "I think, if you want to wait."

"Thanks," he said, finding a chair. Black leather; his hands passed over it, knowing it.

"Just a minute." Her back to him, at the other wide archway, the far room. Drapes.

"I'll be fine," he said, seated.

"You're sure?"

"Yes," he said. "Thanks." He stared at the floor. Then, in his hands, balanced, a china cup of coffee, spoon and all. He stared at it in horror; it flopped and slid and returned. A single black drop, as large as gum, shot down the side of his leg, streaking the pants; he fixed his eyes on it, nodding. Out of sight. What you don't know. He crossed his leg to hide.

"Don't you worry," the woman said.

"Oh hell no," he said, keeping himself from laughing. "Don't you worry about me." He rocked from side to side.

It's the way I am. Like a boat.

You'll get used to it.

Al Miller said, "Honor is the thing you must have. Like credit in the financial world. A check goes through twenty hands before any real money is involved. My point is that honor has to be taken for granted the same way we take the check as being good. Otherwise the whole system falls apart."

Stretched out in his bathrobe, his eyes hidden by his dark glasses, Chris Harman gazed up at the midday sky. He did not respond; he seemed to be meditating.

"You mean within an organization," Bob Ross said.

"Exactly," Al said.

Harman, raising his head, said slowly, "But someone can get into an organization, Al. Someone who has other purposes." Reaching, he located his drink. "You can't go on blind trust. You have to protect yourself. I don't think you understand how close they are to us all the time."

"Pardon?" Al said, not following.

Supporting himself on his elbows, Harman said, "Most of what we net—or should net—has to go back in. Reinvestment; but for this purpose: to protect ourselves. I suppose you read where S.P. has been quietly buying up Western Pacific stock. The first W.P. knew about it was when S.P. suddenly announced they already had ten percent and so help me God, they were applying to the I.C.C. to acquire the remainder. My God, they'd be taking over."

"Really dreadful," Ross said.

"But that's not the only way an organization is penetrated," Harman said. "There are also spies and informers and plants, as in the auto business, where all secrets are swiped."

"I can testify to that," Al said. "From my experience."

"Absolutely," Harman agreed. "You're canny. But I've seen other things, Al, which you may not know about. Let me give you an example. Keep this to yourself, of course." He glanced toward Ross. "Bob knows about this."

"Oh yeah," Ross said soberly. "That contact."

Harman said, "We were sounded out."

"Who by?" Al said, trying to make it sound as if he followed; but in fact he had long ago lost the thread of the discussion. Both Harman and Ross seemed to take the thing for granted.

"By them," Harman said. "They were—let's face it—probing for a weak link in us. They didn't find it. But they'll keep on trying. They've got a lot of money ... they're not S.P., of course, but they're also not the pipe-tobacco shop on the corner. By that I mean they're not fly-by-night in any sense; they're here to stay."

"I see," Al said.

"You have to know your friends," Ross said.

"Exactly," Harman said. "Now, we're all friends here, the three of us. But you'll be approached." Removing his dark glasses he gazed directly at Al. "You will. One of these days."

"For Christ's sake," Al said.

"And you won't even know it," Ross said.

"No," Harman agreed. "Not off the bat."

"Tell him about the contact," Ross said.

Harman said, "I knew right off. But only because it's happened before, and because I've made out their line, their logic. Mainly, they operate from out of town, probably from Delaware, through a holding company. Assuming they have a legitimate front at all, they probably control all their own retail outlets."

"They sell to themselves," Ross said.

"But what they actually want or do," Harman said, "we don't know. They've been out here on the West Coast for at least eleven months, I would judge, gathering by the changes in the picture, especially in Marin County. You read, probably, about the enormous new public housing that opened in Marin City; really elaborate structures. The taxpayers are paying. And Berkeley's ruined by them; they've practically taken over the city in toto. It's taken fifteen years, but it's done now." He grimaced at Al.

"Who?" Al said.

"Negroes," Bob Ross said.

Harman said, "That was what gave their contact away. Even on the phone the voice was recognizable. The Negro intonation."

Al stared at him.

"They had a deal," Harman went on. "A very calm, direct one. I played along." His voice now seemed to shake. "I acted as if I had no idea what they were talking about. You see? So it misfired." Again he grimaced; it was almost a tic. "I'm still tense thinking back to it," he said. He sipped the rest of his drink. "Anyhow," he said, "they had hold of some factor they thought they could use to make their entry; we'd have to come to terms. Then they could absorb us. And run us."

"That'll be the day," Bob Ross said.

Harman shrugged. "You never know," he said. "They've got a lot they can bring to bear. Time will tell. Up to this point they've soft-pedaled it. Maybe they're groping around in the dark a little, too."

"Or maybe they're letting us dangle," Ross murmured, "to get more kicks out of it."

"It's a dirty business they're in," Harman said. "Blackmail. A dirty approach to the market." He became silent.

"Why Negroes?" Al said.

"It goes back a long way," Harman said. "There was a particular Negro folk-singer; we were operating on a shoestring, back around 1940. Just before the War, in San Francisco." He glanced at his wristwatch. "Someday when we have the time I'll tell it to you, the whole story."

"But we've got a job to do right now," Ross said, rising to his feet and setting down his glass. "We've got a trip ahead."

"I wonder if he's still alive," Harman said.

"Who?" Ross said.

"Shoeless Lacy Conkway. Five-string banjo. He was in the same prison as Leadbetter—Leadbelly, as you know him. I met Leadbelly a number of times, before his death. In fact, we did a couple of Leadbelly albums."

Ross said, "And a Shoeless Lacy Conkway album."

The two man glanced at each other somberly.

"You mean this raccoon banjo player is after you?" Al said. "All this time?" It was the call from Tootie Dolittle, all right. They had imagined it was someone else, for obvious good reason. "Why don't you have him plugged?" he demanded.

They both laughed, Ross and Harman. And then Harman, in a slow, introspective voice, said, "Al, they may be after me, but we will get to them first. As you suggest. Don't kid yourself on that score. There's too much at stake."

The door from the house opened, and a woman came out onto the patio, a stately gray-haired woman whom Al Miller identified at once as Mrs. Harman. Going up to her husband, she said, "Chris, there's a man to see you who's waiting in the living room now. But he's acting very strangely." Her voice had a tense quality; she smiled briefly at Ross and then at Al. "Maybe you'd better—" She leaned down to confer with Harman, and her voice become blurred.

"All right," Harman said, getting to his feet. "What kind of man?" He glanced at Ross. "Have you ever seen him before?"

Ross said, "Maybe we'd better not take off just yet." He shot a glance at Al.

"I've never seen him before," Mrs. Harman said.

"This is Al Miller," Harman explained to her, indicating Al. "He's working for us currently. This is Mrs. Harman, Al." Rubbing his chin he said. "What did he come for? What did he say?"

"There's something wrong with him, I think," Mrs. Harman said to Bob Ross. "It may be that he's drunk." She added, "An older man. About sixty."

Harman started into the house. But at the door he paused and turned to say something more to Al. "You'll see a lot," he said. "From now on. It'll be good experience. You'll see what I mean.

About the problems we were discussing. The problems the organization faces and has to keep so constantly in mind."

"We'll come inside with you," Ross said.

"I wish you would," Mrs. Harman said.

The four of them walked through the house, to the living room. It was a beautiful house, and Al's attention was caught by first one aspect of it and then another. He trailed behind and was the last to arrive in the living room; he had to peer past the others to see.

There, seated on the couch, wearing a suit and tie, with a cup and saucer on his knee, smiling straight ahead of him, sat Jim Fergesson. He did not seem aware of them; he continued to stare fixedly ahead. His suit, Al saw, had mud on it. And his face was inflamed and streaked with sweat.

At once, seeing him, Harman began booming out cordially, "Jim. I'll be God damned." He made a motion, and Mrs. Harman at once withdrew. Ross moved off to one side, to become inconspicuous.

The old man turned his head and saw Harman. With tremulous slow care he set down his coffee cup and saucer; they clinked together. He rose to his feet and came a couple of steps toward Harman. Holding out his hand, he said in a hoarse voice, "Hello there, Harman."

"For Christ's sake," Al said. "You here?" He was taken completely by surprise.

The old man made out Al. He pointed his finger at him and began to laugh. His face, red and puffy, lit up as he laughed; he tried to speak but seemed unable to. He continued to point at Al, his finger wavering, as if there was something he kept wanting to put across, but the harder he tried to express it the further it eluded him.

"I'll be God damned," the old man managed at last. Spitting, wiping his mouth, he again broke into laughter, mostly convulsions of his face, with very little sound. "Listen," he said, moving toward Al. "Did you write that letter?"

"What letter?" Al said.

"That—" He paused, choking. "That anonymous letter."

"Hell no," Al said. "I don't know anything about any letter."

Harman, in a pleasant, conversational voice, said, "Was there an anonymous letter, Jim? Concerning me?"

"Yes," Fergesson said.

Ross said something unintelligible and began pacing around, off by himself, clenching and unclenching his fists.

"Well," Harman said. He continued to smile. "But why should it have been written by Al, here?"

"It wasn't," the old man said. "I knew it wasn't. I was just ribbing him." He dug Al with his elbow; his hot, wet breath blew into Al's face, stunning him. It had a dreadful clammy quality and he retreated reflexively.

Indicating the couch, Harman said to the old man. "Sit down again. Please."

As he reseated himself, Fergesson said, "I can't get over old Al Miller being here." He shook his head, still with the fixed grin on his face, the laughter that he could not seem to control.

Harman, also seating himself, said, "Al's working for the organization, Jim."

The old man's eyes flew wide open and bulged. "No," he said. He seemed overcome with wonder and delight.

Al said, "That's the way the ball bounces. I mean it's all the same. It's in the game."

"Hey," the old man said. Again he lumbered to his feet and made his way over to Al; nudging him again, he said in a loud voice, "We're all part of the same bunch." He looked around at them all.

"Yes," Harman said, smiling. "I guess we are." He had a genial, tolerant expression on his face.

"Listen," the old man said to Harman, going up to him and taking him by the sleeve. "Harman, you know, Al and me weren't speaking for a while; you know that?"

"I didn't know that," Harman said.

"I was really sore at him," the old man said. "But I'm not anymore. He really let me down, but I don't care. I went by his lot, and it was hard for me to get over it, but I did. He was in pretty thick with my wife; they're a pair, the two of them." He went on, but Al lost the sense of it; the words became jumbled. But anyhow they were not directed to him. The old man was confiding to Harman, standing close to him muttering away in a wet, sputtering monotone.

Coming over to Al, Bob Ross said, "Who is this old guy?"

Al said, "He owns a garage."

"Oh," Ross said, with a knowing expression. "I remember. Chris mentioned him. He's retired, isn't he?"

Al said, "No, he's just getting started."

"I think I recall," Ross said. He puffed several deep puffs on his pipe. "Well, I guess we don't get up to Petaluma today."

13

Seated in the middle of the couch in Chris Harman's living room, the old man talked on and on. Al had never heard him rattle away like this before; his face shone, his eyes fixed first on Harman and then on Bob Ross and then back to Harman, and then on Mrs. Harman, and, for an instant, on Al Miller himself. He winked at Al.

"I tell you," the old man said. He had been discussing dry and wet heat. "People say you can't live up in Sacramento, but that's valley heat; that's okay. You can stand it up to a hundred and twenty if it's dry like that. What you can't stand is in Texas, on the gulf; that gulf wind—" He waved his hand. "That's terrible down there."

It was a little like the way he had buttonholed customers, Al thought. He groaned.

"What's that from you?" the old man said at once, halting. "I mean Al Miller, there." He gaped at Al, waiting.

Al said, "Amarillo isn't so bad."

Excitedly, his words tumbling over one another, the old man burst out, "That's in north Texas, with no wind, no gulf wind. That's exactly what I mean; that's dry."

"When were you ever there?" Al said.

"I was born there, around there—in Kansas. You get the same wind crossing Kansas; it's so hot it heats up your car no matter what speed you go. You know I grew up in Kansas."

Al said, "Yeah, but you haven't been there for a long time."

"It's still the same," Bob Ross said. "We were down that way recently to get some tapes made. At Oklahoma City."

"Hey, Al," the old man said. "Remember that old Packard you were driving around in when I first met you? What was that, a '37?"

"Yeah," Al said. "A Packard Twelve."

"That's how I met Al," the old man said. "Al wanted me to fix up that Packard and keep it running forever for him. He liked that car pretty good. Didn't you, Al? Remember that time those teenagers challenged you to a drag race? And you went up to the Black Point Road; it was around two in the morning. And you raced them in that old Packard, and you got it up to—what was it?—around ninety miles an hour, and it threw a rod. And you had to have it towed all the way back to Vallejo. How much did that cost you? You tried to get me to come and get it; I remember that. What became of that Packard, finally?"

"You know," Al said. "The rear mains went."

"That's because you drove it cold."

"Hell it was," Al said. "It was because I took it in to you and you balanced the crankshaft wrong."

"That's a lot of bull," the old man said loudly. "There isn't anybody else in the whole world who could have kept that Packard running except me, the way you were mistreating it.

Hey, you know what? Remember that kid who stole that Ford coupé off your lot? I saw him the other day. He was driving a new Olds."

Grinning at Harman, he said, "I have to tell you about that, Harman. Al had this beat-up Ford coupé that some guy had used to haul sacks of cement and lumber; it was one of those utility coupés. It came in all battered and dirty—what'd you get it for, Al? Around seventy dollars. Anyhow, Al got it in on trade. And he took it down to this body shop—I wouldn't touch it; he knew what shape it was in—and he paid them to repaint it. It cost him thirty dollars for that. And then he tried to get me to patch it up mechanically, but it was no good at all; the rings were completely gone—it was leaking oil all over. So anyhow, Al was determined to sell that car. He stuck it out there in front with one of those signs of his on it. Didn't you even put an ad in the *Tribune*? Everybody that came onto the lot, he tried to peddle that wreck to them, but nobody'd take it. So old Al started having more and more work done on it. He took it over to some garage and made a deal with them; he had them put in new rings and regrind the valves. That must have cost him another fifty bucks. He had around two hundred in it by then. So still it didn't sell. So he got seat covers for it. It didn't sell. So—" The old man paused. "I think he even had a set of retreads put on it finally. Anyhow, you know what happened to it? This kid stole it and smashed it up. Nothing was left of it. Just junk. What'd you get finally, Al? Ten bucks for scrap?" He winked.

"Your brains are scrambled," Al said. "There was no such car."

"The hell there wasn't," the old man stammered, blinking.

Leaning back in his chair so that he could face Al, Chris Harman gave him a long searching glance but said nothing.

Al rose to his feet. "Pardon me," he said.

"What is it, Al?" Harman said in his cultured voice.

"I have to go to the bathroom," Al said.

After a pause, Harman said in the same tone, "Follow the hall. The second door to the right. Past the picture."

"Past the Renoir," Bob Ross said, chewing on his pipe.

"Thanks, Chris," Al said, going down the hall.

As he shut the bathroom door and locked it, he could still hear the old man. Even in here, he thought, as he unzipped his trousers and slid them down and seated himself on the toilet seat. The sound still reached him, above his own sounds.

For a long time he remained in the bathroom, doing nothing, merely sitting with his hands together before him, hunched over so that he was comfortable. He had no thoughts in his mind, nor any awareness of time; the old man's voice had become vague to him, with no individual words.

A rap on the door startled him; he sat up straight.

"How long are you going to be in there?" Harman said, close to the door, in a low, sharp voice.

Al said, "I don't know. You know how these things are." He waited, but Harman said nothing. In fact, Al could not tell if he was still there, just beyond the door. "Is this the only bathroom," he said.

"You better get back out here," Harman said, in the same insistent, tense voice.

"Why?" Al said. "I don't mean to contravene your authority and judgment in this matter, Chris, but these things take time." Again he waited. Harman said nothing. At last Al heard the man going away down the hall.

"Hey, Al!" the old man called, so loudly that Al jumped. Again there was a rap on the door, a great bang that visibly shook the door. It was the old man this time. "Hey!" he yelled; the knob turned and rattled. "Get off the pot. We got a lot to do, buddio. You going to spend the day in there?"

"I'll be out in a minute," Al said, gazing at the tile of the shower.

The old man, his voice right at the door, said, "You in there playing with yourself, Al?"

"I'll be out in a minute," Al repeated.

The old man went off. Once more, in the living room, his talk resumed. Then, after a time, there was silence.

"Listen," the old man said, once again at the bathroom door. "You hear me, Al?"

"Yeah," he said.

"We're going down to a restaurant I know and have lunch," the old man said. "We're going to conduct our business down there. So get out of there and come along, or you're going to get left behind."

"I'll be out," Al said.

"We're going in the Mercedes," the old man said. "Listen, Al. You can drive. Chris says he wants you to drive."

"Okay," Al said.

"Are you coming out?"

Al got to his feet and flushed the toilet. The old man said something, but it was lost behind the racket of the water.

When he opened the door he found the old man still standing there.

"I never did get finished," Al said.

The old man clapped him excitedly on the back as they walked up the hall to the living room. "I'll buy you lunch," he said. "I'm treating."

"Okay," Al said.

Harman glanced at him without expression. He had put on a black Italian knitted sports shirt and slacks and crepe-soled shoes while Al had been in the bathroom; he was ready to go. "I hope we can all fit in the Mercedes," he said, leading the way.

"If not," Al said, "one of us can follow in the truck."

Harman said, "Is that supposed to be a joke?"

"No," Al said.

To that, Harman said nothing. They stepped down a short flight of stairs and into the garage, where the Mercedes was parked. Harman got out his keys and unlocked the car door, holding it for the old man to enter.

"Al has an old Marmon," the old man said as he seated himself on the black leather seat in the back, his hands on his knees. "Don't you, Al? Sixteen cylinder."

"Is that so?" Harman murmured as he and Ross got in. "That must be quite a car. A collector's item. Here." He handed Al the keys.

"I can't drive," Al said.

"Why not?" Harman said in a slow, calm voice.

"I lost my license," Al said.

After a pause, the old man said, "Hey Al, you're spoiling the fun. You're always so God damn gloomy and sore." To Harman he said, "He's always this way. He's got a grudge against the world."

"I didn't really lose my license," Al said. "I just don't feel like driving."

"That's what I mean," the old man said. He was breathing rapidly, and he sat with his hand pressed tightly against his coat. His face had a pinched, flat cast to it, an inertness. Speaking as if he were in pain, he said, "He put me on his shit list because I sold my garage. He wanted me to support him the rest of his life." He halted, grimacing. "Fix his wrecks for him."

Harman sat thoughtfully plucking at his lips. He did not seem ruffled or at a loss; he pondered, looked for a moment at the old man and then at Al, and then, swinging around, he opened the car door and stepped out. "No problem," he said. "Mrs. Harman will be glad to fix us lunch. We'll finish our business here."

Still seated in the back of the Mercedes, the old man said in a strained voice, "I—hate to put her to any trouble."

Ross said, "We could even send out for a caterer." He, too, stepped from the car. Finally the old man, holding on tightly to the car door, got out. Only Al remained in the car.

"It's no trouble at all," Al said.

"What?" Harman said.

"I said it's no trouble at all." Al climbed from the car. "I'm starved," he said. "Let's pitch in. Tell her to bear down and really whip up something nice."

"Sure," the old man said, panting. "You won't do anything for anybody else, but you want them to wait on you." To Harman he said, "Isn't that human nature? I tell you, it's really funny. This guy ought to be grateful to me. He sure got a good low rent from me on that desirable lot. That's why he's so sore; he knows he'll never get anyone else to solve all his problems for him, the way I did." Starting on back through the house, he said over his shoulder, "I don't know why you want to go out and hire anybody like that. You really made a mistake."

As they entered the dining room, Harman drew Al off to one side. "This enmity between you two," he said. "I have no desire to mix into anybody's personal situation, but it might have been better if you had given me some inkling in advance. Don't you think? Simply from a practical standpoint."

"Maybe so," Al said.

"In any case, you probably ought to bear in mind that he's an old man. And he's been seriously ill. It's not my place to give you advice, of course."

"There's something to that," Al said.

"I think it's a good rule," Harman said, "to keep one's private life and one's business life separate. It strikes me that you've got the two muddled together, to the detriment of all of us. Now let's try to get things back on a civil footing, and then later on—"

Al said, "It's no use, Chris."

After an interval, Harman said, "What does that signify?"

"The jig is up," Al said.

For a long time Harman scrutinized him. Ross appeared, but Harman waved him away. The old man, at the far end of the dining room, was chattering with Mrs. Harman about food; his voice penetrated the whole room. He seemed to have gotten back most of his energy.

"We placed that call," Al said.

"What call?" Harman said. His forehead had become as white as tusk. There was no hair on it at all, Al noticed; it was absolutely polished and smooth. It shone. "Miller," he said, "do you know what I'm beginning to think about you? You're a bullshitter. I should have been on to you from the start. You've been bullshitting me the whole way." He did not seem especially disturbed; his voice was controlled.

Al continued, "The colored individual who called asked about the 'Little Eva' record. Did he not?"

Harman's head moved up and down.

"Your response," Al said, "was an offer to sell him some. But we weren't fooled. It took a long time, Chris, but we did do it."

"Did do what?" Harman said.

"We got inside," Al said. "We penetrated your organization. You were right. We're here, now." He paused. "Aren't we, Chris?"

Still Harman's eyes showed no reaction. It was, Al thought, as if the man actually did not hear him. Had not heard in the slightest.

"And him," Al said, pointing at the old man. "We reached him, too. You heard what he said. About the letter."

Turning, Harman walked away from him. He walked over to Ross, Mrs. Harman, and the old man.

"You can't get away," Al said.

Harman did not stir. But the old man ceased talking. The room was silent. The old man, Bob Ross, Mrs. Harman all gazed at Al.

"We've watched your activities for a long time," Al said. "In the main, we've found you a shrewd operator. You've interested us. But even good things can't go on forever. And you've had quite a good thing going for you. Haven't you, Chris? But now the time has come." He walked from the dining room, into the hall. "We're going to blow the whistle. On all of you."

At the telephone he dialed, watching the three men and the woman. They remained where they were, in the dining room. Harman was saying something to them. Al could not catch it. He did not try.

The phone receiver clicked, and then, in Al's ear, a woman's voice said, "Good afternoon." A warm, familiar, reassuring voice. "Lane Realty. This is Mrs. Lane."

Al said, "This is Al." The people in the dining room had stopped talking now. Their sound had died away.

"Oh yes," Mrs. Lane said. "How are you today, Mr. Miller? I been wondering about you, how you been getting along. Actually I been a little worried about you, but I suppose you know what you're doing."

"Could you come and pick me up?" he said.

Hesitating, she said, "I—you're not at your lot, I know. I can see down there. Where you at?"

"I don't have a car," he said. "I'm up in Piedmont." He gave her the address. "I'd appreciate it," he said.

"Well," she said, "by the tone of your voice I can perceive something is going on. I know you wouldn't call me. Okay, Mr. Miller. There ain't any bars in that neighborhood, so it ain't that again. I'll be there. As soon as I can. Should I just honk or—"

"No," he said. "Come on up to the porch. If you will."

"I'll get out of the car," Mrs. Lane said. "But I won't go any further than the sidewalk. You have to come down. Goodbye now." She hung up then.

He put down the phone and walked back into the dining room. The four of them watched him silently as he approached.

"This is it," he said.

Pressing her hands together, Mrs. Harman said, "Chris, is something dreadful going on?" She moved over to stand by her husband.

Bob Ross had relit his pipe. He seemed completely at sea; he started to say something and then, grunting, wandered off. Perhaps, Al thought, it was too much for him.

"Do you want to do business?" Al said to Harman. "With me?"

The old man said in a squeaky voice, "Listen, Al—you're jealous of me and I wish you'd get the hell out of here. Isn't that a fact? You're doing this out of spite." He, too, seemed confused; his hand, pressed against his coat, now scrabbled and then dug into the inside pocket. He brought out an envelope, and from it took a checkbook and a passbook; he studied them, his lips moving. "You know what I got in here?" he said to Al. "Want to know? Listen to this." His head bobbed up and down, trembling. He swallowed, cleared his throat.

"That passbook is a fake," Al said.

They all stood rigid, their eyes fixed on him.

"Didn't you know that?" Al said to Harman. "Did you get hooked on that, too? God, he hooked me years ago, when we went into business together originally. That book's been around since

1949. Eleven years. He uses it to establish credit; he waves it around. Like he's doing now. With you."

Bob Ross laughed.

Swiveling his head, Harman said, "What's funny, Bob?"

"I just have to laugh," Ross said. Again he laughed. "I'm not laughing at you," he said, but he obviously was; he moved into the next room. They could still hear him laughing.

Very slightly, Harman smiled.

"Maybe he's nuts," Al said, nodding toward the old man. "I've wondered about that. He may very well think he's really got all that money. Here's what became of his garage. He went into bankruptcy. They took it over. That's why he retired. He got nothing out of it. In fact, he owes his brother-in-law seven thousand and me five hundred; he borrowed up to the hilt."

After a time, Harman said in a casual voice, "Well, we don't have to dwell on it now." He moved toward the kitchen. "We'll have another round of drinks and then lunch." To his wife, he said, "What about baked ham sandwiches and coffee? And possibly you could fix a salad." To Al he said, "We've got some good French bread."

As Mrs. Harman went past him and into the kitchen, Harman smiled at Al. He had completely regained his composure. Or, at least, he showed nothing but composure. This is really a smart man, Al said to himself. He knows that it can be checked on in half an hour. He needs to do nothing but put in a couple of phone calls to banks here in town, and then he'll know all there is to know about the old man's financial situation. He won't waste his time trying to battle it out in words. There is no showdown in words, not with this.

I almost had him, Al Miller realized. I almost plugged him with words. But he knows too much about words. He knows they are nothing.

The old man had said nothing; he still stood holding his passbook. Then he put it away in his pocket and started from the dining room, back toward the front part of the house. Al walked after him. As he came into the living room, he saw the old man get the passbook out once more, glance at it, and then again put it away in his coat pocket.

"Fuck you," the old man said, seeing him.

"The same to you," Al said.

They were both silent.

There's no use telling him I saved his money for him, Al said to himself, because he wouldn't care anyhow. And I haven't saved it because tomorrow or tonight or next week he will sign it over to Chris Harman anyhow. So it doesn't matter. But, he thought, at least I didn't have to stand there and watch it.

"This is a nice house," the old man said hoarsely.

"Yeah," Al said.

"Must cost around seventy-five thousand," the old man said.

"I don't know," Al said. "The stucco's beginning to crack. I think he's let water get behind it. That's what ruins stucco."

From behind them, Harman said, "No water has gotten behind the stucco of this house. I can assure you of that, gentlemen."

"Al knows everything," the old man muttered. "No use arguing with him; he's a know-it-all."

"Evidently," Harman said. "Well, the world can use that, too. Any ability can be useful, depending on what it's applied to." He gave Al an amiable smile.

There're no hard feelings there, Al said to himself. That man can afford to be magnanimous; he knows what I know, that what he failed to get today he'll get tomorrow anyhow. And he knows, too, that I've done everything I can; I've completely exposed myself, laid myself out bare, and accomplished nothing. I've shot my wad. Whatever menace I posed to him was over when he asked his wife to fix baked ham sandwiches and coffee; he had the situation back in his hands at that moment, and he will never lose it again.

To Harman, he said, "How about a raise?"

Startled, Harman said, "For—" He gasped and turned red.

"I think I'm worth more than I'm getting," Al said.

"We'll see," Harman murmured, in an automatic manner; he had no other response, evidently. And then he collected himself. "I tend not to agree," he said to Al. "No, I can't agree at all."

"Then I quit," Al said.

To that, Harman had no response at all.

Outside, from the street, came the sound of a car horn.

"I'll see you," Al said. He walked to the window and looked out. There, on the sidewalk beside her old dun-colored Cadillac, stood Mrs. Lane, wearing a long heavy coat and peering up at the Harman house. Her hair was tied up in a silk scarf; she had not had time to dress as fully as she usually did. Seeing him, she gave a sign of recognition. He did the same, and started toward the front door of the Harman house.

Coming from the kitchen, Mrs. Harman said rapidly, "I'm glad to have met you, Mr.—" Her voice faltered.

Over in the corner Bob Ross stood smoking, saying nothing, watching everything with an ironic expression.

Harman walked to the window and glanced out; he had started to speak, to say goodbye to Al, perhaps. But then he made out Mrs. Lane.

"We'll be seeing you, Harman," Al said to him. "Again."

He opened the door and stepped out onto the porch. A moment later he was going down the flagstone path to the Cadillac. He did not look back. He's probably signing over his money right now, he thought. Even before I'm gone. But there was nothing he could do about it, so he went on, to the parked car. Mrs. Lane had gotten back in behind the wheel; as soon as he opened the car door and seated himself, she drove out onto the street.

"I know who house that be," she said presently.

"Yes," Al said.

"Crazy Al Miller," she said. "Coming back from that house, like some I don't know what. Do you know?"

"No," he said.

"Did you get it done?" she said. "Whatever you had to get done? Did you do it to your satisfaction?"

He said nothing.

"You didn't," she said.

"No," he said.

"Too bad," she said. "That really too bad. But anyhow you out of there. That something."

"I hope so," he said.

"Just don't go back. Promise me, Mr. Miller. As one small West Oakland businessman speaking to another."

He did not answer.

"Otherwise," she said, "it going to get you finally."

"Maybe so," he said.

"I know so," Mrs. Lane said.

They drove on until they had reached the Broadway business section.

"Where you want to go, Mr. Miller?" Mrs. Lane asked. Her voice had softened somewhat. "To your lot? Or home?"

"I want to go home," he said.

She drove him to the building, the gray three-story old wooden building, in which he lived.

"Thanks," he said as he got out of the car. He felt weary and run down.

"Get a good rest," she said. "And tomorrow you see things with a new eye."

He went on and up the stairs to his apartment, too tired even to say goodbye.

That night, very late, he was awakened by his wife pushing at him and calling insistently in his ear. He had taken two phenobarbitals and for a long time it was impossible for him to come fully awake; he sat upright in the bed, resting against the wall, rubbing his forehead.

"Didn't you hear the phone?" Julie was saying loudly.

"No," he said.

"And me talking? And trying to get you to wake up and talk to her?"

"To who?"

"Lydia," his wife said.

"He's dead," Al said. "Isn't he?" He got out of bed and went to the bathroom to wash his face with cold water.

While he washed his face, Julie sat on the edge of the tub; she had on her bathrobe and slippers and seemed fully awake and rational. "He had a bad heart attack about ten-thirty in the evening," she said. "They rushed him to Alta Bates Hospital and put him in an oxygen tent. He died, I think she said, at three o'clock. It's five now."

"Five," he repeated, drying his face.

"Lydia said it was the strain of some big check he wrote out. He told her when he got home at around six."

"So he did write it out," Al said.

Julie said, "They argued about it, but she said she could see he was unnaturally tired, so she didn't try to reason with him but let him go to bed. Around nine. He went right to sleep and seemed to sleep soundly. Until the attack."

"She can stop the check," Al said. "I know God damn well he

couldn't have put it through." But he did not know it; he only hoped it.

"That's what she said," Julie said. "She's going to stop it, she said. It apparently was an enormous check. All their money. In the tens of thousands."

"Good," he said.

"You don't seem very upset," Julie said.

"Hell," he said, "I saw it coming. We all knew it was coming."

"Lydia wants you to meet her at her attorney's office at seven-thirty," Julie said. "She begged me to have you do it."

"Seven-thirty a.m.?" he said.

"Yes. So they can be sure of stopping the check."

"Christ," he said, going back toward bed.

"You will," she said, following. "You have to, with all that involved. She has to have someone she can lean on. I wish you could have talked to her. It would have made her feel better, and you would understand more. It's really dreadful. They've been married for almost thirty-five years."

He got into bed and pulled the covers over him.

14

At seven-thirty the next morning, Al Miller showed up at the address he had been given. It was an office building on Shattuck Avenue, and in front of it he found Lydia Fergesson standing with a small round bald-headed man who carried a briefcase and wore an old-fashioned double-breasted suit. Lydia introduced him as Boris Tsarnas, her lawyer. She herself was dressed as he usually saw her; she did not look especially different on this occasion.

As soon as she saw him, she came swiftly toward him, calling out to him, "The man whom you know, that criminal person, has possession of the check. What is his name? That we need to know at once."

The lawyer explained that by eight o'clock he could be in touch with an official of the Bank of America. If the check had not cleared, it could be stopped, even though it might have been cashed somewhere, even at a branch bank. He spoke very rapidly, in an accented monotone. Al decided that he was Greek, too; certainly from the Balkans.

"If it's a legitimate investment venture," Tsarnas said, "this Mr. Harman can take legal action to force payment. But if he's the confidence man that you and Mrs. Fergesson seem to feel, then he won't dare go into court. He'll know the situation. Probably he has no idea that your husband, Mr. Fergesson, passed away during the night, so we have at least half a day's jump on him in connection with closing the account, if we decide to do that. It was a joint account, this commercial account on which the draft was made, is it not?"

"Yes," Lydia said.

From Al, the lawyer got information about Harman's business, his residence, the situation under which the check had been written. He seemed to be satisfied, and yet, throughout, he had an oddly neutral attitude. At last Al realized that this man had been Fergesson's lawyer also, and, if the investment were on the level, he meant to see that the check was finally released. He took an abstract view of the whole business; to him, no persons were involved, only legal issues. His attitude amazed Al.

Scarcely anyone was up this early; only a few cars moved along Shattuck Avenue. The air was cold. All the shops remained shut from the night. Many neon signs, Al noticed, were still on. Pale in the morning sunlight.

"Now what?" he asked Lydia, after the lawyer had gone off in his own car. He and Lydia remained on the sidewalk together.

Lydia said, "I have God knows so much to do. It is all like some dream. You have been a great deal of help to me, Mr. Miller. Boris has the will. I know its contents. However, it must be formally read. You are not in it."

"I guess I'll survive that," Al said. "Are you in it?"

"The law requires it to be," Lydia said in a firm voice, the same voice she had used from the moment he had met her this morning.

"It was quite a surprise," Al said.

"It was a fortunate thing that he died right then," Lydia said, "because even a day later it would be too late to stop the check."

Her matter-of-factness overwhelmed him. It was as if he were seeing the original peasant person showing through from beneath all the culture and learning. The same practical worldly dedication that he had seen in the old man; they were two of a kind. But, on final analysis, it did not strike him as wicked. It seemed perfectly natural. Even, he thought, what the old man deserved.

As they walked toward Al's car, Lydia said, "This individual who has the check, this Chris Harman, will harbor ill-will toward you as a result of what you have done for me."

He shrugged. "Maybe so."

"Do you concern yourself with that?"

He did not know if he did. It was too early; too early in the day.

"You can count on my gratitude," Lydia said. "I know that in a situation unforeseen now, perhaps I can return for what you did."

To that, he said nothing.

She patted him on the arm. "Be of good cheer."

"Why?" he said.

"Only God can know why," Lydia said, and started off in the direction of the taxi which was waiting for her.

Now I have no job, he said to himself as he got groggily into his own car, a Chevrolet from the lot. Nothing. The old man is dead and I'm not in the will; not that I expected to be, or even gave it a thought. I am finished with the Harman organization. My lot is ruined beyond any doubt, not two months from now but right now. All the old man's property will be tied up in court. And the lot belongs to him; it is part of his estate. Of course, when the courts look it all over, they will conclude that it was legally sold. But that will take time.

I guess I killed him, he realized. I got him yesterday, at Harman's house. When I said that about his bankbook being a fake. It took him a while, though. Thank God he didn't drop to the floor then and there. Thank God the machinery ran on awhile longer, probably out of habit rather than intent.

Al thought, He always expected to get pinned under a car in his garage. That's how he anticipated it. But that's not how it worked out. He was killed by a flock of words. My words.

Starting up his car he drove off in search of a coffee shop where he could get breakfast.

On Sacramento Avenue he found a coffee shop which he knew, and there he ordered breakfast. Most of the customers were men; they read the sports section of the morning *Chronicle*, drank their coffee and ate their fried potatoes, bacon and eggs. The place was warm, yellow with light, and it cheered Al up. It made him feel less alone.

While he was eating, a Negro customer came up and seated himself beside him. "Ain't you Mr. Miller?" the man said.

Al knew the man slightly; he had passed by the lot a couple of times. So he nodded.

The man said, "The doctor looking for you."

"What doctor?"

"Doctor Do," the man said, and then slid from his stool, and sidled on out of the coffee shop, onto the sidewalk.

As soon as he had finished eating, Al went to the pay phone booth and dialed Tootie's number.

"Hey, man," Tootie said, when he recognized Al's voice. "They looking for you."

"Who?"

"Them guys. What don't mean you not a bit of good."

"Sheoot," Al said, falling into the vernacular.

"You better not say that," Tootie said. "You better get it into you crappy head you in trouble."

"Name the guys."

"I don't know whom them is. I just heard them looking for you to get you. Didn't you done them something in? Be frank. They not pick on you for nothing."

"Beats me," Al said.

Tootie said, "What I hear, you kill someone."

"Balls," Al said.

"And that cost them a lot of money. Somebody I hear say it cost them people around a hundred thousand dollar."

"There ain't no hundred thousand dollar," Al said angrily, caught up in spite of himself in Tootie's mad account.

"What you going to do?" Tootie said.

"Nothing," Al said.

"You better buy yourself a gun and lay low."

"Balls on that," Al said.

"Anyhow, I warn you," Tootie said. "I hear this kind of stuff and it always prove out to be correct. I think whether you know it or not, you up against the big."

"Okay," Al said. He started to hang up.

"I hear you scratching around there," Tootie said. "Getting ready to ring off."

"I'll go to the district attorney," Al said, "and tell him all I know. They won't touch me."

"Who you kill?" Tootie said.

"I don't know."

"Sure you know."

"Just some guy that got in my way."

"You daffy," Tootie said. "I ring off myself." The phone clicked. Presently Al hung up his own receiver and left the booth.

Good of him to warn me, he said to himself.

Maybe he's right, he thought. I should buy a gun and lay low. But where can I go? The Harman organization has my complete record, all the facts about me: every place I've lived, where I was born, where my wife works, what I've done since I was in grammar school. They can probably turn it over to a psychologist and he can predict exactly what I'll do. They'll know exactly where to find me, what street, what number, which particular room. That's what modern industrial technology can do.

He bought a *Chronicle*, and, reseated at the counter, began to read over the "men wanted" ads. There were no jobs worth talking about. I could be a salesman, he decided. Or service penny-gum machines. He read the personals then, and after that the personals in business. Look how some guys stay alive, he thought. I will come into your own home and hypnotize you into not smoking. Or if you want, I will show up at your kid's birthday party and entertain with puppets. His game went back to the personals. "Inside dope on bughouse," he read. "Thank St. Jude for saving my heirloom furniture." Christ. He put the paper away.

Early in the afternoon Julie showed up at their apartment. He had been taking a nap. Astonished to see her so early, he sat up. But before he could speak, Julie said, "I've been fired." She began taking off her shoes and stockings.

"Why?" he said.

Julie said, "Some customer called in and told the office manager that I didn't believe in God. He had me come into his office and he asked me and I told him it was so, but it wasn't any of Western Carbon and Carbide's business. But he said the morals of the employees were Western Carbon and Carbide's business. And he also said that they never found that college girls worked out. They're never satisfied with their jobs. They're always trouble-makers." She hung up her coat in the closet.

So Tootie was right. They were out to get him.

"Listen," he said. "How would you like to leave the Bay Area?"

"And go where?"

"Beats me," he said. "But we'll work it out."

"There're lots of jobs in the Bay Area," Julie said, going into the kitchen and beginning to pile dishes into the sink. "I won't have any trouble. I've already listed myself at some of the employment agencies. You have to expect this sort of thing. Anyhow, you have your job."

"No," he said.

"No what? What do you mean? You mean after one day you're not working there anymore, for that man?" She ceased working with the dishes and came into the bedroom to stand facing him. "How come you're home? Why aren't you at work?"

Al said, "We're in trouble."

"You held that job just one day, didn't you?" Julie said. "That good job."

He nodded.

"You quit?"

"Yes," he said finally.

"Will you tell me why?"

"I don't know why," he said. "I know what happened, but I don't know why. You have to take my word. There wasn't anything else I could do." He faced her, his hands in his pockets. His wife had folded her arms tightly before her, as if she were cold. Her face had a withered, old expression, and all her features, her nose and eyes and mouth, became by degrees smaller. The bones themselves seemed to shrink. As if, he thought, the life-force inside her were thinning out. Turning to air. Vanishing. Puffing away as she breathed in and out. Maybe that was all it was any-how, merely air. Air in all of them, that kept them alive.

"I'm going to divorce you," she said.

He made a move toward her, to reassure her. To warm her back up to some kind of life. But she drew away. She avoided him.

"This is no time for this," he said. "This sort of thing."

"I suppose you're going to hit me," she said. "Like you did that poor man."

"What poor man?"

"That drunk who got onto your lot, and you hit him."

He did not remember. He had no idea what she was talking about. "We're both out of work," he said, "and we're going to have to start over, probably somewhere else entirely. But we'll make it back up. I learned a lot from this."

"No," she said. "We're through."

After a time he said, "I'll tell you what. I'll make a deal with you. Give it one month. If we—" He hesitated.

"Yes," she said with bitterness. "If *we* don't find some sort of job. We. Not you."

He said, "If I don't have something worthwhile in a month, then we'll break up."

"I can't make a deal with you," Julie said, "because—do you want to know why? Can you face the truth? You're not honest. You can't be trusted." She moved farther away, as if afraid. Dreading his reaction. But he did nothing. "Now hit me," she said. "And prove how reliable you are. How honest you are."

The phone rang.

As she went past him to answer it, he said, "Let it go."

"It's probably one of the agencies," she said. "For me." She picked up the receiver, said hello. Then she put her hand over the receiver and said to him, "Do you know somebody named Denkmal?"

"God no," he said.

"Anyway it's for you," she said. She held it out to him.

He shook his head no.

Julie, her hand over the phone, said to him in a soft voice, "I'm not telling your lies for you. You'll have to do it yourself from now on." Again she held the phone out.

So he took the phone from her and said hello.

A man's voice said, "Al Miller?"

"Yes," he said.

"Say, Miller, my name's Denkmal. I own the barbershop. You know, across from you. Listen, I can see your lot from here. You better get down here."

He hung up, ran past Julie and out of the apartment, downstairs and across the sidewalk, to the Chevrolet.

When he pulled up at the curb before the lot, the barber in his white uniform came across the street, through traffic, and up beside him. They stood together, facing the lot. Nothing stirred.

Denkmal said, "I don't know what they did. I thought they were customers, looking at cars."

"Did they go in the back?" Al said. He walked onto the lot, and the barber followed. The cars in the first line seemed okay.

"They were doing something," the barber said.

It was the Marmon, in the back. They had broken all the glass, slashed the tires, ripped the seats, smashed the gauges of the dashboard. When he lifted the hood he saw that they had cut wires, torn parts loose. And the paint was ruined. They had gouged and scratched it, and with a hammer, dented the hood and doors. The headlights had been wrenched loose and broken. Looking down he saw that water was leaking out in a pool. They had smashed the radiator.

"You better call the Oakland Police Department," Denkmal said. "You had it almost completely rebuilt, didn't you? I've been watching you; good Lord, you've been working on it for a couple of years."

"The motherfuckers," Al said.

Denkmal said, "It didn't look like juveniles. Usually it's juveniles that do vandalism."

"No," he said. "It wasn't kids."

"The police will say it was kids," Denkmal said.

Al thanked the barber for calling him. The barber went back across the street to his barbershop. Al remained on the lot, standing with his back to the ruined car, watching the traffic pass. Then he went into the little basalt blockhouse and shut the door and sat down, by himself.

What else can they do? he asked himself. They got my wife's job; mine was already gone. They got my Marmon. Maybe Tootie was right; maybe they'll stick a shiv into me, or beat me up. Or rape Julie. Who knows? He did not know. He had cost Harman forty thousand dollars at least; perhaps more.

He remembered how, as a kid, he had used a gun. The only time. He had had the job of feeding the chickens and ducks in their pens. He had gone down there and found field rats galloping around; so his dad had given him the .22 rifle and he had clambered up on the roof of the chicken house and sat cross-legged, above the pen, watching for the field rats to come out of their burrows. He had shot one. He had hit it in the hindquarters and it had spun around like a gear in a clock, its feet flailing. Around and around it had gone, and then, just when he thought it was going to die, it bolted for its hole, made it, and disappeared.

In his mind he tried to picture how a man would look, hit somewhere, spinning around and around. I can't make it, he thought. Fuck it. I won't buy a gun.

For an indefinite long time he remained there, at his desk, in thought. And then he noticed that several cars were parked at the curb a little way down. The garage doors had been opened, and Lydia Fergesson was coming out of the garage. With her were several men in business suits, all looking grave.

Seeing him in the little house, Lydia came across the lot toward him. "Mr. Miller," she said, opening the door of the house. "We were able to stop the check. The money I have taken out and put for safekeeping in a safety-deposit box." Her eyes flashed as she spoke. Her face had heavy makeup on it, and she wore a fur neckpiece, black coat, dark stockings, and carried a big leather purse. Her whole body vibrated with tension, almost a kind of excitement. Near even to frenzy.

"Good," he said.

"The body lies in state at this mortuary. *Qui tollis peccata mundi, miserere nobis.* Eh, Mr. Miller?" She put down a white embossed card on his desk. "The service will be tomorrow in the morning, at eleven. Then he will be cremated."

He nodded, picking up the card.

"Do you wish to go to view the deceased?" Lydia said.

"I don't know," he said. "I can't decide."

"There is always the problem of what clothes," she said. "They contacted me in that matter. He had new ties he had bought, but it was my conclusion not to use anything but what we are all familiar with. The minister is Unitarian. Do you know songs he enjoyed?"

"What?" Al said.

"They play on the organ songs he enjoyed."

"No," he said.

"Then they will play hymns," Lydia said. "Worse luck."

Al said, "I hastened his death, by arguing with him at Harman's house. Did you know that?"

"You were doing your duty."

"How do you know?"

"He gave me a complete account of the proceedings. He recognized that you were attempting to save him from himself."

Al stared down at his desk.

"He did not hold it against you."

Al nodded.

"Please go and view the remains," Lydia said.

"Okay," he said.

"Today," she said. "Because if you do not do it today there will be no remains to view."

"Okay," he said.

"You're not going to," Lydia said. "Why not?"

"I don't see any point in it," he said.

Lydia said, "No one can make you do anything, Mr. Miller; I recognize that about you. You do exactly as you want. I have been thinking about you today; you are very much in my thoughts. I want to bestow on you enough money to get you started again."

He glanced at her, taken utterly off guard.

"Your economic existence is in ruins," Lydia said. "Is it not? Because of your obedience to duty. Someone must restore you by stepping in and aiding you, someone who can. I have the money."

He did not know what to say.

"You are thinking," she said, "that you would be sharing in the loot."

At that, he laughed.

"Wash your conscience clear," Lydia said. "You have nothing to feel guilty for."

"I want to feel guilty," he said.

"Why, Mr. Miller?"

"I don't know," he said.

"You want possibly to share in his death."

Al said nothing.

"Instead of viewing him," she said, "This is what you do. It is your system."

He shrugged, still gazing down at the desk.

Opening her big leather purse, Lydia searched and then put out her hand with something; he saw that it was a five-dollar bill. She pushed the bill into his shirt pocket. As he stared at it, she said, "I want you to buy flowers to send to the mortuary for display."

"I can buy flowers," he said.

"No you can't," she said calmly. "Can you? Have you ever done that? Not in your life, my good young friend. Nor have you ever gone to a funeral. You do not know how. There are so many things in this world which you personally do not understand how to go about doing. You are, I would say, if it does not hurt, a barbarian."

"A barbarian," he repeated.

"But you have instincts," she said. She was moving out of the little house, shutting the door after her. "Good instincts which will save you, if they have not already. You must depend on them, and also, my good young friend, on letting someone else show you how to get about in this cruel old world of ours which, alas, you understand so very little. So dreadfully very little."

"God in heaven," he said, looking up at her. Her peculiar choice of words, for a moment, frightened him.

She smiled. "What do you think? What do you feel? Tell me now, what your instincts say to you about how to live. How you should begin your life, really for the first time."

To himself he thought, They tell me to kill myself. But he did not say it aloud; he said nothing.

The door closed. Lydia had gone. He remained where he was, glad to be alone again; glad she was gone. But a moment later the door once more opened. "Mr. Miller," she said. "I notice that the superb old car of yours is in tatters. What happened to it?"

Al said, "They took it out on the car."

"That was my impression," she said, "upon seeing it with broken glass and the fabric ripped." She re-entered and seated herself at the desk, facing him. "What I will do for you," she said, "is buy that from you. I know from what I heard in the past, mostly from you, what you expected to get from it. About two thousand dollars. Did you not?"

He nodded.

"Then I will buy it for that." She laid out a checkbook, and, with a fountain pen, began carefully to write out a check.

"Okay," he said.

She smiled as she wrote.

"Aren't you surprised I'm taking it?" he said. It had surprised him, his reaction. His acceptance. "I need the two thousand dollars," he said. It was as simple as that. With two thousand dollars he could get away. Otherwise, he could not. Probably the two thousand dollars would save his life and his wife's life.

As soon as Lydia had left, he locked up the lot and drove to the bank on which the check was drawn. The bank cashed it without making any trouble for him; he had the money converted into traveler's checks, and then he drove quickly back to his apartment.

When he entered he found Julie in the bedroom, packing her clothes in one of their suitcases.

He said, "I have enough money for us to get out of here and make it somewhere else."

"Do you," she said, continuing her packing.

Seating himself on the bed beside the suitcase, he laid out the books of traveler's checks.

After a long time, Julie said, "Where do you intend to take us?"

"We'll get started," he said, "and then decide along the way."

"Right now?" She watched as he got the other suitcase and began to pack his own things.

"We'll get on the bus as soon as we're packed," he said.

To that, she said nothing. She resumed her packing. They both worked together, side by side, until they had gotten as much as was practical to take.

Julie said, "While you were gone, there was another call." She showed him the pad. "I wrote it down. The man said for you to call him back as soon as you could."

The number, he saw, was Harman's home phone.

"He talked very strangely," Julie said. "I couldn't make half of it out. At first I thought he had the wrong number; he acted as if he were speaking to a company."

"An organization," Al said.

"Yes, he kept saying 'you people.'"

Al said, "We're ready."

Picking up her suitcase, she started toward the door. "I hate to leave all this stuff here." She halted to touch an ashtray on the coffee table. "It won't be here when we get back; we'll never see any of these things again."

"Sometimes you have to do that," Al said.

Still lingering, she said, "I like the Bay Area."

"I know," he said.

"You did something really dreadful," she said, "didn't you? I knew it when I first got home today. Does it have to do with Jim Fergesson's death? I've been thinking about that. Maybe you tried to get his money. I don't know." She shook her head. "You'll never say. I guess things like that happen all the time. I never liked him. He really had no right to the money anyhow. I say what I said before: I wanted him to die. He treated you very badly." She eyed him.

Picking up his own suitcase, he moved to the door, guiding his wife along ahead of him, out into the hall.

* * *

Rather than taking their own car, they went by taxi to the Greyhound bus station. He bought tickets for Sparks, Nevada. An hour later, after waiting in the station, they were on their way by airconditioned double-decker bus, traveling on Highway 40, through the great flat Sacramento Valley.

It was early evening and the air had cooled. The other passengers dozed or read or looked out. Julie looked out, now and then saying something about the fields and farm houses which they passed.

When they reached Sacramento it was still light. The bus stopped long enough for the passengers to eat dinner, and then once more they were in motion. Now it was dark. The bus began to climb the winding, older highway that led from Sacramento into the Sierras. Most of the other traffic was large trucks. Gazing out, Al saw roadside diners and closed-up fruit stands and gas stations. The fields were behind them now.

"This part is sort of depressing," Julie said. "I'm glad we can't really see it. But I wish we could see the Sierras."

"These are the Sierras," he said. "It's like this all the way. Advertising signs and bars."

"What's it like on the other side?"

"We'll find out," he said.

"Anyhow," Julie said, "the air smells nice."

15

At Sparks, Nevada, he bought tickets to Salt Lake City. They spent a few hours wandering around Sparks; it was close to Reno and very modern and well cared for. And then they were on their way across the Nevada desert. It was three-thirty in the morning.

Both of them slept. There was nothing beyond the bus, no lights, no life. The bus roared along without stopping.

When Al awoke the sun had come up; he saw all around them the rocky lands, hills of broken rock, scrubby gray plants, and, here and there along the road, discarded human debris. The time was eight-fifteen. According to the schedule they were almost to the Utah border.

At Wendover the bus stopped so that they could get breakfast. This was the last stop in Nevada, the last gambling machines. The town lay along the highway, spread out with space between each house and shop, sandy soil on which nothing grew. To exercise their legs, he and Julie walked the length of the town and then back to a café for hotcakes and bacon.

"We could be almost anywhere in California," Julie said, looking around the café. "The same booths, the same cash register. Jukebox." The café seemed to have been newly built; everything was freshly painted and stylish. "The only thing different," she said, "is the newspaper. And the funny-looking dirt outside."

Several other passengers were eating in the café, too, so they had no fear of being left.

"Are we going to stay in Salt Lake City?" Julie asked.

"Maybe," he said. It seemed to him as good a place to relocate themselves as any. At least, from what he had heard of it.

"It's sort of exciting," Julie said, "an adventure like this . . . not knowing where we're going, just moving on, not stopping. Cutting ourselves off from our past. Our families." She smiled at him. Her face was wan from lack of sleep, and her clothes were rumpled. His were the same. And he needed a shave.

Suddenly he had a premonition. Salt Lake City was too big a town. They would have a representative there.

He said, "I think we'll go on as soon as we get to Salt Lake." Getting out the map, he examined the possibilities. A town small enough to be unimportant to the Harman organization, but large enough so that he could get a job or go into business. Open a used-car lot, he thought. There would be enough money, just barely enough, if he bought wisely.

"I'd like to see Salt Lake City," Julie said. "I've always wanted to."

"So would I," he said.

"But we can't." She studied him.

"No," he said.

"I have no say-so in this?"

He said, "You better let me decide."

Julie went on eating then. So he did too.

After they had left the café they walked slowly back in the direction of the parked Greyhound bus. They could see the driver; he was off talking to two middle-aged women. So they did not hurry.

"This is a very pretty little town," Julie said. "But there's nothing doing here. We've seen it all. It's just a place for people to stop and eat and get their cars fixed and do a little last gambling." Turning toward him, she said, "Do you feel safer here? Probably not. You'll never feel safe. It's really inside you."

"What is?" he said.

"The conflict. The thing you're running away from. Psychologists say we carry our problems with us."

He said, "Maybe so." He did not feel like arguing with her.

They came to the bus. The door was open, and he started to ascend the metal steps.

"I don't believe I'll get on," Julie said.

"Okay," he said, stepping back to the ground.

"At all." She did not flinch; she met his gaze. "I've decided I don't want to go any farther. I think there's something you're not facing in yourself; that you've never faced. And you're dragging me along. If you try to force me to get on the bus, I'll scream and they'll stop you. I see a highway patrolman or somebody over there." She nodded her head; he saw the parked patrol car with its antenna.

"You're going to stay in Wendover?" he said, in agony.

"No. I'm going to take the next bus back to Reno, and I'm going to stay there a few days and do some shopping, and then if I like it there I'll stay there and get a Nevada divorce, and of course get a job there. And if I don't like it, I'll go on back to Oakland. And get a California divorce."

"On what?"

"Won't you give me part of the money?"

He was silent. Other passengers, seeing them at the bus, were beginning to come, afraid they might be left behind. The driver was winding up his conversation with the middle-aged women.

"I want you to come back with me," Julie said. "But probably you won't; you'll go on fleeing."

He groaned.

"Yes," she said. "Groan, because you know it's the truth."

He said, "It's crap."

"Just give me some of the money. Not even half. Just, say, five hundred dollars. I know how much there is; that leaves you almost fifteen hundred. Under California joint-property law, half of it is mine. But I don't care. I just want to end this—pathology. This—" She broke off. Other people were going by them and up into the bus.

Al said, "I'll have to sign the traveler's checks or they won't be good."

"Fine," she said.

Holding the checks up against the side of the bus, he signed five hundred dollars' worth. He gave them to his wife.

"Well," she said quietly, "you did just give me five hundred. I thought maybe you'd volunteer half. Well, it doesn't matter." Tears filled her eyes, and then she turned to the driver, who had come up, and said, "I'd like my luggage; I'm not going on. May I, please?" She held out the claim check. The driver glanced at her, then at Al, and then accepted the claim check.

Al got onto the bus and reseated himself, alone. Below, on the outside, the driver was unloading Julie's suitcase. He slammed the metal door shut after the suitcase and then hurried up into the bus to seat himself at the wheel. A moment later the motor roared on; gray smoke poured from the exhaust. The remaining passengers got quickly on and found their seats.

Seated in the bus, Al saw his wife walk away with her

suitcase, into the bus depot. The door closed after her. And then the doors of the bus shut and the bus began to move.

He felt the rift, the ghastly, purposeless rift. What did it matter now whether he went on or not? But he was going on; he was on his way alone to Salt Lake City and whatever came after that. Maybe this is better, he thought. For us to separate. At least they won't get both of us. It was hopeless from the start to try to make her go along. He thought, You can't force people to do anything. I can't make Julie do what I want her to do, any more than Lydia Fergesson could force me to send flowers or go to the mortuary. Each of us has his own life to live out, for better or worse.

The Great Salt Lake was enormously hot, white and unsteady. Toward midday the bus had crossed it and had reached the fertile green part of Utah with trees and small lakes; once more he saw countryside not much different from California. There was quite a bit of traffic on the highway. He saw, ahead, the beginnings of a large city.

He found Salt Lake City as crowded and busy and built-up as the Bay Area; it, like Oakland, had other smaller cities so close to it that they merged. Residential and business districts, he thought as he gazed out the bus window, were about the same everywhere. Motels, drugstores, gas stations, cleaning establishments, dime stores . . . the houses seemed to be mostly of brick or stone, or, if of wood, unusually substantial. The streets were well maintained and noisy. He saw a lot of teenagers and their cars, the modified hot rods that he saw all day long going back and forth along San Pablo Avenue.

In many ways, he decided, Salt Lake City appeared to be an ideal town for a used-car business. Everyone seemed to drive, and there were plenty of older cars to be seen.

When he got off the bus in downtown Salt Lake City, two plainclothes policemen took hold of him and led him off to one side of the depot. "Are you Allen Miller of Oakland, California?" one of them asked him, showing his badge.

He was so completely cut down that he nodded yes.

"We have a warrant for your arrest," the plainclothes policeman said, showing him a folded paper, "and return to the State of California." They began to move him, between them, toward the curb and their parked police car.

"What for?" Al demanded.

"For fraud," one of them said as they pushed him into the car. "Obtaining money under false pretenses."

"What money?" he demanded. "Who says so?"

"The litigant signing the complaint in the County of Alameda, California; Mrs. Lydia Fergesson." The policeman started up the car, and they drove off into downtown Salt Lake City traffic. Meanwhile, in the back of the car, the other policeman was searching Al; he offered no resistance. "You'll be here a couple of days and then you'll be on your way back."

Al could think of nothing to say.

"You know this Mrs. Fergesson?" one of the policemen said to him, with a wink at the other.

"Sure," Al said.

After a time one of the policemen said, "Is she a widow?"

Al said, "Yes."

"Fat? Middle-aged?"

Al said nothing.

"What's your stated occupation?" one of the policemen said.

"Car salesman," Al said.

"You've gone up in the world," the policeman said, and chuckled.

Transportation arrangements were made the next day. With another male prisoner of the State of Utah, he was sent back to

California in the custody of a sheriff's deputy; they made the trip by air, and within a few hours after leaving the Salt Lake City airport they were landing at the Oakland airport. There, a police car met them and they were taken to the Oakland Hall of Justice.

Only two and a half days had passed since he and Julie had started on their trip. I wonder where she is, Al thought as he sat on a bench in one of the courtrooms, waiting to be arraigned. Did she go back to Reno? Is she there now? Strange he thought, to be back here. He had never expected to see Oakland again. Through a window of the courtroom he could make out the public buildings of Alameda County, and somewhere, not far out of sight, would be Lake Merritt. Where, many times, he had gone canoeing.

Coming back by air made the distance seem short. I didn't get very far, he decided. A few hours away; that's all, for those who travel by air. It had never occurred to him to take a plane. That must be the kind of thing Lydia meant, he thought. When she said I understood the world so little.

Someone, evidently an employee of the court, came over and told him he should have an attorney.

"Okay," he said. The whole thing seemed vague to him. "I will."

"You want to phone?"

"Maybe later," Al said. He could not think of anyone to phone. He wished that he had his pills with him. Perhaps he did; he began fishing in his pockets, but without success. No, he realized. The Anacin tin was in another pair of pants. Or the police had taken it away; they had gone over all his things. Maybe that's what happened to me, he thought. Somehow I got cut off from my pills.

The next he knew, a short, bald, foreign-looking man in a double-breasted suit had come into the courtroom. I know him, Al said to himself. Maybe he's my lawyer. But then he remembered him. It was Lydia's lawyer, whatever his name was.

Several people conferred with the lawyer, and then Al found himself being moved out of the courtroom, down a hallway. I'm really in their hands, he said to himself. They guide me around wherever they want. A policeman pointed to an open door, and Al entered a side room, a sort of office with chairs and a table.

"Thanks," he said to the policeman. But the policeman had already gone on.

The door opened and Lydia's short, bald, foreign lawyer entered with his briefcase; moving rapidly, in an important manner, he seated himself facing Al and unzipped his briefcase. For a moment he glanced over papers and then he looked up. He smiled. They all smile, Al thought. Maybe that's how you can tell them.

"I'm Boris Tsarnas," the lawyer said. "We have met."

"Yeah," Al said.

"Mrs. Fergesson didn't want to see you, at least at this time. I'm her counsel, you understand, in this matter." His voice dropped to a drone. "As well as other matters involving the estate of her deceased husband and so forth." He studied Al for so long that Al became uncomfortable. The man had bright, intelligent eyes, small as they were. "The investment," Tsarnas said, "was perfectly reputable."

That was it then. That explained it. Al nodded.

"We had all the financial records, all the statements from the accountants, gone over. The net return on her investment will probably be very high; at least ten percent, possibly more. Possibly as high as twelve. Harman was acting without any recompense. He has no involvement with the enterprise, save that he knows both Mr. Bradford and the deceased Mr. Fergesson. It appears that he was doing precisely as he indicated, offering his informed guidance in securing for the deceased a premium investment which now becomes advantageous to the heir, Mrs. Fergesson. And so I have advised her." He snapped his briefcase shut. In a friendly manner, he said, "I thought you would be interested in knowing. You seemed to have some concern over Mr. Harman's reliability. When the check in question was stopped at Mrs. Fergesson's insistence, Mr. Harman proceeded to make good on it himself. That is, he advanced forty-one thousand dollars of his own money to Mr. Bradford to cover the sum, until such time as the check would be made good. So he risked a good deal of his own cash to be sure the investment opportunity was secured and therefore not lost to the widow of the deceased."

Presently Al said, "Lydia knows all this?"

"As soon as we had gone over the financial statements, we so informed her. This Marin Gardens place is well thought of, in Marin County real-estate investment circles. A number of sanguine people on the other side of the Bay, and a few here, have bought in."

Al said, "What's that got to do with her having me arrested?"

"You obtained a large sum from Mrs. Fergesson under false pretenses. You alleged that while working to protect her interests you encountered a severe loss, and you intimated that she was responsible and so should make good. As soon as she told me what she had done, I advised her to start action to stop that check." The man's eyes danced. "But of course you put it right through. Mrs. Fergesson then wished me to advise her concerning further action. You had, as we discovered, left California as soon as you had cashed the check." His smile grew. "The bank informed us that you had converted the two thousand dollars into traveler's checks. And we found that both you and your wife had packed and left together. In fact she had packed while you cashed the check." He continued to smile at Al, almost as if he admired him.

"I sold her a car," Al said.

"A thirty-year-old car completely in ruins. Worth no more than a few dollars as scrap."

It was true. He had to admit it. "But they wrecked the car," he said.

"Who?" Tsarnas's eyes blazed up briefly.

"Harman and his goons."

"Nonsense. Yes, you told her that. The Oakland police have the vandals. The car was wrecked even before Mr. Fergesson's death, by some kids who've been vandalizing property up and down West Oakland for months."

"Juveniles," Al murmured.

"Yes," Tsarnas said.

Al said, "Harman got my wife fired."

"Your wife wasn't fired," Tsarnas said.

Al stared at him.

"If it's important to establish this, and I don't quite see why it is, we—that is, the Harman organization—checked with your wife's employer. She quit, sir. She said that her husband now had a decent job and she had been wanting to quit for quite some time. It was not unexpected. They had no idea where she or you might have gone; she simply quit and left the office. Her check is being mailed to her. She didn't even wait to pick it up." The lawyer studied Al. "You were interested in Fergesson's money, I take it; the accrual from the sale of his garage. Or was it a grudge because he sold his garage? Why did you go to so much trouble to bilk Mrs. Fergesson, deceiving her regarding the investment arranged through Mr. Harman, and then settle for two thousand instead of the—"

"I have nothing to say," Al said. Somewhere he remembered that statement; it seemed to be right. It seemed to be what he wanted.

Considering, Tsarnas at length said, "Mrs. Fergesson is interested in having her money restored to her. Not in persecuting you. Do you have the money?"

"Most of it," Al said.

"It can be arranged," Tsarnas said, "that if you make full restitution, no charges will be pressed. There are innumerable expenses connected with your arrest in Utah and your return here; probably something would have to be worked out with both states. I don't know. Anyhow, if you are willing and able—"

"I am," Al said. "Willing and able. I can sell my lot and the rest of my cars. To get the money."

"You have no record?" Tsarnas said. "No history of bunko stuff of this kind?"

"No history at all," Al said.

"Were you working alone?" Tsarnas said. "I'm just curious. I know Mrs. Fergesson had great fondness and admiration for you, up to the moment she realized—and don't imagine she wanted to realize—that you had bilked her out of two thousand dollars. My Lord, didn't you work with her husband for a number of years?"

"Yes," Al said. "I worked with her husband a number of years."

"You really must have been nursing a long-term grudge," Tsarnas said, "to become active so soon after his death. That man was just cremated."

"How was the service?" Al said.

"I didn't have the opportunity to be present."

Suddenly Al realized that he still had the five dollars that Lydia had given him to buy flowers. It was still in his shirt pocket; he got it out and held it between his hands. He had bilked her out of this, too. So he handed it over to the lawyer. "This belongs to Lydia," he said.

The lawyer put it in his briefcase, in an envelope.

"How did you know which way I went?" Al said. "How did you know I headed for Utah?"

"You were cashing those traveler's checks all along the route. Every time you stopped to eat. And you paid for your ticket at the Sparks Greyhound ticket-office with a traveler's check. There was a bulletin out just after that, and they got in touch with the police."

Al said, "What about my wife?"

"She got in touch with us," Tsarnas said. "From Reno. She had noticed that you were acting erratically, and she feared to travel any farther with you. So under a pretext she disembussed at some small town along the way. Wendover."

"Of course I was acting erratically," Al said. "Everyone was against me. Plotting to kill me."

"So she probably is back here by now," Tsarnas said, half to himself as he rose to his feet. "She felt you needed psychiatric aid. Possibly you do. If I were your attorney, I'd advise you to place yourself under county or state medical care. You certainly could obtain it, and private care is frightfully expensive."

"Harman's after me," Al said. "He's brought everyone else into it on his side. I'm surrounded. That's why I had to leave the state."

Eyeing him, Tsarnas said, "You might consider this. Mr. Harman has an airtight case he could bring into court against you, if he really wanted to hound you—as you seem to believe. Defamation of character, in as much as you accused him before witnesses of being a criminal, a swindler. And it can be shown that it damaged him in a financial way; it affected his business interests, did it not?"

"Who'd I say that in front of?" At the Harman house he had said nothing against Harman; he was sure of it. "Who's the witness?" The old man, who had heard him say that, was dead.

Tsarnas said, "Mrs. Fergesson."

It was true. He nodded.

"I have no reason to believe he contemplates any civil action against you," Tsarnas said. "I'm only pointing it out in order to bring you to your senses, so perhaps you can be made to listen to reason."

"I'm listening to reason," Al said. "All the time."

"Did the grief and shock of Fergesson's death temporarily drive you to derangement?" Tsarnas said. "Under the emotional pressure did you lose the ability to distinguish what you were doing, from a moral standpoint? Well, it doesn't matter; if you behave yourself, and keep your head, you won't be coming up before the judge anyhow." He nodded goodbye to Al and left the room. The door shut after him.

An hour later Al was told that he could go.

He left the Hall of Justice and stood outside on the sidewalk, his hands in the pockets of his cloth jacket.

They really gave me a demonstration, he said to himself as he watched the people and traffic going by, the heavy downtown Oakland traffic with its buses and taxis. They showed me they could whip me back here any time they wanted. And they could tell it their way, make their account of it work and demolish mine. The same way they demolished my Marmon. And, he realized, they got everyone in it, even my wife. Although, he realized, she doesn't know and never will know.

Who does know? he asked himself. Lydia Fergesson? Probably not. That lawyer? Too shrewd; I'll never be able to tell about him, one way or another, if he believes it, or if he knows it's nothing but a mass of interlocking and carefully polished shit. The police? They don't care. They're just a machine that does what the wires make it do, like a vacuum cleaner that sweeps up whatever's in front of it, and whatever's small enough.

Harman knows, he said to himself. That, perhaps, is the only one I can be certain of. Not Bob Ross for sure, not Knight, not Gam, or any of them working for Harman; not even Mrs. Harman.

But Chris Harman himself; that's the difference between him and the rest of us. He knows what's going on; he knows what makes the thing run. And, Al thought, I know.

Hands in his pockets, he walked over to the bus stop to wait for a bus that would take him uptown to his apartment.

They prey on the weak, he said to himself. That is, the sick, such as the old man. The helpless, such as me. The widows, such as Lydia Fergesson. And they have us. There's no way we can fight back, because the language itself works against us. The very words were manufactured to explain their situation so it looks good, and ours so it looks bad. Looks so bad, in fact, that we're relieved to be let out of jail; we're relieved to be allowed to walk the street.

He thought, I guess they'll let me go back into the used-car business. Where I was. I wasn't offending anyone, there. I was in my place, the way Tootie Dolittle is in his place.

But the difference between me and Tootie, he realized, is that Tootie knew the boundary; he knew how far he could go before he was stepped on. And I didn't. I thought if I used all the words, the same type of talk as Harman and Ross and Knight and Gam and the rest of them, I could make it, too. As if the only thing that separated me from them was the talk.

The yellow Key System bus came. Along with the other people at the stop he pushed onto it; the doors wheezed shut, and the bus started up. He was on his way back to his apartment in the three-story building where the McKeckneys and the young Mexican couple lived. Where he had begun his effort, his life of lies and crimes.

I wonder if Julie is home, he asked himself. He did not feel like coming home to an empty apartment.

16

The door of his apartment was unlocked, and, as he opened it, he could hear voices from inside. So she was home, he thought. He pushed the door so hard that it banged. But it was not Julie. In the living room of the apartment stood Bob Ross, smoking his pipe and looking at a motor magazine that he had picked up from the table. And, in the other room, was Chris Harman. He was using the phone.

Seeing Al, Harman finished his phone call and hung up. He came into the living room and said, "We were just checking now, trying to locate your wife."

"I see," Al said. "Did you find her?"

Ross said, "Apparently she's somewhere in Nevada, or possibly on the California side of Lake Tahoe. She may be at one of those Lake resorts, such as Harrah's Club."

"She'll turn up," Harman said, in his easy, friendly voice; he smiled at Al, the smile that Al was familiar with. "But probably broke. But glad to be home again."

"What do you care?" Al said.

Harman said, "You've suffered a lot of unnecessary loss in this, Al. I personally am very concerned that it be made up to you."

Beside him, Ross nodded in agreement as he put down the motor magazine.

Al said, "What loss?"

"The humiliation," Harman said. "For one thing." His hand moved. Ross, seeing the motion, ducked his head and started from the apartment, out into the hall. "I'll be along in about fifteen minutes," Harman said after him.

"I'll be in the car," Ross said, and shut the door after him.

"I haven't suffered any humiliation," Al said. "Show me where I have."

"Perhaps the word's the wrong one. Pardon me if it is. I get a little clumsy sometimes when I try to express my deeper feelings; bear with me. You don't deserve what happened to you, Al. You know it and I know it. Bob is aware of it. In fact we were all discussing it last night, when we learned that you had been picked up in Salt Lake City and were being held. My wife, Bodo, was especially concerned that something be done for you. I got in touch with Mrs. Fergesson's lawyer . . ." Harman paused and grinned, almost a grimace. "She's an incredible person, that Lydia. I had never met her before, of course. Until this business. I must say it's a real experience to be around her for any length of time. But surprisingly, we found we had a great deal in common in terms of interests. She's educated well beyond her external manner; once you get down to the authentic person—it makes you anxious to know her much better."

Al nodded.

"She could hold her own in any salon," Harman said. "Any-where on the Continent."

Al nodded.

"What's your attitude toward me?" Harman said.

Al shrugged.

"Not too unfriendly," Harman said. "Not something you can't get over, in time. Although God knows you have no valid basis for any enmity toward me. But we'll let that pass. The mind is a strange instrument." He reflected. "At any rate," he said, pac-ing around the living room of the apartment, "I want to rehabili-tate you."

Al said, "I see."

"I feel," Harman said, "that it's my responsibility. In many ways. Some that you wouldn't understand."

They both were silent.

"How do you mean, 'rehabilitate'?" Al said. "You mean send me to a psychiatrist?"

"Oh hell no," Harman said. "What kind of rehabilitation is that? A perfunctory social means of providing custodial care, or some crackpot Freudian religion to make money off neurotic women. I mean through a decent job that will give you back your self-respect and dignity. By harnessing your ability." He added, "Of which you have plenty. Perhaps more than you realize."

"Would I work for your organization?" Al said. "Or do you mean you'd put in a word for me somewhere?"

"Frankly," Harman said, meeting his gaze directly, "I'd like to have you with me. But if you don't cotton to the notion—" He shrugged, still smiling. "It's okay with me. I'll see that you're put on somewhere else." He glanced at his watch.

"You have to go?" Al said.

"Yes. In a minute. Jim's death was a terrible ordeal for all of us. God, he was so—" Harman gestured. "Lively. Animated. Full of his old good spirits. Like he was when I first started taking my cars to him. Cracking jokes."

"Full of the old Jim," Al said.

"As if," Harman said, "what was left of him all sort of—how would you put it? Boiled up at once. And was consumed. There was nothing left, after that."

"Really sad," Al said. "And thought provoking."

"Will you be thinking it over?" Harman said. "About going back and picking up? I mean the job."

"Oh yes," Al said. "Sure."

"Good boy," Harman said. "You know, Al, you always have to be able to pick up again. If you can learn that you have it. If you can put adversity behind you and resume. Resume and resume; never stop resuming. Because—well, here's how I see it, Al. Nothing is that important. Not even death. You see?"

He nodded.

Harman's hand shot out and they shook. Then Harman opened the hall door, waved, smiled a short, penetrating, official smile at him, and was gone. But then, almost at once, the door flew partway open, and he was back. "You have no fundamental hard feelings toward me, do you, Al?" he said sharply.

"No," Al said.

Nodding, Harman shut the door. This time he was really gone.

For a long time Al stood at the window of the empty apartment, by himself, watching the street below. Julie had not come back, even by six, and by then he was becoming too hungry to stay any longer. He went into the kitchen and fooled with dishes and cans, but it was no use. So he wrote a note to her and left the apartment.

As he came out onto the dark sidewalk he saw a shape at work off in the shadows, bouncing up and down. At first he thought it was an animal. But it was Earl McKeckney, busy with some matter of his own, toiling as silently as usual. The boy raised his head as Al passed him. They looked at each other, said nothing, and then Al went on down the sidewalk, his hands in his pockets.

A flapping sound made him pause at the corner. Behind him, at top speed Earl McKeckney came running along the sidewalk backward. He did not bump into anything, but veered as he came to each telephone pole and wall; he reached Al, danced around in a circle, and continued on, still backward, still avoiding all things.

"Hey," Al said. "How do you do it?" Perhaps the kid had memorized the position of every object in the block.

Not stopping, Earl yelled, "I got my ring." He held up his hand; on his finger was a ring with a bit of glass in it, a mirror. "My Captain Zero Secret Periscope Ring." Eyes fixed on his ring, facing Al, he departed, hurrying deeper and deeper into the darkness, until he at last was gone.

Really weird, Al thought. Can't make it out at all.

He continued on until he reached an Italian restaurant where he and Julie had often eaten. She was not there, but he went in and ordered dinner anyhow.

After he had eaten dinner he roamed around the evening streets for a while. And then he turned in the direction of Tootie Dolittle's apartment.

"Hi," he said, as Tootie let him in. The Dolittles were still eating dinner; he saw the table with its dishes and pans and silver. Leading Tootie off to one side, he said, "Listen, I want you to do something for me. I want you to get me something." He wanted Tootie to get him a gun.

"That thing?" Tootie said. "That we were discussing you should have?"

"That's right," Al said.

Glancing at his wife, Tootie said in a low voice, "You can walk into a hardware store and buy one, man."

"Oh," Al said.

"Only it'll be registered, and you know how they can do with those bullets." Tootie's voice was virtually inaudible. "You mean a gun what got found somewhere. That nobody bought."

"Yes," Al said.

"I don't know," Tootie said. "Anyhow, come in and have some dinner," He moved Al toward the table.

"How do you do, Al?" Mary Ellen Dolittle said, as he seated himself. "Welcome, and have something with us, please."

"Hi," Al said. "Thanks." He had a little of the dumplings and lamb stew. Tootie had already put a plate, silver, a napkin, plastic cup and saucer in front of him; Al stared down in bewilderment. The objects seemed to materialize out of nothing.

"You look really tired," Mary Ellen said, with sympathy. "I think I never seen you so tired-looking, Al."

Tootie said, "They still after you?"

"No," Al said.

"They give up?"

"No," he said. "They got me."

Tootie's eyes widened and then narrowed. "Then you not here. You dead."

Picking at his dumplings and lamb stew, Al did not answer.

"I like to inquire," Mary Ellen said, "what this be about. But I know neither you boys ever going to say, so I save myself the bother. You going to go on the rest of your life like this, Al Miller? You not change, as a result of the big time job you got I hear of?" She waited, but he did not answer her either. "No," she said. "You not."

"Al don't have the big-time job anymore anyhow," Tootie said. "So lay off him."

Mary Ellen said, "Well, Al Miller, eat up your dinner and then go on."

He glanced at her. She was serious.

"She mean it," Tootie said. "She given up on you. I see her give up on people before, but I surprised at her at this point. Is that the true way of God, to throw a man out? I say to hell with that, and all the Uncle Tom religion you spout." Tootie's voice rose until the dishes rattled; Mary Ellen shrank away, but she did not try to break in. "I really sick of you," Tootie shouted at her. "You the hopeless one. You get out, you hear? You hear me?" He yelled with his face close to hers, until at last she scrambled to her feet. "Go on," he yelled, jumping up. "Leave here and don't come around again." Then he dropped back down into his chair; he grabbed his coffee cup, squeezed it between both his dark palms, and then he slammed it from the table, skidding it across the floor so that it burst against the wall. Streamers of coffee appeared on the wall, as high as the picture of Jesus which Al had seen there as long as he had known them.

"You through?" Mary Ellen said presently.

"What do you know about old Al?" Tootie said. "Nothing." His face had a stern, brooding expression. He shook his head. "Nothing at all."

"I didn't mean to stir up trouble," Al said, going on with his eating. It had shaken him, that Mary Ellen had ordered him out; he could not bring himself to look at her. But now she came over and put her hand on his shoulder.

"Maybe I did done wrong," she said. Her fingers caressed his shoulder, guileless fingers. "Listen, Al," she said, drawing her chair over so that she was seated so close to him that her knees pressed against the rungs of his chair. "I see it, what Tootie said, and I saw it when you came in. All over him," she said to her husband. "In him and around him."

"See what?" Al said.

"That you going to die soon," Mary Ellen said.

"Oh," Al said.

"It don't even bother you," Mary Ellen said softly.

"No," he agreed.

"Do something," Mary Ellen said.

He went on eating. When he had finished he got up from the table. "How about it?" he said to Tootie.

Still brooding, still clasping and unclasping his hands, Tootie said, "Naw."

"Really?" Al said. "You won't get it for me?"

"Naw," Tootie repeated.

"So long then," Al said.

"I tell you why," Tootie said. "You think you want it for getting back at them. But when you get your hands on it—" He studied the remains of the coffee cup and the spilled coffee. "Then you take it and stick it against your head and you give it to yourself. You not know that now. You not admit it or face it. But it still true."

Is it? Al wondered. Maybe so.

"You haven't seen anything of my wife, have you?" he asked them. "She hasn't called here?"

"No," Mary Ellen said. "Don't you know where she is?"

Tootie said, "Did she leave you, man?"

"Maybe," Al said.

"You just a humpty dumpty," Tootie said. "You just stand there, stand around, while it all happen to you. You just perch and watch. So now you don't even have a wife. A nice wife like that."

"Why don't you go and look for her?" Mary Ellen said.

Tootie said, "I bawled Mary Ellen out because she asked you to leave. Now I think she right. You ought to leave. You ought to go out and make it. And then come back and sit here. Okay?"

Putting on his jacket, Al left their apartment. They were both watching him as he shut the door after him.

He stood by the ruins of the Marmon, kicking at a cylinder that had been part of the ignition system. Most of the lot lay in darkness, but the neon sign of the coffee shop across the street gave him enough light to see again what he had already seen before; there was no hope of restoring the Marmon. Whoever had wrecked it knew what he was doing. The idea that had come grotesquely into his mind: it couldn't be done, at least not without several weeks of work, and by then it wouldn't matter. He had seen himself driving the ruined Marmon down the freeway, late, in the part of the night when there was the least traffic. All the way to the Richmond Bridge, and then at seventy-five miles an hour, into the steel and concrete side of the bridge and through and down into the water. But it was out of the question, and anyhow it was only a vision, a dream of his own death.

A hearse, he thought. All this time, all these months; was that what I was restoring it to be? A black, big, heavy, silent hearse wheeling along the deserted streets with me in it, on my back with my hands folded, my eyes open wide. My tongue, possibly, sticking out a half-inch, stiff, swollen; unless the undertaker pushed it back in or snipped it off. Me sticking out my tongue as they dragged me up the street, my tongue out at them even in death. The sons of bitches.

And then he had another dream, another vision; this one was so clear that he at once began to work on it. He did not hesitate. He hurried to the little basalt blockhouse, unlocked the door, and began searching around until he had found a paper bag left over from a lunch. He carried the paper bag outside, and, stooping down, began to sweep up sand from the lot. The sand had been put there to collect grease dripping from his cars. He swept it with his hands, pushing it into a pile, and then he dumped the sand into the paper bag.

Maybe I can get both of them, he said to himself. The Mercedes-Benz and the Cadillac. Unless, he thought, they have locks on the gas tanks. He could not remember.

While he stood there at the edge of the lot, holding the paper bag of sand and trying to remember, a car horn honked. He turned and saw an old but polished Cadillac at the curb. It had stopped, and the driver was watching him; he saw, in the reflected streetlight, the driver's eyes.

Rolling the car window down, the driver leaned over and called out to him, "Hi!" It was a woman. For an instant he had it that she was his wife; he leaped all over and started toward her. But it was not Julie, and he knew that. It was Mrs. Lane. He went on toward her anyhow, more slowly, taking his bag of sand with him.

He stood on the sidewalk, saying nothing.

"Hello there, Mr. Miller," Mrs. Lane said, her lips drawing back to show her carved golden teeth; the club and diamond sparkled. "What you doing down here in the dark? You appear to be having to pick up something you drop."

He said nothing.

"You want me to drive up on the lot so my headlights make it show up better?" she said.

"No," he said. "Thanks."

"Guess what I doing," she said, still leaning toward him. Now he could smell her perfume: it was so intense that it came out of the car and around him where he stood. "Here, I show you." She shut off the motor of the Cadillac, squirmed over, opened the door on his side, and stepped out. She had on a knit dress and high heels and a hat; she was dressed up, obviously going out somewhere. "Don't you think I look good?" she said.

"Yes," he agreed. He had never seen her so spruced up, so sleek. Her hair, her skin, her eyes, everything about her shone. She had one single piece of jewelry on: a brooch near her collar.

"I been on a diet," she said. "I don't even have a, if you don't mind my saying it, a panty girdle." She patted her stomach. "I flat," she said. "Flat as a griddle pan. After all these years. I flatter than a lot of those high-school girls that go by eating those Popsicles and sticking out and hunching." She laughed. Turning in the streetlight, she showed him, with no need of comment, that she had on no bra, either. "Fact is," she said, "I need nothing under this, and that exactly what I got on." She raised her arms and skipped a step or two.

"Nothing at all," he agreed.

"Whee," she said, her eyes glowing.

"Where's your husband?" he said.

"Oh him," she said. "He gone. He a contractor. Up in Shasta County seeing about a important public building. He be back in another week. I going to a party." Her voice lilted and rose. "Goodbye," she said, reopening the car door. "I got to scoot. I just see you working away and I stop to show off. Don't get a chance every day."

"You look fine," he said.

She said, "Mr. Miller, you sound so bad. Where all your usual jokes and ironic style of humor?"

He shrugged.

"No more," Mrs. Lane said, regarding him. "Is that it? I hear about Mr. Fergesson. Now where you go? What you do?"

"I'm looking for my wife," he said.

"She gone, too? Everybody gone? Nobody want you, it seem. No wife, no friend, no job. You in a bad way. How did you get that way, Mr. Miller? Life perplexing in certain regards. One day you have all those things, the next day not. And what you done in between? Far as I can see, you not done nothing at all. Sometime it make you ponder if those church people not right. But I, myself, I never go to church and believe nothing. I already had that, and it just the same as all the rest. I think you and I both be crazy to go back to that, as much as we wish we could, like other folk."

He nodded.

"What in the package?" she said.

He did not know what she meant. He looked around.

"In your hand," she said.

He showed her.

"Sand," she said, looking into it as he held it open. "You picking up sand like a little boy." She took the sack of sand away from him and set it down by one of the parked cars. "That all you get out of this? At your age, thirty-something years? No wonder you got nothing joking to say. And here I going out to my party. I going to get in and drive off leaving you. And I even take your sack of sand away from you. I a bad woman if I do that. I really bad; I see myself in my jangly skin laughing out. My mean jangly skin."

"That's okay," he said. "I wasn't getting anywhere. Forget it."

"You not begrudge me my party," she said. "I know that, Mr. Miller." After a moment she reached out and took hold of his wrist. "I think I take you with me," she said.

"Where to?" he said.

"Not to no old party. I take you home with me." She pulled him, and he went along, across the sidewalk to the car. Opening the car door, she sat him down on the seat and then she went around to the other side and got in behind the wheel. "I drive," she said to him, "because I know the way." She started the motor.

He reached out and put his arms around her.

"Yes," she said, "I really look good tonight. I don't think I look this good ever in fifteen years." She drew him against her, holding him against her shoulder and patting him. Then she put the car in gear and drove, holding the wheel with her left hand. "It a good thing I got automatic transmission on this," she said, "or long before now I run into somebody while changing gear."

Soon they were traveling through streets he had never seen before. Streets that he did not know.

"I never hit anybody yet," Mrs. Lane said.